LEGACY OF LIGHT

A War For Magic

D1528409

For all the authors who've inspired us, allowing us to disappear into their worlds. For the ones who have yet to pick up their pens and write books that change our lives. We're glad to be able to breathe life into words.

We write of magic, but maybe the real magic is in our ability to live many lives within the pages of a book.

Glossary

The world of Dreach-Sciene and Dreach-Dhoun was created using a combination of words from Old English and Gaelic. In these two languages, words didn't only have one meaning. They had many. They became ideas rather than just singular objects. That's why we chose to blend the two. Deep meanings can be conveyed in a single beat. Even our location names can hold more power.

Aldor – (All-door) Old English for life. 'Aldorwood' means the wood of life.

Bràthair – (Brah-thair) Gaelic word for brother.

Dhoun – (Doon) Old English for dark. 'Dreach-Dhoun' means dark magic.

Dreach – (Dray-ach) A simplified spelling of the Gaelic term 'draiocht' meaning magic.

Isenore – (Eesen-oar) Old English for iron mine.

Scíene – (Scene) Old English for beautiful, brilliant, light. 'Dreach-Sciene' means light magic.

Sona – (So-na) Old English for hope. The Isle of Sona means the Isle of Hope.

Tá sé in am – Gaelic for 'it is time'.

Tenalach – (Ten-eh-lahct) – An Irish term for a deep connection with the earth.

Toha – (Toe-Ha) An old English term meaning the leader of an army, but also a leader of people.

Tri-Gard – Gaelic for the three guards.

Trúwa – (True-wah) Old English word for trust, fidelity, promise.

Uisce – (Ish-ka) Gaelic for water.

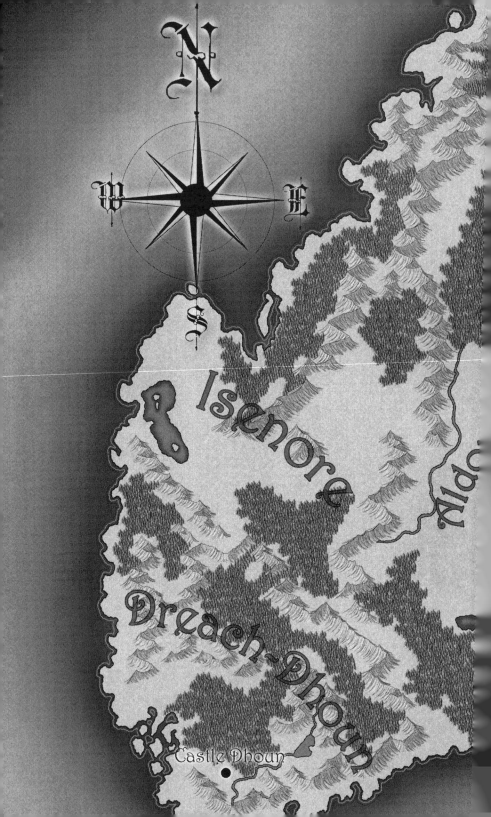

reach~Sciene

Palace of Sciene

The Sea of Uisce

hitecap

Isle of Sona

Feet pounded across the marble as the young messenger ran as fast as his legs would take him. The home of the King of Dreach-Sciene stretched out in front of him, a symbol of forgotten prosperity in a dying world. His damp boots slid to a halt with a loud screech as a young boy cut in front of him.

"Excuse me, Your Highness," the Messenger said, bowing as the boy nodded his head solemnly and continued on his way.

Once the little prince was out of sight, the Messenger took off faster than before. He had an urgent need to see the King. It'd been five years since anyone had news of this magnitude and he didn't know what it meant.

Silk tapestries adorned the stone walls, giving the palace halls an air of importance. They were important, he supposed, for only someone with immense power could regain what the kingdom had lost. Their only hope was the King.

The Messenger stopped outside of an ornate mahogany door. The carvings were elaborate, beautiful representations of the kingdom's three realms – majestic trees for Aldorwood, lavish iron armor for Isenore, and a ship for the Isle of Sona - a replica of what had once been the most powerful kingdom in the southern hemisphere. He studied the images as he calmed his frantic breathing, knowing he had to control himself in the presence of the King.

For the first time, he realized there should have been guards standing watch at the door. Turning his head left then right, he couldn't see them. Unable to wait any longer, he grasped the metal knocker and pounded it against the door once, then twice. Nothing happened, so he did it again.

Thinking the King was out, his shoulders sagged. What was he to do? The matter was urgent, important.

Just as he was about to give up, the door swung open and the Messenger stood face to face with two guards in full armor. The silence stretched for what felt like an eternity.

Finally, the Messenger cleared his throat. "I need to speak with the King."

The soldier on the left eyed him up and down. "The King meets with his people every day at noon."

He was about to slide the door shut when the Messenger stuck his foot out. "I come from the village on a matter of importance."

"Let the young man in," a voice called from inside.

Quick to obey, the soldiers grabbed him by the shirt and pulled him in before shutting the door behind them.

The King sat at a long, rectangular table covered with unrolled scrolls of parchment. A handful of other men surrounded him.

King Marcus Renauld was a large man, both in stature and in personality. His gaze, though not harsh, had a way of making people squirm. He was intense, but there was not a more respected man in all the kingdom.

"Speak your business." The King inclined his head to the Messenger who promptly bowed.

"Your Majesty," he began. "I've come on an important matter of utmost secrecy." He looked around at the gathered men and the King followed his gaze.

"Leave us." The King's tone was not to be argued with. Chairs scraped against the floor as they were abruptly slid back and abandoned. The door shut with a definitive slam that echoed off the vaulted ceilings. Only the two guards remained. "They can be trusted."

The Messenger swallowed hard, giving a single nod of his head.

"There's a rumor among the people of something, or more like someone, I think you'd be very interested in."

"I'm listening." The King leaned forward and folded his hands together on the table.

"There's talk of a seer in the village."

The King shot to his feet, his chair clattering to the ground behind him. "Are you certain?"

"I believe it to be so, Sire. My source is one to be trusted."

"How is this possible?" He stepped back from the table and began to pace. "It's been five years. The war took every last bit of magic. I was there. I saw it happen."

The Messenger shifted from one foot to the other uncomfortably. He knew what this could mean, but was happy it was now in the King's able hands. The King stopped moving and fixed him with another of his scrutinizing looks.

"You know where this person is?"

"Yes, Sire."

"You will take me there." He turned to his guards. "Have someone fetch me my coat and ready me a horse."

"Your Majesty," one of the guards stepped forward. "Surely you'll take the carriage."

"A man on a horse can disappear in a way a man in a carriage cannot." He rubbed at the graying whiskers on his chin absently. "No, I don't think it would be a good idea to be seen tonight." He reached up and removed the golden circlet from atop his head, setting it on the table.

The guard who had yet to speak stepped close to the King and whispered, "Are you sure you trust this man?"

"Trust is only necessary when you can afford to do without that which is offered." He placed a hand on the guard's shoulder. "You may come if it makes you feel better, but the armor stays here."

A short time later, the four men sat atop their horses, cantering down the path from the castle. A rain drizzled down, dampening everything in their way. The night was cold, despite the summer month, making the Messenger pull his cloak tighter around his shoulders as his icy fingers went numb on the reins. He glanced behind him where the King seemed unaffected by the weather, only determined.

The path led them through a dense part of the forest surrounding the castle. Trees loomed over them, a web of shadows in the dark. Insects and frogs inundated the air with their nighttime song, joining the steady drumming of their horse's hooves.

By the time they'd reached the village, mud had splattered up the flanks of their large beasts and onto the men who rode them. The rhythm of their travels changed as forest paths gave way to cobblestone streets.

They slowed to a walk so as not to attract attention. The Messenger led them past row upon row of squalid houses, the fruit of poverty evident in their wretchedness. They took a turn at the end of the road, into an alleyway where they found the entrance to a non-descript tavern. A wooden sign above the door proclaimed it as The Hunter's Inn. The rowdy noises from inside grew louder as they got closer. The Messenger pulled his horse to a stop and motioned for them to do the same.

"The woman you are seeking is being housed by the matron of this establishment," he said. "Her name is Lorelai. I have fulfilled my mission." He bowed his head. "With your leave, Sire."

The King didn't remove his gaze from the door before him as he waved the Messenger away and dismounted. "Stay with the horses," he told his guards.

"You shouldn't go in alone," one of them responded.

"I need to know." The King, having been desperate for answers for five years now, stepped forward just as the door opened, spilling golden candlelight onto the street.

He left his guards behind and walked forward, at once both apprehensive and excited. He knew what this would mean if it were true. A plump older woman held the door for him but showed no recognition in her eyes.

"Are you daft, man?" She narrowed her tiny eyes. "The cold is gettin' in."

The King swallowed the natural urge to chastise her for speaking to him in such a manner. Tonight, he wasn't the king. He didn't look at her as he scooted by into a room lined with long tables where men and women alike sat behind large mugs of ale.

He unclasped his soggy cloak, letting the warmth of the nearby fire dry him for a moment. His eyes scanned the groups of people, but not one of them gave him a second glance. Too involved in their own transgressions.

A woman brushed up against his back. "What can I get you, sir?" she purred. He shifted away from her ample bosom and kept his eyes trained on hers. She stood still, seemingly unable to look away.

"I need to speak with your mistress." He kept his voice low and even, knowing she'd do what he asked.

"Right away." She flitted away as he stayed rooted to his spot by the fire.

A moment later, a different woman appeared. This one was older, carrying herself as if she was once a thing of beauty. She still had an attractiveness about her, but her hair was streaked with gray and rouge no longer covered up the deficiencies on her face.

King Marcus Renauld was not a cruel man, but his shrewdness allowed him to see a lot about a person the moment they appeared.

"How can I help you?" There was no melodic quality to her voice as he'd come to enjoy in most women. Instead, it was rough, gravelly. This was a woman who'd seen many of the harsher realities of life. To his utter dismay, that could describe most of the people in his kingdom since the war.

"I've been told to seek a woman named Lorelai." The King straightened himself to his full height and towered over the woman in front of him. To her credit, she didn't flinch. Her hands flew to her hips in defiance.

"There ain't no one here by that name."

The King leaned down and looked her directly in the eye. Her pupils dilated as she blinked rapidly. "I don't believe you," he growled.

They were still staring at each other as another woman approached. "It's okay." She put a hand on the older lady's shoulder and the woman instantly relaxed. "I've been waiting for him."

The King turned to find a young girl, not yet into adulthood. Ash-white hair hung all the way to her waist and icy blue eyes regarded him with a maturity beyond her years. She was as tall as the other woman but thin and willowy.

"Your Majesty." She dipped into a curtsy.

The King grabbed her arm and pulled her up, looking around to make sure no one else took notice of her display. "But you're only a girl," he muttered, more to himself than to her.

"I'm sixteen," she responded, yanking her arm out of his grasp and squaring her shoulders. Her voice was like a song, holding every note the older woman's lacked. She turned to the other woman who now stood with a bewildered look on her face. "I told you the King would find me." She turned on her heel and marched towards a door at the other end of the room.

The King didn't know if this girl thought him being here was a good thing or a disaster, but he followed her anyway. He knew there'd be raised eyebrows as he followed her into the private room, but as long as none of them knew who he was, it was okay.

He soon found himself alone with his could-be seer. She looked young and fragile, not how she should look if touched by magic.

A single bed stood along the back wall with a table and two

chairs in the center. Other than those essentials, the room was sparse.

Lorelai waited for the King to sit as was customary and then took the space across from him.

"I'd ask for refreshments," she began. "But, something tells me you don't want to be interrupted."

"Seer's intuition?" he asked hopefully.

"Common sense." Her soft laugh echoed throughout the room.

The King couldn't remember the last time someone laughed at him. He grimaced, impatient to get on with it.

"Ask me your questions," she said finally.

"You saw I would come?" he asked.

"I did."

"So, it's true."

"I'm sure I'd be able to tell you if I knew what it was." She held in her laugh this time.

"You see things."

"I have eyes, yes."

"That is not what I mean." He drummed his fingers on the table in agitation. The girl was playing with him.

"You must speak plainly, Sire."

"You can see the future." It sounded crazy coming out of his mouth in light of the world they were living in – the one without magic.

"That is not how it works exactly. I can see what certain people are capable of and the paths open before them. Sometimes I can see an event will occur, but I don't know who will be involved."

The King leaned in eagerly. "How is this possible?" he asked. "Magic was taken from these lands when we lost the war."

"I have no magic, Sire." Surprise laced her words. "Before the war, people obtained their magic from the earth, it was a gift. The sight is different. It's who I am. A part of me. It was not given and therefore can't be taken away. Seers have remained true, but have been forced into hiding by those who are desperate for their perceived magic."

With just a few words, the hope he'd placed on her was gone. He was no closer to regaining their magic than he was five years ago when it was stolen.

"Don't fret, you haven't come in vain for I've seen something that will aid you in the future."

"Speak," he commanded.

She closed her eyes and breathed in deeply. "There will come a time when a noble man will rise and only he will have the power to defeat the darkness."

"We will win? We will defeat Dreach-Dhoun?"

"An outcome no one knows." She opened her eyes. "He may succeed in his mission or he may fail."

"A noble man will rise," he whispered. "Trystan, my son. He's the one, yes? Of course, he is. It couldn't be anyone but the prince."

She stood up and moved towards the door. "I can't say, Sire. All I know is his destiny intertwines greatly with Dreach-Sciene's survival."

Her words did nothing to damper the spark of hope growing in his heart as she led him back through the tavern. He'd always known his son was different, special somehow. She opened the door to the cold night. The rain was coming down more heavily now.

"Ah," she said, stepping outside, seemingly unaware of her quickly dampening hair. "Davion." Her voice had taken on a sweet, almost motherly fashion.

The boy she was talking to currently had one arm in the tight grip of one of the King's guards.

"Caught this boy trying to steal from the saddle bags, Sire," the guard said, thrusting the kid forward.

He couldn't have been any older than Trystan's five years, but here he was on a night like this in the streets.

"I was just wanting something to eat, Sir," the boy cried softly.

"Let him go at once," Lorelai commanded of the guard, stomping her feet. She hit a puddle, splashing muddy water up onto her dress.

The King nodded to his guard who released the boy. He ran directly into Lorelai's arms. "I was looking for you, Davion," she cooed. "I wanted you to meet my new friend." She eyed the King warily and then spun the boy around to face him. "This is the king, Davi, isn't that grand?"

To the boy's credit, he fumbled through a bow.

"He's going to take you with him," she said.

"What are you going on about, girl?" the King asked.

Lorelai left Davi by the side of the building and stepped closer so only the King could hear her. "I don't understand it. I've known Davi for over a year. He's an orphan living on the streets and his future is unknown to me. What I've seen is he's important. Whenever I see images of your son, it's Davion by his side. He will be his greatest protector and most loyal friend."

The King didn't know what to say. He trusted what this girl said to be true. He had no choice.

Turning to his guards, he shouted, "The boy comes with us."

His gaze reverted back to the girl. "Thank you. You have given me hope. I may be able to restore life back to my kingdom."

"Be careful, my king. It is a fool that believes everything pertains to one's self." Lorelai fixed the King with her piercing gaze. When she looked at him, it was as if she saw all, knew all. Nothing could be hidden, nothing protected.

THE KING HANDED Davion up to one of his guards and mounted his own horse with more questions than he'd had before.

It seemed to take them longer to get back, but as soon as they reached the castle, the servants took their horses and ushered them inside to get warm. The King handed off his sopping coat. If he hurried, he could still make it to his children's rooms before they drifted off.

Putting a hand on a lost looking Davion's shoulder, he ushered him through the halls. The child didn't speak and the King suspected it was because he'd never been in surroundings such as these. Torches along the walls lit their way, reflecting in the boy's wide eyes.

The King looked down at the filthy boy with mud matted in his dark hair and sighed. This was not how the night was supposed to go.

Rissa's room was first. She was his curious little three-year-old who was forced into the cruelest fate of all – growing up without a mother. Her maid, Ana, was exiting the room when he arrived.

She curtsied upon seeing him.

"Ana." He nodded. "I need you to take Davion here and get him cleaned up, fed, and tucked in somewhere warm."

She looked at the boy curiously, but didn't ask any questions as she ushered him away.

The King glanced down at his muddy boots and wet clothing, realizing there was nothing he could do about it. After the night he'd had, he just wanted to look into his little girl's innocent face and give his son a long hug.

Rissa and Trystan were both laying on Rissa's bed. On stormy nights, Trystan slept in there to keep her from being scared. It warmed the King's heart to see them together.

"Father," Trystan called when he saw him.

"Da," Rissa piped up.

The King smiled more cheerily than he felt and moved further into the room to sit on the corner of the bed, careful not to get it muddy.

"Tell us a story," Rissa said.

"Which one would you like to hear?" he asked.

"Trystan the bold," Trystan said.

"Again?" The King laughed. "Okay then. Over a hundred years ago Dreach-Sciene and Dreach-Dhoun were one. The kingdom was called Dreach until a powerful sorcerer rose to defy the King. His magic was like nothing anyone had seen before. He pulled enormous amounts of energy from the earth and unleashed it. The King of Dreach and his son Trystan wouldn't let him seize the throne. They fought battle after battle, combining their magic to fight this other sorcerer. There was to be one final battle to take place in the mountains of Isenore. This would decide their fate. The battle lasted two days until both armies were weary. All seemed lost for Trystan and his father. On the second night, Trystan went out alone to pull magic from the earth. Now, a person can only hold so much before their body starts to break down. He went past that point. By the time he returned to his camp, he was stumbling and babbling. It was plain to everyone what he'd done. Some thought it bravado or ego – until the fight began again.

Trystan lurched forward to grab a spear. He then hurled it into the air with every bit of magic he'd absorbed. He pushed it through the protective barrier set up by the other sorcerer and directly into his heart. But he couldn't recover. Both men died at the exact same moment. The battle ended, allowing Trystan's father and his people to retreat with their lives and the kingdom was split in two."

"What about my name?" Rissa asked.

"You, my darling girl." He reached out to run a hand lovingly over her fire-red hair. "Are named for the greatest hero I've ever known. Your mother."

He watched as his children drifted off, safe in their castle. He thought of the boy he'd brought home, who was alone and scared; who had a destiny, just like his son. Trystan was the man Lorelai had spoken of. He was sure of it. What nobler man was there in the kingdom than a prince? If he was going to rise, the King knew what he had to do.

He went to his rooms and wrote out a note, dripping wax onto the paper and pressing his ring into it. Walking into the hall, he went to find a messenger who was still awake. He came upon a girl who would do just fine.

"Take this to the Duchess of Sona." He pressed it into her hands along with a pouch of coins. "For your ship's passage."

She dropped into a curtsy before hurrying away.

He hoped he was doing the right thing. His brother, Geran, might be volatile and scheming, but he was still a member of this royal family and Trystan was going to need them all behind him – the entire force of the Renauld name. The Duchess of Sona had been hiding him for too long. It was time for him to come home.

13

He wasn't going to lose this fight.

The sword sliced the air missing Trystan's ear by a split hair. Lurching to the right, Trystan whirled just in time as the second attack came. Raising his heavy broadsword, it collided against his attacker's blade with a metallic clang, stunting the blow. The contact reverberated up his arm, into his shoulder. He grimaced in pain as sweat beaded on his brow, threatening to drip into his eyes. He didn't dare take the time to wipe it away.

His opponent was skilled and eager, already bouncing back from the jarring blow. The Prince's numerous years of practice took over. Bending his knees, he straightened his back to keep his hips aligned with his shoulders. This fighting stance was ingrained in him and he did it without thought. His instinct to stay alive.

The steel blade glinted in the morning sun as it thrust his way again and again. The prince parried the attempts, slapping the edge away with ease. A tiny grin of victory escaped as he deflected blow after blow. His attacker was tiring, he could tell. Victory was near. Deciding to end this fight, Trystan delivered a powerful low slash to his opponent's abdomen. The other swordsman evaded it easily enough, but it knocked him off balance and he hit the ground with a loud grunt. Trystan's blade hovered above the man's chest, a mere inch from his heart.

"Concede or I will run you through."

His opponent knocked the blade away and leaped to his feet with a nimble backwards roll.

Feinting hard to the right, Trystan fell for the ploy as his nemesis attacked from the left and the hilt of his blade connected with the Prince's ribs. His opponent took advantage of the slight stumble. The Prince's feet were swept out from underneath him and he crashed onto his back, his sword flying out of his grip.

The point of a blade was thrust under Trystan's chin, against the vulnerable hollow of his neck.

"You concede?" The shadow above him growled as it blocked out the sun. The two men stared at each other, breathing heavy from their exertion.

Finally, Trystan grinned as his head fell back to peer up at Davion in amusement. "Quite impressive, my friend. Avery would be proud. That was a heck of a fight."

Davi held a hand out to the prince and pulled him to his feet, clamping a friendly hand on his shoulder. "Either I'm improving or you're slipping in your old age, Toha-to-be. I bested you in no time. Hope you're not too exhausted, else those fine maidens over there will be sorely disappointed."

Davi nodded to the two pretty young maids who'd been watching their match with wide-eyed admiration. They giggled behind their hands in response to Davi's flirtatious wink and one even had the gumption to smile back at him and drop a little curtsy. They straightened abruptly when they heard the irritated voice from the other side of the courtyard.

"Millie, Jalis, you're both needed inside."

The girls scurried away as a slender redhead in a sky-blue dress gracefully descended the stone steps into the courtyard. Her hair glinted brightly in the sunlight, matching the blaze of censure in her moss-green eyes. With the chastised girls out of her view, Princess Rissa's disapproving glance settled on the dark-haired Davi.

"Truly, Davion. Can you not go a day without flirting with the maids?"

Davi's smile grew wider, not the least bit concerned at Rissa's wrath, and flung his arms out to the sides in jest. "I could, but why deny them the pleasure of all this?"

Rissa's unladylike snort of exasperation belied her regal bearing as she crossed her arms. "Careful. Your head swells bigger as we speak. Soon you will not be able to lift it."

"Then I shall enlist the aid of the maids, Princess. I'm sure they would be more than happy to help me carry it around."

"Sadly, you speak the truth. They do seem to find your appearance undeniably appealing. No doubt once you have charmed them into being alone with you, you break the illusion by opening your mouth and allowing your idiotic words to flow out?"

"Oh, trust me, Princess," Davi's grin reeked of mischief as he leaned on his sword and winked her way. "When the maids do find themselves alone with me, we are too otherwise occupied for conversation."

Trystan laughed out loud at this, but his sister was not as amused. The flippant comment only appeared to increase her exasperation. Her irritated gaze moved to Trystan. "I'm glad you can find time to laugh, brother, since I'm here on behalf of the King. He's summoned you to his quarters. If I were you, I would not make him wait."

Swirling her skirts, Rissa pivoted on her heel and stormed away. Trystan watched his sister depart with a knowing smile. "Davi, why do you love tormenting her?"

"Because it's so much fun."

TRYSTAN FELT many eyes on him as he marched down the marble hall with Davion by his side. His heavy steps echoed off the stone walls, but he seemed to be the only one who could hear the pounding keeping time with the rhythm of his heart. All other sounds dissolved into the cacophony of daily palace routines.

Only it wasn't like any other day at the palace. He hadn't expected to be summoned so soon. If he'd known, he wouldn't have practiced so hard with Davi. He was well aware the dukes and other various nobles had started arriving the day before, keeping the staff busier than usual. There were more people to feed, rooms to sweep, linens to clean. Extra nobles meant more guards walking the halls, their servants cleaning armor and sharpening swords. No, it wasn't just any day. It was the last day before their beloved prince gained his birthright. The day Trystan moved one step closer to the crown - to be prepared to step in if anything were to happen to his father.

And he smelled like a lathered horse.

He'd been having fun only minutes before, but a weight had

settled in the center of his chest ever since Rissa had summoned him and it wouldn't ease up. He knew what tomorrow meant for him, but something told him today would be important as well.

A maid scurried to a stop in front of them, dropping the basket she'd been carrying.

"Your Highness," she gasped, dropping low and fanning out her skirt to hide the once clean and folded linens that now lay wrinkled at her feet. She dipped her head, her long blond braid falling over one shoulder. "I'm so sorry. I didn't see where I was going."

Davi glanced at him and chuckled.

"It's fine," Trystan said more harshly than he'd intended. His nerves were getting the better of his manners.

"Let me help you," Davi said in his easy tone. "Don't mind the prince. Even royals can have sticks up their asses. Theirs are just made of gold."

She met his eyes across the basket they were both piling linens into and gave him the tiniest smile before straightening up and hefting the basket into her arms. She gave one more final dip and then hurried off.

Davi turned back, still chuckling to himself and met Trystan's glare unflinchingly. "Come on." He clapped his friend on the back. "Your father is waiting."

"For me." Trystan started walking again. "I don't recall him summoning you."

Davi shrugged. "Everything is open to interpretation."

"No, it's really not."

Davi didn't turn back and Trystan didn't make him. If truth be told, having his friend at his side helped ease some of the Prince's nerves. He knew leading the kingdom was his destiny, not Davi's, but he felt like a brother, like he too was a prince and heir, making Trystan feel less alone.

The halls grew quieter the closer they came to the King's quarters. It was a more isolated and protected part of the castle. When they were children, Trystan, Davi, and Rissa hated these parts because they felt official, formal. They'd much preferred the stables, the kitchens, or the training yards where people would talk to them and teach them.

Down this way was the council hall, a room which had always been secretive and off limits to those not on the council, including the realm's only prince. They passed by its door and stopped in front of the two guards standing outside the King's office.

The wooden doors were pushed open without hesitation revealing the King standing with his back to them as he looked out the window onto the woods below.

The two young men waited patiently until the King turned. "I don't remember summoning you, Davion." He leveled him with an unblinking stare.

"Sire," Davi began.

"No, it's not open to interpretation."

The corner of Trystan's mouth twitched, but he hid his smile with a cough. Davi bowed with a sigh. If it were anyone else, Trystan knew his father would chastise them, but Davi was a favorite of his and he could get away with just about anything.

The door thudded to a close upon Davi's exit, and Trystan almost choked on the stifling air as he moved to stand beside his father at the window.

"How are you holding up, son?" The King put a hand on his shoulder, squeezing lightly.

"I'm okay," Trystan grunted, shrugging off his hand. "I can handle it."

"You're about to become Toha. It's a lot of pressure whether it's your rightful position or not. That is why you don't come of age until you've passed twenty winters. Do you know what being the Toha means?"

"Of course, I do. I become head of the army, the symbol of strength across the kingdom."

"Trystan." He locked his eyes onto his son's. "You become the symbol of hope." He paused to scratch his chin and regarded his son thoughtfully. "The Toha is more than a general, more than a soldier. And that is why only a prince can hold the title. Tomorrow, when the sun is high, you will pledge to be the people's protector, their warrior for justice, their light in the darkness."

Trystan didn't know what to say in response and his father sighed. "There's still much you don't know. Come, the council is waiting."

"The council?" Trystan's eyes grew wide and he glanced down at his sweaty shirt. Even the prince was usually kept from the council meetings and this was how he'd arrive at his first one?

"Tomorrow you become more than a prince. A Toha must know his kingdom and all happenings in it."

The two guards fell in step behind them as they left the room and walked the short distance to the council chambers.

Trystan's childhood mind had imagined some grand room with tall tiers of chairs filled with important dignitaries who stood when they wanted to yell, their voices echoing through the room. He imagined chaos amongst nobles who didn't always see eye to eye.

Instead, he was led into a circular room with no windows

and only the single door. Torches hung along the walls to cast light onto a long, round table with high backed chairs. The room was bare, simple, unlike the men and women inside of it.

The group of people already present jumped to their feet when they saw them enter. The King smiled wide.

"Coille," he boomed. The rest of the group looked unfazed by the King's lack of formality. It was no secret Lord Coille, the Duke of Aldorwood, was the King's oldest friend.

"Marcus." Lord Coille clasped his hand. "It's good to see you, even under the circumstances."

"Yes, even then."

"Father," Trystan whispered. "What did he mean?"

"You'll find out soon enough."

A small woman who couldn't have had more than ten years on Trystan walked towards them. "Sire." She bowed.

"Lady Destan." The King gave the Duchess of Sona an affectionate smile. She turned her dazzling blue eyes on Trystan and her smile grew.

"My prince." Her voice was soft and melodic. "I'm happy you have been invited to join us."

"As am I, my lady." He inclined his head towards her.

"Is everyone here?" the King asked.

"We're missing Lord Eisner." The King's brother, Lord Drake, walked up behind them. "But we can start without that old fool."

The door burst open and a portly, swarthy-faced man ran in. He pulled a handkerchief from his pocket to dab at the sweat on his brow. "I'm sorry, gentlemen. My daughter has been causing problems again. I swear, show me a compliant woman, and I'll show you dice that can roll themselves."

A few men chuckled uncomfortably. Lady Destan took her seat quietly, her face showing no reaction. Trystan, on the other hand, couldn't hide the scowl as he looked at the Duke. The kingdom was made up of three realms – Aldorwood, the Isle of Sona, and Isenore. Trystan had always thought they were better off without the last of those and its Duke Eisner.

"Gentlemen," the King said, breaking the tension. "We have much to discuss. Let's get started, shall we?" He looked sideways at his scribe as the dukes took to their chairs and nodded. "We've begun receiving reports on this year's crops and can expect the yields to be down from last year."

"This is the third year in a row," Lord Coille interjected. "As most of the kingdom's farms are in my realm, we've been monitoring the situation closely. This year we had record freezes followed by extreme heat; flooding followed by drought."

"Our orchards on Sona have suffered as well," Lady Destan spoke up.

"What are you all saying?" Lord Eisner asked. "Are you trying to tell me we won't be getting our shipments in Isenore?"

"Food will have to be rationed," the King said.

"It was already rationed." Lord Eisner stood and leaned over the table. "In Isenore, we've been getting our jobs done. Our mines are booming and your iron shipments have been increased. If you think for one minute you can shorten our food supply –"

"Sit down, Eisner," the King boomed. "We all know your mines aren't as mighty as you say."

"If food is scarce," Trystan said, gathering his courage to speak. "Then why are we feasting tomorrow?"

"It's an important day," the king answered.

"What will the people think of us when they see dancing and gorging? It isn't right."

"The people," the King started, narrowing his eyes at his son. "Will see their prince taking his rightful position as Toha. We must give them pride in their kingdom, in their royal family."

"But -"

"Trystan," the King snapped. "Enough. It's too late to cancel it." He looked to Lord Drake who gave him a tiny nod and sighed. "We must keep up appearances. Everything must seem okay here at the palace."

"Who cares about appearances?"

The King slammed his fist down on the table, making Trystan jump. "The King of Dreach-Dhoun cares." He unclenched his fist and massaged it with his other hand. "We have reason to believe the King across the border has managed to put spies within these walls."

"What reasons?" The Duke of Isenore asked accusingly. "Why was I not told of this?"

"Our troop movements near the border have been compromised as if King Calis himself got a look at our maps. There have been small attacks. He's testing us. More than a few shipments have gone awry."

"None of this is anything new." Lord Coille scratched his thick beard. "Calis has been one step ahead of us for more than a decade, it seems."

"He grows bolder as we grow weak," Lady Destan said quietly.

"Speak for yourself, woman," Lord Eisner snarled.

She didn't rise to his bait. Her voice was calm, logical. "Of course, we're growing weaker. Every year we cut food rations. What happens when there are no more rations to cut? We can't let our people starve. Our world is falling apart. It snows when there should be heat. It's dry when it should rain. And it's not only the weather. Rivers have dried up while others have been created right where houses stand. I was only twelve when we lost our connection to the earth – our magic – but I remember what life was like with that bond. The earth took care of us, now it's dying and threatening to take us with it."

"Tomorrow marks the twenty-year anniversary of that dark day," Lord Coille said, forgetting talk of spies for just a moment.

Trystan leaned forward, wanting to hear more. He knew the day of his birth had been tumultuous for his people. He still found it hard to believe in magic. Everyone who was old enough to remember told stories of the time when anything was possible, but stories were all it was to him, imaginary.

"I remember it like it was yesterday," Lord Coille continued.

"We don't need to discuss this," Lord Eisner snapped.

"Of course, we do," he replied. "We must remember always." He looked to Trystan. "Now, son, there's something you need to understand, something young people need to be told, lest it be lost. It's spelled out in the Realm's name. Dreach is an ancient word for magic. It was the magic keeping the balance in the world. It came from the earth, but it was only there because of the Tri-Gard."

"I know all of this," Trystan said. "My tutors instructed me well. The three members of the Tri-Gard used their crystals to infuse the land with power."

Lord Coille nodded. "The three were a force for good until they were coerced into stripping the land of its power. Without being able to draw from the trees, the rocks, the very ground we walked on, our abilities disappeared. We were superior to Dreach-Dhoun in every way. We would have won the war. But, to this day, parts of their lands still hold immense power while ours are barren."

"This is a council meeting, not a history lesson," Lord Eisner interjected.

"Oh, do shut up." Lady Destan winked at Trystan before turning a scowl on Lord Eisner. "The difference between the two realms is in our intentions for the magic. Dreach-Sciene translates into light magic, but Dreach-Dhoun only means dark magic."

"I don't understand what this has to do with anything we're discussing," Trystan said, honestly curious.

"Oh, my boy, it has everything to do with it." Lord Coille leaned back in his chair and glanced at the king who gave him a nod to go on. "Our light magic kept our world in working order. It put clear distinctions between the seasons, allowing crops to thrive. It imbued nourishment into the soil. We've survived without it for twenty years, but each year has been worse than the one before it. We're at the end of our luck, I'm afraid."

"Has anyone been sent into Dreach-Dhoun to try to recover what was stolen?" Trystan looked to his father.

"If it were only so simple." The King sighed. "In order for power to be restored, the three guardians must be reunited. We know where one of them is." The King glanced towards his friend, Lord Coille. "He's in the dungeons of Dreach-Dhoun. The other two are in hiding and we have no way of finding them."

Trystan still wasn't sure if he believed, but looking around the table, he saw that they did and it was enough for him. A swell of duty inflated his chest as he thought of his people and his need to save them. "Send me, Father. I will find them."

"No." The response was quick and finite. "Absolutely not."

"I can do it," Trystan stated.

"We don't doubt you, Your Highness," Lord Coille said after

a moment of stubborn silence from the king. "But we're not even sure it can be done. Dreach-Dhoun is not the place for a prince."

"There's no negotiating, Trystan." The King's tone was not to be trifled with. "I have other plans for you. We're sending a contingent of our best soldiers to survey border defenses. Dreach-Dhoun is preparing for something. We need to root out their spies. You will remain here where you can prepare the troops who are about to be under your command. We must be ready."

It wasn't what Trystan wanted to hear, but he was a prince and he must follow the orders of the king. He lowered his gaze to the table, the weight of the title of Toha ever growing. "Yes, Sire."

When he looked back up, he met the Duchess of Sona's sympathetic gaze before looking beside her to where Lord Drake, his uncle, sat smirking. He sunk lower into his chair and listened attentively to the rest of the meeting, feeling deflated and angry.

"Nothing said here today is to get out." The King surveyed his council. "Not until we find the traitors. Understood?"

The dukes nodded as they trickled out, leaving Trystan with only his father and his uncle.

"Why was I not told before of the extent of the problems our people are facing? I still think it's wrong to feast when the people are set to starve." Trystan clenched his fists down by his sides and tried to keep his tone even. The King may have been his father, but he was still the king.

It was his uncle who answered. "Dreach-Dhoun must not see us in such dire straits, Your Highness."

Trystan blew out a long breath. "And what about what our people see?"

"Son." The King tried to put a reassuring arm around him, but he moved out of reach. "The matter is done."

"Unbelievable." Trystan yanked the door open and marched out into the hall, almost colliding with Davion.

Davion stumbled back as if hit and then dropped into a low bow. "I'm sorry, my prince. Next time you're charging around the castle like a headless horse, I'll be sure to stay out of your way." There was a twinkle in his eye as he raised his head.

"Idiot." Trystan crossed his arms over his chest and glanced behind him to make sure his father or uncle hadn't followed him out.

"Why are you in such a foul humor?" Davi asked. "I thought it was your lifelong dream to sit in with the dull and duller."

"I should have you whipped for insolence."

"Could work, if your father allowed whipping."

"We could always start." Trystan shrugged.

"You wound me, Your Highness." He held his hands over his heart and threw his head back.

"Can you be serious for a moment?"

"What is it?"

"Nothing," he sighed. "Just a prince following his orders."

"Well, soon you'll be a Toha following his orders." Davi smirked.

"Don't remind me." Trystan ran a hand over the top of his head. "I need a drink."

A slow smile spread across Davi's lips. "You're a mind reader. I'll bet you some of the guests are in the main hall. I was trying to find Alixa earlier."

"Who?" Trystan asked.

"She's the Duke of Isenore's daughter. We have yet to meet. The rumor is she's a true beauty, but a wild thing."

"Sounds like your kind of woman."

Davi shrugged. "Female is my kind of woman."

"I'll be sure to pass that on to my sister." Trystan laughed, letting it release some of the tension he'd been carrying.

Davi sighed. "Rissa only likes the familiar. She's young, she doesn't know any better."

"She's only two years younger than us."

"Ri is special, Trystan. You know it as well as I. But she's a princess. I'd never let myself go down such a route."

They entered the hall where many of their guests were playing dice, drinking, and listening to the fiddler.

"That's a good thing." Trystan nudged him. "Because it looks like she's hitting it off with one of the young noblemen who arrived today."

Davi followed Trystan's gaze and when he stiffened beside him, Trystan patted him on the back before going to grab a drink.

Rissa was sitting in the castle gardens, her favorite place to be, even if they were no longer lush and green. The loss of magic affected the castle grounds as well, and that which once thrived now lay brown and dull. Even so, the gardens had a calming effect on her; a soothing balm to her raw nerves. She seemed to suffer from nerves more and more these days after being around Davion. Deep in thought, a wrapped parcel clutched tight to her chest, she didn't hear footsteps approach until a quiet cough interrupted her. Turning around, she found her good friend, Willow, whose father was the Duke of Aldorwood.

"Hi Willow," Rissa said cheerfully. "What brings you out here so early?"

"I wanted to find you actually." She shifted from one foot to the next and it was only then that Rissa noticed she was carrying something.

"Well." Rissa laughed. "Why are you all jittery? It's not like you, unless ... oh, this has to do with my brother, doesn't it?"

The other girl's cheeks reddened and she looked down, her blonde curls falling in her face. Willow was the most beautiful girl she knew. Her perfect skin was pale and unmarked by the sun. Her soft hair was long and smooth. Gowns tended to hug her slender waist to perfection. And yet, Trystan never seemed to notice.

Their father and Willow's had been hoping for a wedding, officially combining the two families. Willow had the poise and intelligence to sit beside Trystan on the throne. Still, something had always been missing and it was obvious to everyone besides Willow.

"I have a present for him," she said shyly.

Rissa's grin widened. "Let's see it, then."

She held it out and Rissa uncovered a beautiful portrait of Trystan sitting atop his horse, his armor gleaming in the sun. He raised a sword above his head.

"Did you paint this?" Rissa asked.

Willow nodded.

"You've gotten so good." She looked up and met her friend's eyes. "He's going to love it."

"You think so?"

"Of course. Honestly, you could've left him out of it and just painted the sword." She laughed. "He loves that thing."

Willow laughed finally, relief rolling off her in waves. "You'll take it to him?"

"You don't want to come to his rooms with me? I'm going now."

"Of course not." Willow's eyes widened in shock, completely scandalized. She'd been raised by one of the most conservative women in the realm. Rissa was raised by men. That was the difference between them.

Rissa stood and brushed off her skirt before giving her friend a wink and heading towards her brother's room.

She knocked as she always had. Two raps. Pause. Three raps. He didn't answer so she pushed her way through and found him sitting on the end of his bed with his head in his hands.

He groaned and she laughed, crossing the room to throw open the curtains.

"Ri –"

"Stop your moaning," she said. "It's not my fault you drank enough to fill the sea last night and today's a big day."

"Don't remind me."

"Where's Davi?" she asked. "Passed out in some random girl's bed, I assume."

"Jealousy isn't flattering, sis."

"I'm glad you're always telling me where my heart lies," she snapped. "After all, I'm just a poor woman who can't decide anything for herself."

Trystan started to laugh and couldn't seem to stop himself. He leaned back on his bed, trying to catch his breath, and shut his eyes.

Rissa grinned at him. "Happy birthday, big brother."

Opening one eye, he looked at her. "You know, I think you're the only person who thinks of today as my birthday and not just the day I become Toha."

"Not the only one." She sat across from him and handed him the painting when he sat up fully.

"Willow?"

"Yup."

"It's beautiful."

"You better remember to tell her."

"I will. Now, what'd you get me?" he asked.

"Greedy, greedy." She tossed the parcel at him, laughing when it hit him in the chest.

He unwrapped it. "A book of stories?" he asked.

"I figured everything from here on out is going to be about your duty to the people." She met his eyes. "I wanted to remind you to forget about it sometimes. Disappear into something else and do something for you. Do you remember, you used to love storybooks? You were obsessed with Trystan the Bold."

"Thank you," he said quietly, looking down at the book and then back at her with unspoken emotions crossing his face.

"What's wrong, brother? And don't tell me it's nothing because you look like I've just thrown your favorite sword down the well or something."

He chuckled and leaned forward to bury his face in his hands again. "Just thinking."

"A dangerous endeavor."

He tilted his head to glare at her and she sighed.

"Trystan."

He opened his mouth to speak but seemed to rethink his words. "I can't tell you."

"And why not?"

"Council stuff."

She huffed at that.

"Just … it's bad, Ri. There are things happening that none of us can control." He groaned. "What if I'm not enough?"

"Of course, you are."

"I'm about to become the commander of the army and I've never been in battle. How am I supposed to help if we are to go to war?"

War? She didn't know what he was talking about, but she

did know her brother. She touched his shoulder lightly. "You've been preparing for this your entire life. Just because your sword has never drawn blood, doesn't mean you aren't the right person to lead us."

He sighed. "After today, I wonder if the Toha is all I'll be. How will it change me?"

Rissa scooted forward and wrapped her arms around her brother's solid shoulders, squeezing as hard as she could.

"It is the title which must bend to its bearer," she said, leaning back. "Not the other way around."

DESPITE THE TRADITIONS and expectations of being a royal, Trystan was never one to allow servants to help him dress. He figured if he couldn't dress himself, then he wasn't fit to lead his men to war. Because that's what would be asked of him eventually. It was always there, right on the border, the threat. Eventually, they'd be forced to fight just to survive because the land was no longer providing for them.

His elders said it was the lack of magic creating difficulties for their people. Fairy tales. That's what it sounded like to him.

He didn't know magic. He knew the tip of a sword, the taut string of a bow. He knew a starving people and a garden that struggled to bloom.

He pulled the silk shirt over his head. It was blue with gold embroidery. The sleeves puffed out when they reached passed his elbows. Together with the tight-fitting trousers and green jacket, he looked like a popinjay. He glanced at himself in the looking glass as he tied the belt at his waist and shook his head.

He'd rather wear his armor.

But he was a prince, not merely a soldier. He was soon to be Toha, guardian of the realm. Every firstborn son or daughter of the royal family held that title until the day they became king or queen. A day he hoped was a long way off.

The Toha led the realm's fighting men and traveled far and wide to keep an eye on the defenses.

He sat on the edge of his bed and pulled on his black leather boots. It was almost time. A servant entered the room and attempted to bend down to tie the Prince's laces, but Trystan waved him away. "Go," he ordered.

The servant issued a quick bow and practically ran from the Prince's harsh tone.

With a sigh, Trystan finished tying his laces and stood. He attached his sword to his waist and breathed deeply before stepping from his quarters. Three guards had been waiting outside his door and they formed up behind him without a word.

The halls were quiet as even the servants were in the hall for the ceremony. Rissa came running towards him, her dress twisting about her legs. Its green matched his jacket and set off her deep red hair like a blaze of fire as it danced around her shoulders.

She was out of breath when she caught up to him.

"Ri." He'd have laughed at her panting had he not been so nervous.

"I wanted to catch you before you reached the hall." She fell in step beside him and straightened her dress.

Trystan shook his head. His sister was the only woman he knew who would run through the palace in a gown and heels. She was crazy and he was thankful to have her at his side.

"Are you nervous?" she asked.

He just stared at her.

"Right." She laughed. "Stupid question." Her feet slowed before they reached the hall and she gripped his arm to make him stop. "You're going to do great." She pulled him into a hug and he was quick to return the gesture. "I believe in you."

When she finally pulled away, there were tears in her eyes. She did her best to wipe them away, but Trystan grabbed her hand. "Sis, don't cry."

"It's just …" She paused and looked him in the eye. "After today, we won't be just the prince and princess anymore. Just us. Everything's about to change, isn't it?"

"We are always changing, Rissa."

"But I don't want us to change." She pointed her finger at herself then to him.

He put a hand on each of her shoulders and bent his head to meet her gaze. "Never. You'll always be my little sister."

She smiled and wiped away the remnants of her tears. "Let's go make you Toha."

Their father was standing outside the hall with the two dukes and one duchess of the realm. The Duchess of Sona flashed a brilliant smile when she caught sight of them. The Duke of Aldorwood stepped forward to clasp a hand on Trystan's shoulder. The Duke of Isenore turned to ready himself for their entry.

"Are you ready, my boy?" Lord Coille asked.

"I was born for this," Trystan answered. It was what they all expected, what they wanted, and the nervousness drifted away as he realized he was stepping into the role he was always meant to play.

His father beamed as he pulled Trystan and Rissa away for a private word. "Son," he began. "I'm so proud of the man you are becoming. Don't let anyone ever say you're not worthy."

Trystan lifted his chin to meet his father's eyes and straightened his shoulders, pride giving him a boost of confidence. "Thank you, Father. I will do my best for you. I promise."

The King smiled and turned to Rissa reaching out to cup her cheek. "And you, my darling girl, are precious without the title." He looked her from head to toe and smiled. "You look so very much like your mother."

The King entered the hall first and a hush fell over the audience. Trystan stood in the doorway with his sister by his side. He wished Davi had been allowed to stand with him as well, but only those of noble blood were allowed to take part in the ceremony.

Rissa gave his hand a final squeeze before dropping it and walking forward in time with him. A soft melody drifted through the large hall as every person in the room rose to their feet and trained their eyes on their prince and princess.

Trystan looked straight ahead as the walk seemed to go on forever. His father's beaming face from before had now turned into the stoic face of the king.

The dukes and duchess followed in close behind with Lord Drake and they all stopped when they reached the front. The entire ceremony was choreographed perfectly. Rissa stepped back and Trystan kneeled on the ground in the place where the stone floor was broken, revealing a small patch of earth.

His knees hit the dirt and he knew he should have felt something, but he didn't feel the connection with the earth his sister did – no matter how hard he tried.

Once upon a time, all of the people of the realm had a connection – or so he'd been told.

Now it was only symbolic, a relic from long ago.

The dukes, duchess, royal uncle, princess, and king formed up around him.

"We are here today to celebrate our prince taking on a sacred duty," the King said, raising his voice for all to hear. "The Toha is the second highest position in the land. He controls the armies, but that is the least of his responsibilities. He protects us from those who would destroy our way of life. I held the position of Toha before becoming king, but it was a different time, and I failed. We lost a lot in my time and it's time I pass the mantle to one who is worthier than me – my son."

The King looked down on Trystan. "Are you prepared to take on this responsibility?"

"I am," Trystan answered.

"Will you do what is necessary to keep the people safe?"

"I will."

"Are you prepared to sacrifice and give everything to the role?"

"I am."

"Even if it means your life?"

"Yes."

"Will you trust those in your command? Will you listen and reason?"

"I will."

The King finally smiled. "Prince Trystan Marcus Renauld of Dreach-Sciene, you are charged with providing hope, guidance, and skill. You are charged with the guardianship of this realm, from the Isle of Sona to the mountains of Isenore to the forests of Aldorwood. You knelt as a prince. Now rise as Toha."

Trystan patted the earth and got to his feet.

The King pulled a sword from the scabbard at his waist and held the blade in his palms as he extended it towards Trystan.

Trystan sucked in a breath as he took the sword. It was magnificent. It was balanced perfectly - sturdy, yet light. The hilt was made of gold that snaked up the blade. On the gold hilt was the image of a tree surrounded by symbols he didn't understand.

Trystan removed his own sword, the one he'd had for years. It too was a beauty. He knew the next moment was crucial. He was supposed to choose someone to bestow his sword upon, a prince's sword. A man who would become his second in command. There were no rules, but tradition stated it would be someone with noble blood in their veins. His father had suggested the Duke of Isenore's son, as he'd one day be one of the most powerful nobles.

That was the plan, anyway. In that moment, Trystan knew there was only one man worthy. Only one man he wanted at his side.

His feet carried him across the hall, past the Duke of Isenore's son. Past the other young nobles who had been given seats near the front of the hall. The servants sat further down and among them was the man he considered his brother.

He was loyal and skilled, honest and brave.

A gasp reverberated around the room as Trystan stopped and stepped around a girl sitting on the end of the row. He extended his old sword towards Davion.

Davi's eyes widened and his mouth tried to form words. If he accepted, no one would question his blood again. He wouldn't need to be a noble, he'd be respected as the Toha's second. He'd no longer be the orphan boy, the charity case.

"Do you accept?" Trystan asked.

His friend's eyes glassed over, but he did a good job of holding it together.

Trystan nodded in encouragement. "Truwa, Brathair." The words were for Davi's ears only.

Davion grasped the hilt of the extended sword. "Trust." He grinned. "Brother." He raised his voice for the audience to hear and cleared his throat. "Yes, Toha. I accept."

Trystan held his own sword out and Davi raised his to cross their blades.

The prince turned and marched back towards the front as the crowd's murmuring continued. He formed up with Rissa on his right and his father on his left. Together, they left the hall.

Once outside, Trystan could finally breathe again. It was done.

"Trystan," his father said. There was no chastisement in his voice, only resignation. "You could've secured a powerful noble's full support in there and yet you chose a commoner."

"I promised you in there I would trust my men, Father. There isn't anyone I trust more than Davion."

The King nodded slowly. "Whenever I see images of your son, it's Davion by his side. He will be his greatest protector and most loyal friend."

"What?" Trystan asked.

The King seemed to shake himself out of a trance. "One day, Son, I will tell you about the night I brought Davion home and the woman who convinced me he was worth it." With those words, he walked away, leaving Trystan alone with his sister.

Rissa stood on her toes and gave Trystan a kiss on the cheek.

"What was that for?" he asked.

"You did a good thing in there."

He studied her sadly. He may be able to choose Davi as his

man, but Rissa would never be able to choose him in the way she wished.

"Come on, Brother," she said, attempting a smile. "We have a ball to prepare for."

"Don't remind me."

The grand ballroom was filled to capacity with royalty, high-born nobles, and knights, the crème de la crème of Dreach-Sciene society. The perfume of flowers, wine, and delectable food drifted on the warm air, along with the flourish of a violin and the laughter of those in attendance. Chandeliers glowed overhead and sparkled off of the crystal and jewels scattered throughout the room. The ball was being held in Trystan's honor, and he was well aware it was part of the Toha tradition and had been since long before his time. The knowledge did nothing to alleviate the guilt brewing in his gut ever since finding out the true indigence of his kingdom or the desire to be anywhere else but here.

"Smile, Trystan," Davi whispered at him from behind his own grin and goblet of wine. Both men stood at the front of the room near the King's table, affording them the best view to overlook the guests as they danced and chatted to one another. "This is an important day for our kingdom and you. You've finally been made Toha. And because of your insanity, I'm to be your second in command. I guess the good thing is it's quite literally an invitation for the ladies to throw themselves at our feet."

Trystan laughed behind the guise of taking a sip from the goblet in his hand. "Really, Davi? You have a one-track mind, my friend."

Davi raised a dark brow in puzzlement. "And what else should I be thinking about at the moment? The fact that the sword you gave me comes with the weight of responsibility on its blade?" He clapped Trystan on the shoulder. "I'm honored you chose me, Brother. But our duty can wait until tomorrow. The night is young and so are we. The room is filled with beautiful women, drink, and food. What more could we ask for?"

Trystan sighed as he tugged at the constricting collar of his silk shirt. Normally Davi's enthusiasm amused him, but tonight it only fueled his irritation. Davi noticed the annoyance and regarded his friend in confusion.

"Seriously, Trystan. This is supposed to be the most important day of your life. I've heard you whine about this day for years. Yet here we now stand and you act as insolent as a scorned wife instead of a newly titled Toha. What is wrong?"

Trystan let his gaze slide around the room. "Does this indulgence not bother you, Davi? There's enough food here to feed the villagers for a week. Does it not raise concern that we will gorge ourselves tonight while the rest of the realm lives in poverty? And that it will only get worse?" He pointed to the table laden with silver dishes filled to overflowing with rich fruit, spicy meats, and sweets of all sorts. His father had spared no expense, despite the royal coffers being nearly empty. Servants in livery bearing large trays of food and drink moved about the room, tending to the guests every want. Women clustered in groups, sneaking glances at Trystan from behind their fluttering fans; clad in a rainbow of silk gowns adorned with brooches and necklaces and jewels all meant to impress the future king. All it did was enforce the brutal reality of dissent burning in his belly.

His new second in command stared at him over the rim of his goblet. "What do you mean, it will only get worse? I know we are in lean times, but we have been before. Surely this will pass like it always has."

It was on the tip of Trystan's tongue to spill the facts discussed in the earlier council meeting. It was second nature to tell all to his friend of fifteen years. They had no secrets. But his father and the other council members had trusted him with grave information and he'd made a promise to keep it to himself. He wouldn't share it with Davi until he had permission and now was not that time.

"Forgive me, friend. I've been Toha for a matter of mere hours but already I worry about the realm like some old mother. You are right. This too shall pass."

Davi laughed in agreement as he slapped Trystan on the back. "Spoken like a true leader. Why worry yourself over things you can't control? Soon you will have enough worry on your plate as general of the guard. But not tonight. Tonight, we have fun. Look about the room. You can have your pick of any of these beauties. They would fall over themselves for the chance to dance with the future king. So, which one will it be?"

"Davi…"

"Just humor me, Trystan. Pick one."

There was no use arguing. Once Davi's mind was made up, there was no changing it. Giving in, his eyes moved about the room once more, passing over the peacock-mimicking ladies of the court. He found Rissa standing with the Duchess of Sona, Willow and one other, all deep in conversation. Willow glanced up and caught his eye, her face flushing a bright red at his perusal before she looked away. His gaze moved past Rissa and the Duchess to the one he did not know. Against his better judgment, his eyes stopped on this person who appeared even less thrilled to be here than he was.

She was dressed in a simple yellow gown, the clean lines and high waist emphasizing her shapely figure. Her caramel-colored skin highlighted the light eyes in the heart shaped face, and errant strands of dark curls escaped from the pile adorning the top of her head. No jewels or brooches to be seen. She didn't need them. She met his curious gaze head on and instead of dropping her eyes like Willow had done, this one stared back with a look akin to hostility.

"Who is the one in the yellow gown with Ri?" he asked with interest, even though his false look of indifference had already moved on.

"Ah, she, I believe, is the infamous Alixa, daughter of the Duke of Isenore. You have good taste."

Trystan turned his eyes Davi's way. "She's the duke's daughter? Why have we not met before?"

Davi shrugged. "She's never been to court. It's said her father and brother are overbearingly protective of her. I can see why. She's as fetching as they say, but they also say her temper is just as magnificent." He raised one brow in question. "Shall we go over and find out for ourselves if the rumor is true?"

Trystan was as surprised as Davion when he found himself agreeing.

They made their way across the floor, Trystan pausing occasionally to graciously accept the smiles and murmurs of congratulations. As they approached the women, all conversation ceased and four sets of eyes greeted their arrival, some holding more warmth than others. The Duchess, as welcoming as always, was the first to speak.

"Congratulations, Your Highness, on becoming Toha. You honor us and the realm with your courage and ability. "

Trystan inclined his head in acknowledgment. "Thank you, Lady Destan. May I not let you or the realm down in your expectations." Bowing his head to Willow, he continued, "Willow, a pleasure as always. Thank you for the thoughtful birthday gift. It will hang in my chambers with honor." He ignored her giggle of girlish pleasure as his eyes fell on the duke's daughter. Before he'd had a chance to speak in any way, however, Davi interrupted with his usual tact.

"Princess, Lady Destan, Lady Willow. You are all visions of loveliness tonight as usual. But this new vision isn't one I'm familiar with. Rissa, why don't you introduce us to your new friend?" He smiled at the raven-haired beauty and grasped her fingers in his, placing a light kiss on the back of her hand. "I'm Davion, by the way, the Toha's second in command."

Rissa rolled her eyes as she stepped Alixa's way, placing herself between Davi and the girl and forcing him to drop her hand. "Trystan, is it too late to rescind the appointment? Because if I have to listen to that line for the next year, I swear I will rip off my own ears." She countered Davi's indignation with an irritated frown. "Alixa, this is my brother, Trystan. Trystan, this is Lady Alixa, daughter to the Duke of Isenore."

"A pleasure to make your acquaintance, Lady Alixa. Welcome to Dreach-Sciene." Trystan wasn't sure what to expect as he took the girl's slender hand in his. Maybe a shy smile. A nervous laugh. It certainly wasn't the look of disdain in the hazel eyes as they traveled over Trystan's face with an insolence he was not accustomed to.

"Your Highness," she said, but the words sounded as if they had to be pulled from her lips. "Thank you for our invitation to such a lavish affair. I don't think I've ever seen so many delicacies or so much food offered at once. I'm pleased to see your kingdom is so bountiful while others are not."

The words were innocent enough, but the tone left no doubt as to their intent. It was a reprimand rolled up in polite conversation. If Trystan wasn't so shocked and amused at the blatant scolding, he'd have been fascinated someone else saw this whole unnecessary affair from his point of view.

None of that showed as he responded in true prince fashion. "Davion informs me this is the first time you have graced us with your presence. I hope you're enjoying your first visit to court, my lady. I'm surprised your father hasn't brought you before this. He's quite a frequent visitor."

"Indeed, he is," the girl responded back, keeping her sham smile in place. "My father is, shall we say, a connoisseur of court life. I, on the other hand, prefer to stay in Isenore with my people. I'm a true believer in earning the respect of one's subjects by working side by side with them. Toil the land with them. Break a sweat with them. Earn a blister or two from the hard work." She turned Trystan's hand, still holding hers, palm up and dropped her eyes. Lightly, she ran a finger over the slight calluses on the otherwise smooth skin "Something I see you yourself aren't familiar with…. Toha."

She added the word of respect almost as an afterthought as if she knew she'd gone too far with the insult. And it was a flagrant insult. Four heads swiveled back and forth following the exchange between the prince and the dark-haired girl with intense interest.

A spark of irritation ignited in Trystan's chest. He pulled his hand out of Alixa's grasp as he studied her with narrowed eyes. Who did this girl think she was? She knew nothing about him or his beliefs, yet she presumed to judge him without any proof or evidence.

"A fine sentiment indeed. I'm sure you've had much experience with slaving in the iron mines of Isenore yourself, yes?"

Alixa flushed, but didn't respond so he continued.

"And you are correct. My calluses are caused by my sword and not a farm hoe. But pray tell, fine lady, what use would knowledge of crops and cattle do a Toha in battle? Would blistered hands and dirty nails help prevent an army invasion? Or perhaps the enemy could be turned away with talk of crop rotation or fertilizer?"

"That knowledge is more important than you seem to be aware, Your Highness. Swords and arrows may keep out an army but they can't kill poverty or hunger. Death is death no matter by what means you approach it." Her smile hardened as if she was preparing herself for battle. This was obviously something she felt strongly about and Trystan found himself intrigued by her passion.

"Here now. No talking about death," Davi interrupted with his usual contagious laughter. "You may not be aware of this, Lady Alixa, but it's Trystan's birthday as well as his Toha commencement. Talk of armies or death isn't allowed. Not tonight." He glanced to the center of the room where people were congregating as the music started flowing again and dropped a hand on Trystan's shoulder. "I think the pressure of the day has gotten to you, Your Highness. You're way too uptight. I think you need to let loose. Dance a little. And we all know there's no better dancer in court than our very own

Willow. Toha, why don't you escort the beautiful Lady Willow onto the dance floor?"

Typical Davi, never one to be serious about anything. Trystan sighed as Alixa dropped her gaze from his and looked away, her lips sealed in a tight grimace. The conversation was over. He was strangely disappointed. Even more so when he noticed Willow's excited look of hope at the dance suggestion. Freaking Davi. He knew better than to encourage the girl's infatuation. Trystan was quite aware of Willow's expectations for their future together. For some reason, he couldn't find himself a portion as excited. But he couldn't leave the poor girl dangling at the moment. So, being the chivalrous gentleman he was, he bowed slightly in Willow's direction.

"Davi is right. There's no one I'd rather have accompany me on the dance floor. Shall we?"

THE OTHER FOUR watched them walk away and Davi chuckled as Trystan threw a 'you're so going to pay for this' look over his shoulder.

Rissa couldn't help the laugh that escaped her as well. "Consider yourself warned, Davion. It's a good thing he thinks so highly of you, otherwise, he'd have had you put to death long ago."

"He wouldn't dare."

"You seem very confident." The smile Alixa threw Davi's way seemed much more genuine than the one she'd favored Trystan with, and Davi -never one to ignore any sort of female attention- responded by puffing out his chest in exaggerated importance.

"As the Toha's second in command" -he ignored Rissa's

49

MICHELLE BRYAN & M LYNN

slight snort of derision- "as his second in command, I need to be confident. I need to be open and honest. Plus, I've known the prince for so long we're practically brothers. The Princess, too. Right, sis?" He threw a lopsided grin Rissa's way. The Duchess and Alixa laughed at Davi's impudence, but the comment seemed to annoy the Princess. Gathering her skirts up in her hands, she pinned him with a hard stare.

"Don't be absurd. I have but one brother, and it is not you." She walked away, her back rigid with displeasure as his puzzled, "What did I say wrong?" rang in her ears.

His sister? Ugh. Rissa didn't even know if she was his friend right then. She wanted nothing more than to strangle him for the way he made her heart squeeze when he said that single word. Sis.

Davion was infuriating. She'd watched him flirt with the court ladies shamelessly since he was old enough his voice didn't crack. Even the servants were recipients of his attention. Rissa knew his every move. He'd flip his dark hair out of his eyes and puff out his chest. It used to be humorous because there wasn't much chest to puff out. He'd been a scrawny kid growing up.

Then, all at once he wasn't. The Princess didn't know when it happened, it just did. The scrawny boy became the broad-shouldered man. The blue eyes that always appeared wary as if expecting to do something wrong, were now darkly lashed and full of confidence and charm. He became the object of all the young women's desires. They'd do anything for attention. Even

Alixa – who Rissa thought was a stone-faced woman – had softened to a pile of goo when Davi pulled out his charm. Or horse crap. Rissa would rather think they became soft like crap when they fell for it.

But she fell for it, too.

And she was a princess, making it the worst of all.

Her father was actively negotiating with nobles of the realm for her hand in marriage. Trystan's too, but Rissa knew Lord Coille would win that prize for his daughter. She felt sad for her brother. He didn't love Willow. But he would be king and a king doesn't have the option to fall in love. Except their father had loved their mother.

Rissa stood in a darkened corner of the ballroom, trying to avoid all of the people who would do or say anything for a moment of the Princess' time. The lords and ladies seemed to be enjoying themselves. The wine had been flowing freely for hours and rosy-faced pairings pranced around the dance floor.

"Excuse me, princess," a gruff voice said to her right.

She turned her head to look at the hulking man who'd walked up beside her, recognizing him instantly. She'd only met Royce Eisner for the first time yesterday, but it hadn't taken long to see through his arrogant manner. She liked him even less than his ice-queen of a sister, Alixa.

She eyed him warily. "Hello, it's nice to see you again, Royce." Lies.

Even his smile looked creepy. She knew most of the lords expected Trystan to choose Royce as his second in command. Many of them would see it as a comment on Royce's character. Rissa knew the decision had nothing to do with Royce. It was about how much her brother trusted Davion.

But she was still glad it wasn't Royce. It would have meant him living in the palace with them.

Her skin crawled as his eyes scanned her from head to toe. He was an attractive man – with the olive skin associated with the people of Isenore, and wide set amber eyes – but there was something very off about him.

"May I have the honor of this dance?" he asked.

Rissa wanted more than anything to say no, but her father's voice popped into her head. He wouldn't want her offending the future Duke of Isenore. She looked around for a legitimate excuse and her eyes connected with Davi's across the room.

Her lips tilted up and she placed her hand in Royce's. "I would love to dance."

He led her to the center of the dance floor and took her into his arms. Rissa kept a respectable distance between them and let the music fill her mind. She loved to dance and in time she could almost forget who her partner was.

Or at least she could forget until they spun and she saw her father standing with Lord Eisner. They talked as their eyes followed Rissa and Royce around. Rissa glanced up at her partner who was giving their fathers some sort of knowing nod.

No, she thought. *No, no, no, no, no.*

With a suddenness that startled those around them, Rissa pushed away from Royce. He reached for her, but she was already backing away. She didn't look over to see her father's reaction or that of Lord Eisner.

"No," she said. "This is not happening."

Her breath wheezed in her chest as she spun around and pushed through stunned onlookers. Their princess was going crazy and they wanted a front row seat. She had to get out of there. Reaching down, she picked up the ends of her long dress and kicked off her heeled shoes, leaving them where they lay. Then, without pause, she started running. Past the tables laden with food and drink. Past her father, looking on in worry and disappointment. Past the lords and ladies of the realm who viewed her as nothing more than an ornamental princess. And out the door.

Torches lit her path as she ran on bare feet across the stone floor. There were no guards in that part of the palace as they were in the hall where the royal family was supposed to be. She knew a few of them would be along soon – if they could find her.

She ducked off into a side corridor that led to a tiny doorway, only used by the palace gardeners – or gardener, as they only had need for one now. He did the best he could, but Rissa's favorite place still continued to wither away.

She lifted the bolt and slid it to the side to allow the door to swing open. Not bothering to close it behind her, she stepped out into the night air. A shiver ran through her as the cold permeated her skin. It had been warm only days before, but it had been years since the weather patterns were stable.

Rubbing her hands up and down her bare arms, she walked further into the garden. The farther she got from the palace walls, the darker it became. But she didn't need light. She knew the garden as well as she knew any place.

Dead grass crunched underneath her toes and a tear slid down her cheek. By the time she reached the large tree standing in the center of the garden, her sight was blurry with tears.

Her father was going to marry her to Royce. She was sure of it. She'd seen the looks. Royce had never done anything to her, but there was a darkness inside him. All one had to do was look into his eyes to see it. If she were to wed him, her light would wither and die. And then there was the fact that her heart already belonged to someone she couldn't have.

Her eyes trailed up the tree's trunk. She'd been told it used to bloom beautifully. Colorful flowers would hang from its branches. She touched the smooth bark and slid to the ground, letting her dress crumple beneath her.

Auburn curls fell into her face as she bent forward to place both palms on the ground. She hadn't yet been born when the earth was stripped of its magic, but sometimes she thought she could feel a jolt of strength coming from its very core. A hum filled her ears and she gave in to the connection, just wanting to get lost in it.

Her palms vibrated against the earth as a warmth filled her veins. She wondered if that's what it felt like to have magic. She dreamed of it sometimes, of being in total harmony with the land around her.

Tears continued to stream down her face as she looked around at the bleak garden. That was as strong as the earth got, enough to fill her with sadness for what it could no longer do.

"Ri?" A voice broke through her trance. It sounded far away. "Rissa." Closer. "What are you doing?"

As soon as recognition slammed into her, she yanked her hands back from the ground. The humming stopped abruptly. She wiped furiously at her face. The man in front of her didn't get her tears.

Steeling herself, she rose to her feet and did her best to brush the dirt from her dress, knowing it was probably a goner.

"What do you want?" she snapped.

Davion ran a hand through his long hair. She'd told him to tie it back numerous times, but Davi never obeyed.

Rissa crossed her arms over her chest, still waiting for an answer.

"I wanted to make sure you're okay," he finally stammered.

Was he nervous? Rissa didn't believe it. Davion never got nervous.

"Okay," she scoffed. "Why wouldn't I be okay? Doesn't every daughter want their father to sell them off like a fatted pig at festival?"

"What are you talking about?"

"Oh, and that husband of mine is just the greatest." She leaned forward conspiratorially. "You know, if he continues making me want to puke, I may just turn out as thin as those girls you're always chasing. Doesn't everyone want a husband who makes them better?"

"Wait a second." Davi stepped forward abruptly. "You're getting married?"

"I think 'congratulations' is what you're supposed to say." Her sarcasm was not lost on him.

"Who is it?" he growled.

"Royce Eisner."

Davi kicked at a rock on the ground, sending it flying towards the tree. He stepped back and began pacing. "You can't …" He stopped. His fists clenched at his sides. His voice was strangled when he spoke again. "Not him."

Rissa's shoulders dropped as the cracks in her façade of strength widened. Tears welled in her eyes once again. "I won't have a choice. I'm not really your sister, Davi. I'm the princess and as princess, I have a duty to my family." She shivered as the last warmth she'd taken from the earth left her and the cold air made the hair on her arms stand on end.

Davi shrugged out of his jacket and swung it around her shoulders. He bent down to whisper in her ear. "I know you aren't my sister."

"Then why did you say it?" She spun to face him and found him closer than she'd thought. His breath warmed her face and she stood mesmerized by his bright eyes rimmed by long, elegant lashes.

"I don't know," he breathed. "Sometimes, I think we need boundaries. Everything would be easier if I thought of you as my sister."

"But you don't?"

His eyes flicked from her eyes to her lips and back again.

When he didn't answer her, she pulled back. "I'm sorry."

"For what?" he asked.

"I must look like a wreck all tear-streaked and covered in dirt."

"Ri." He reached out to brush a thumb under her eye. A smile curved his lips. "I've seen you in much worse."

Rissa choked out a laugh, relieved some of the tension between them drifted away. Theirs had always been an easy friendship. Only now, it felt as if it was all breaking away.

"You're always beautiful to me, princess."

And then he went and said something like that and the tension snapped back into place. Rissa sucked in a breath as Davi's thumb traveled down to trace the curves of her lips. His fingers found their way beneath her chin and tilted her face up to look at him. He wanted to kiss her. She could see it in his eyes. And she'd kiss him back with everything she had.

Then her heart would break because a kiss was all they could ever have. She was a princess and he was an orphan boy – no title, no land, not even a last name. Tears fell freely and she saw his eyes glass over. He knew as well as she what their positions in life allowed for them.

"I can't marry Royce," she cried. "Not when my heart belongs here with … my family."

He pulled her to him in a firm hug and rested his trembling

chin on the top of her head. "I'm sorry." Just two words, nothing else.

Rissa wished he had more for her.

Pressed against his chest, she felt the pounding of Davi's heart and imagined it pounded for her. But she knew that was all it was. Imaginary. Fantasy. Davi might call her beautiful, he might get close enough to kiss, but she'd seen him do the very same with countless women. He didn't know how to turn it off and she was always forgiving him for that.

But she wasn't a little girl with a crush anymore. She was a grown princess who knew what she could never have. A sigh escaped her lips and she knew Davi would misconstrue the meaning as contentment rather than a soul-crushing realization she would do as her father intended. She'd obey. She'd submit. It wasn't in her to rebel.

"There you are." Trystan's voice broke their moment. "I thought I saw Davi come this way." His footsteps came to an abrupt halt as he looked closer.

Rissa pushed away from Davi as quick as she could. Davi looked towards the ground, the sky, anywhere but at the prince and princess.

"It's dark out here," Trystan said, playing oblivious to what he'd just walked in on.

Rissa was grateful he chose to ignore what he'd observed. "You should be back at your ball, brother." She grabbed Trystan's arm and spun him around to try and lead him away.

"You mean the one you guys left me at?" he asked. "Thanks for that, by the way. I just barely escaped another dance with Willow."

Rissa slapped his chest. "Willow is a perfectly nice girl."

"She is," Trystan agreed. "But she's just …" He couldn't think of the word.

"Boring?" Davi said helpfully. "Hopelessly dull."

"Davion," Rissa growled. "Willow is my friend." She turned back to Trystan. "She's very beautiful."

"Too beautiful," Davi said. "She's like a doll. Play with her the wrong way and she might break. Could have been worse, however, my prince. We could've left you with Lady Alixa. Which would you have preferred? The doll or the ice-queen? I think we chose wisely for you."

"Davi, you're such an ass." Rissa shoved him and he laughed as he pretended to stumble back. Righting himself, he flicked a strand of her hair.

"But an honest one. Now you, little princess, you've got fire."

"I'm sure Royce will love my fire," she said bitterly.

Davi looked at Trystan over her head and each threw an arm around her, wedging her in between them. "You'll just have to make sure he gets burned."

She shook her head, realizing Davi would never understand. He'd never have a duty to his family, not like her and her brother. Trystan stayed quiet and it was because he knew. He too would have to face his duty. The difference was he got to stay when she'd be sent away.

But squeezed in between Trystan and Davion, Rissa felt like it was going to be okay even though in her heart she knew changes were coming. It couldn't stay the three of them forever.

Rissa ran a hand over the familiar, smooth curve of her bow. She knew what she was good at and what escaped her capabilities. She couldn't sew, despite the hours and hours of her governess forcing her to do so as a child. Her embroideries left much to be desired. She wasn't interested in fashion as many of the noble women were.

But she could shoot an arrow as well as any man in the realm's army. That may have been an exaggeration, but she was good. Finally giving up on developing talents suited to a noblewoman, her father first gave her a bow when she turned twelve years old and she'd finally felt like she had something to give.

She'd wanted to learn to fight, but her father said it was not a possibility. It wasn't because she was a woman – there were many women in the fighting forces – but it was because she was the princess. All of the women soldiers were commoners. It was acceptable among them.

Turning her body at an angle to the target, Rissa lifted her bow.

"You should widen your feet a bit more," her brother said, stepping up behind her.

She shook her head and looked back at him. Without moving her feet or glancing back at the target, she nocked an arrow and in one quick movement she'd drawn the string and released. She was still looking at Trystan when she heard the soft thud of an arrow hitting the target.

"Did I hit?" she asked with a smug smile.

"Right in the center."

"See, Toha, stick to what you know." She patted him on the shoulder and shooed him away. He didn't leave as she proceeded to hit the target three more times.

Trystan was an expert with a sword, but he'd never been able to best his sister with bow and arrow.

"I have to go meet Avery for some troop inspections," he said. "It's always a morale boost to the soldiers when you're there. Care to join me?"

She set her bow on the rack nearby and followed him towards the training yard. "Is your second in command going to be there?" She'd been avoiding Davi in the weeks since their emotionally charged moment at the ball. He'd been giving her looks that made it too hard to think about what her future held.

"I've sent him with an important message to Lord Coille," Trystan answered.

"What message?"

"I don't know. It was from Father and was not disclosed to me." The irritation was plain in his voice.

"So, Father sent your second in command on a journey that would take two days each way and didn't tell you why?"

"It's not my place to question the king."

"When did he leave?"

"Four days ago."

Davi hadn't been in the palace in four days and she hadn't noticed? At least she was doing the avoiding thing right.

Avery Payne was already in the training yard practicing with a young man who looked like he was new to the world of swordcraft. The boy danced around the sword-master with wild swings rather than the calculated cuts of his opponent.

Avery sliced at the boy and then spun to swipe his feet out from under him before holding the tip of a wooden sword under his chin.

"You're improving," the sword-master said, reaching down to help him to his feet. "Last time it took me half as long to fell you. The ability to learn is the most important thing. Next is the willingness to make the daring moves rather than only the safe ones. You don't win a battle only by protecting yourself. You win by having the courage to expose yourself to attack in order to take the final blow."

The boy nodded eagerly. Avery gave a jerk of the head to tell the boy to get out of there and he scurried off.

Trystan grinned. "Still the best sword-master we have, I see."

Rissa could remember hours upon hours of sitting there watching Avery train both Trystan and Davi. They wouldn't be as skilled as they were without their teacher.

"Toha." She inclined her head. The short-cropped gray hair had been a chestnut brown when she'd first started training a young Trystan, but in all that time, she'd never dropped the formality of their positions. Only now, Prince had turned into Toha.

"Avery." Rissa walked forward and gave the taller woman a

hug. "I'm glad you're back."

Avery stiffened and Rissa had to hold in a laugh. She'd never been comfortable with the Princess' familiarity and Rissa liked to push boundaries. She finally released the other woman.

"It's good to be back, Toha. The borderlands are a tough assignment."

One of the first things Trystan had done as Toha was send one of his most trusted soldiers to lead the expedition to the border of Dreach-Dhoun. Trystan had never been there himself, but it had seen more activity of late. Dreach-Dhoun had measures in place to keep large forces from crossing into their land, but it didn't stop them from trespassing into Dreach-Sciene to spy on their enemies.

Unlike Dreach-Sciene, Dreach-Dhoun's land still held varying amounts of magic. They'd been the ones to strip the power from Trystan's father's realm, but it also meant they couldn't cross the border without losing their own ability to draw from the earth. It kept Dreach-Sciene safe for the time being, but it also prevented anyone from Trystan's side crossing over as it was warded so only those with magic could cross. Even if the King wanted to send soldiers into Dreach-Dhoun, it was an impossible feat.

AVERY HAD BEEN SENT under the guise of doing the yearly check on the defenses. Really, she was looking for evidence of a traitor feeding information to Dreach-Dhoun. For any sign of clandestine meetings or suspicious activity. The King didn't want to believe the spy was in his own palace so he was looking everywhere else first.

Trystan, Rissa, and Avery walked through the training yard,

watching the pairs fight and giving tips here and there. Trystan inspected stance and readiness. For the past few weeks, he'd been trying to assess the state and capabilities of the realm's soldiers. He wanted to know if they were ready to go to war if the need arose.

They were a fine fighting force and their Toha was proud.

Rissa looked into her brother's stern face as he looked on at two young female soldiers sparring with each other. He stepped forward and as he showed them a more natural way to hold their swords, Rissa thought he looked like it was where he belonged.

She was sure the pride showed on her face when her brother looked at her strangely.

"Toha," a servant came running into the training yard. "Princess. The King would like to see you both."

Trystan nodded. "Avery, assemble the officers. Tell them I would like a full assessment of the men under their command. From you, I want an assessment of the officers themselves."

"Yes, sir." She walked off briskly.

Rissa and Trystan walked into the palace. She didn't know what her father wanted, but nerves always fluttered in her belly when she was summoned to his office.

"Davi," Trystan called as they saw the tall man leaving the King's office.

Davi stopped and a look crossed his face that Rissa would have sworn was infused with guilt.

"When did you get back?" Trystan asked.

"Just now," Davi answered, looking behind him nervously. His eyes left Trystan and rested on Rissa. He pursed his lips and let out a sigh before looking at his friend once again.

"I am travel weary, my friend." He chuckled softly.

"Go," Trystan said. "Avery is handling things for me right

now. Get something to eat and then come report. I'll be in the practice yard."

Davi gave him a nod and lumbered passed them.

The guard outside the King's office opened the door and ushered them in. Their father glanced up from his desk but didn't smile in greeting. "Trystan, Rissa have a seat. We have matters to discuss."

The door slammed loudly, making Rissa jump before she followed Trystan to the wooden chairs in front of her father's desk.

After a suffocating moment of silence, the King finally spoke. "Our realm is at a crossroads," he began. "There are going to be very hard times ahead. Avery returned from the border to tell us Dreach-Dhoun is building up their own fortifications just as we thought. They're preparing for something."

Rissa gasped, but Trystan only nodded. He'd already known.

"Now is the time to strengthen our alliances. The best way to do that is and has always been marriage."

Rissa clamped her lips shut to keep the arguments from escaping, but her brother didn't react.

"Trystan." The King looked at him. "A contract of marriage has been proposed for your hand and I have accepted."

"Is that what you used Davi for?" Rissa couldn't stay quiet any longer. "You used his best friend to negotiate his marriage to a girl he doesn't love?"

The King sighed. "Davion was sent on other business, but the proposal was returned with him."

"So, it's Willow then." Trystan finally spoke.

"She's a lovely girl, son. And Lord Coille is one of our strongest allies. We explored other options, but none would give us access to the extensive trade network and sea-trade options that Willow will. We must begin exploring more of what the sea has to offer in order to keep our people fed. Coille might be our best chance."

Trystan nodded in acceptance, ever the dutiful son. Rissa's lips quivered as rebellion rose up in her.

The King's eyes softened when he looked at her and she understood even he didn't like the deal he'd made for her hand. Before he said it, she knew what his words would be.

"Isenore holds immense power as well. I have secured Royce Eisner as your husband."

"How could you?" she whispered.

"I don't fully trust Eisner to choose the right side in what is to come. I need to do something to ensure his loyalty." He looked truly regretful. "I had no other choice."

Rissa shook her head. Despite knowing this was his plan since the ball, her mind struggled to comprehend how her loving father could send her to a man such as Royce. She looked down to where Trystan had taken her hand in his. When she glanced back up at her father, there were tears in his eyes.

"I do love you both," he said quietly. "We are royals. We must do what is best for the realm."

"What about you, father?" Rissa asked. "You're always telling us you loved mother. Why did you get to choose?"

"Your mother ..." He sighed and rubbed the back of his neck. "Maybe it's time I tell you the entire story." He paused, thinking. "Marissa was the most beautiful thing I'd ever seen. I loved her from the moment I saw her." He chuckled briefly. "Which was as she sat atop a horse leading a contingent of soldiers as part of the Dreach-Dhoun advanced forces."

Rissa's tears had dried up as she leaned forward in shock. Trystan, still gripping her hand, squeezed harder.

"It was about a year before the end of the war. I was Toha, but my father was leading the army himself. I'd been fighting all day – it was one of the bloodier battles. Most of the soldiers were too exhausted to draw more power from the earth so we stumbled around hacking at each other. Then she rode through. She had blood on her face and in her deep red hair. She pinned me with her bright eyes which didn't hold the darkness of most of the other soldiers of Dreach-Dhoun. She slid down from her horse. I thought she was going to kill me. Instead, she put her sword in the sheath hanging on her belt and stuck her shoulder under mine to help me up."

He smiled to himself. "She was the daughter of a very powerful man in Dreach-Dhoun. Prince Calis was in love with her. The night she escaped to our side of the defenses, the King of Dreach-Dhoun was killed and Calis Beirne was crowned."

"You have to understand," he went on. "During the war, the noble houses of Dreach-Sciene were torn apart. We had hoped my marriage to your mother would bring her father onto our side, but he was being controlled somehow. I was lucky enough to fall in love with the woman whose alliance we needed." He looked them each in the eye in turn. "I do wish the same for you."

Rissa squeezed her eyes shut to keep the tears at bay. Before she was born, the people of her realm had given up so much, fought so hard, to create the safety she'd grown up with. She'd do the same for them. She looked to Trystan and knew he was thinking the same thing. It was their turn to sacrifice, their duty.

Trystan gave her hand a final squeeze and let go.

The King stood and moved around his large desk to stand in front of Rissa. "I have something for you, my sweet girl." He opened his hand to reveal a gold pendant hanging on a simple chain. The same image from the hilt of Trystan's sword was carved into it. "This is your mother's family crest."

Trystan leaned forward to see an elegant tree with twisting roots and three symbols surrounding it.

Their father pointed to each symbol in turn. "Magic. Man. Earth. These three things must work in harmony to overcome impossibilities."

She held her hair to the side to allow him to fasten it around her neck.

"Your mother had great power, and you both can have it too. I know these marriages aren't what either of you would like." He glanced at Trystan. "You, my children, can have a profound impact on this world and I truly believe these are the avenues that will get you there. Rissa, you are not yet of an age to marry. The ceremony will be held off for a year."

Rissa breathed a sigh of relief. She knew her father was giving her a small mercy. Many girls in the kingdom married before their eighteenth year.

"But we will move ahead with Trystan's marriage immediately." He still spoke to Rissa. "I will be sending you to Lord Coille's residence in Aldorwood to finalize everything and act as Willow's lady. She's the future queen, after all. You leave in four days with a small contingent of servants, guards, and a wagon to hold the gifts we are sending."

"Yes, father," she said.

"You both may go."

Once outside the office, brother and sister looked to one another. One of them was binding an ally even closer, and the other was ensuring loyalty. The King hadn't said it explicitly, but he had reasons not to trust Isenore.

A fear settled in Rissa, but she pushed it away. A year. She had a year until she need worry. And even though her brother wasn't in love with Willow, Rissa would be glad when she moved into the palace. It would be nice to have a friend around to distract her from what was coming.

She parted ways with Trystan and walked towards her quarters.

Davi was leaning against the wall beside her door. He straightened when he saw her.

"Is it happening?" he asked. "Is your father sending you to Isenore?"

She huffed out a breath. As soon as she saw him, the tears started coming. He stepped forward to comfort her, but she held out a hand.

"Davi …" her voice shook for just a second before she strengthened it. "I need to deal with this on my own."

Hurt flashed across his face. "What does that mean?"

"It means without you." She stepped by him and pushed open the door, stopping on the threshold. "I think you should keep your distance."

"Ri, I don't understand."

She smiled sadly, looking back at him. "That's the problem, Davi. You don't understand because you don't feel the same way. But it's okay. We'll be out of each other's lives in a year."

Tears trickled down her face as she stepped into her room and shut the door, creating a barrier between them. She could still hear him on the other side.

"Ri," he pleaded. "Rissa."

Light streamed into her room as a cool breeze drifted in through the open window, bringing with it the smell of the barns. Rissa didn't bother to close the window since at the moment she really didn't care. Instead, she crawled into her bed and pulled the blankets up over her head. Davi's pleas turned to silence, punctuated only by her muffled sobs.

The forest stretched out for acres, as far as the eye could see - across the realm of Isenore and straight to the mountains bordering Dreach-Dhoun. It was a widespread sea of gray, dying trees and rotting foliage. Alixa stood in the window studying it with a forlorn smile. It hadn't always been this way. She remembered well visiting her mother here in these very chambers and looking out over the majestic canvas filled with greens and reds and shades of gold. She'd thought it, and her mother, the most beautiful things she'd ever seen in her young life. But the life had slowly drained from the forest over the years, along with that of her mother. Now they were both just a fading memory.

It'd been ten years since she lost her mother and she still came to her room often. It hadn't been touched in all that time. Her ivory combs still sat on the dressing table where Alixa would sit for hours while her mother lovingly brushed her hair and sang to her beautiful, lilting melodies in her sweet voice.

Her gowns still hung in the wardrobe and Alixa had convinced herself she could smell her lingering perfume in the air. She knew it wasn't possible, but it was the only way she could hold onto those fleeting memories; memories of the only time in her life when she'd felt loved.

Her father wasn't aware of her visits here. She was sure of that. If he knew of the simple pleasure being here brought her, he'd have most likely had it torn apart. Pleasing his daughter was very low on his list of priorities. Alixa would go so far as to say he derived pleasure from her suffering, just like he'd done with her mother. He was a cruel man, the Duke of Isenore, but that cruelty seemed to be held in reserve for those closest to him. To outsiders, he appeared to be the complete gentleman his status decreed. Alixa knew better. This place had slowly killed her mother, over time. This place, this life, that man. And it was doing the same to her.

Everywhere she looked she was trapped. Not just by the stone walls of the castle, but with legacy and family duty. She felt as a useless object with no purpose but to be at her father's beck and call, running his kitchen and entertaining his guests with mindless pleasantries, only to be told she did it wrong when the guests had finally departed. To be belittled and made to feel stupid just to heighten his own sense of superiority. She hated it. She hated him.

Maybe if she had support from Royce it would have been bearable, but her brother was no better. Cut from the same cloth as their father, he helped make her life miserable. If it hadn't been for her mother, Alixa would not have ever believed herself to be a part of this family. She looked nothing like them and thankfully acted even less like them. Sometimes she truly did think that the Duke was not her father and Royce not her brother. She knew it was wishful thinking, but she was fully aware there was no love between them. There was none of the camaraderie she'd witnessed between the prince and princess of Dreach-Sciene at the Toha ball. She'd met them only briefly, but it was easy to see how fond they were of each other. The idea was foreign to her. If it weren't for her maid, Ella, and a few other servants, Alixa would not even be aware of what kindness was. Hers was a lonely life indeed.

A hawk soared by the window and Alixa averted her eyes from the dismal excuse of a forest. The bird's graceful dance carried it across the evening sky, and she watched with envy as it disappeared into the approaching darkness. If only she could fly away from here as easily and float off to another life.

"God, I hate this place," she muttered as she placed her forehead against the cool glass and a single tear escaped the corner of her eye. Wiping it away with a sigh, she opened the large window and stepped out onto the balcony in anticipation. This was her favorite time of day, when evening turned to night. After the horrible pretense of family dinner was over and her father had retired to his library for the evening and Royce had gone out for who only knew what reason. It was her time to be alone.

She stood still as stone, watching the night sky; enthralled as the stars slowly emerged one by one, like candles being lit. The air on her face was cold with the lingering chill of a northerly wind and goose bumps raised on her skin, but she didn't mind. She didn't want to go back inside. Not yet.

Voices below her cut through her tranquility and she peered over the balcony with irritation. Surely, it wasn't Royce back already? But the wagon and carriage highlighted by the servant's lanterns were not of House Isenore. She was certain of it. These were unfamiliar and her brow furrowed in puzzlement. Her father had guests at this late hour? And coming through the back entrance? Very strange.

Against her better judgement, Alixa left her mother's chambers and hurried down the steps and through the long halls towards her father's study. She hoped to catch sight of the visitors, but instead, she found two unfamiliar guards standing watch outside the double oak doors and she brought up in surprise. She didn't recognize them or their tunics of black and gold. From what house were they and what was their purpose here? The guards stared at her approach in silence.

"Is my father available?" she asked, not that she wanted to see him, but curiosity overrode her distaste.

"No, the Duke is in a meeting. Leave."

Seriously? She narrowed her eyes and scowled, but knew she had no choice. Who gave them the right to order her around in her own house?

She huffed out a breath and turned on her heel, not stopping until she'd rounded the corner and made her way into the library. Its balcony adjoined the one of her father's study. If she couldn't meet who was inside, at least she'd be able to see who it was.

Under the cover of darkness, Alixa crept to the end of the library's gallery. Hoisting her long gown to her knees, she gripped the edge of the stone balcony and clambered over easily, landing in a crouch on the other side. Scurrying for the cover of a marble pillar, she peered into the lamp lit room.

Her father was pacing back and forth in front of the window and she pulled back quickly, not wanting to get caught. Finally, he turned away and the other person in the room came into full view. It was a tall man, similar in age to her father but not near as balding or stout. Although dressed in the same black and gold as the guards outside the door, he was no guard. His noble bearing was unmistakable.

Her father's voice broke the night's silence and Alixa jumped in fright before realizing it just carried from the open window. She leaned a bit further so she could hear more clearly. "Are you sure the King realizes what he's asking of me? I will expect much more in supplies as way of payment."

The mystery man nodded. "The King is very aware. And you will receive more. Much more. But he expects some form of guarantee. Your last bit of information was quite enlightening. It was a start. But he requires more in-depth data."

Information? What sort of information was her father supplying King Marcus with? What would be so important about mining and iron supplies that a messenger would be sent this late into the evening?

"He'll get what I promised. We have another council meeting scheduled a month from now to discuss military action on the border. King Calis should be quite pleased with what I bring back."

Alixa reeled back in shock. King Calis? Surely she heard wrong. Her father couldn't be supplying their sworn enemy, Dreach-Dhoun, with military secrets. But even as her mind refused to believe her father was a traitor to their very own king, her heart was telling her otherwise. The uniforms of the soldiers inside suddenly made sense. No wonder she didn't recognize them. They weren't from any house in the realm she'd ever seen. Her father was a collaborator with King Calis!

Whether it was shock or just bad luck, Alixa failed to pull back in time as her father pivoted on his heel and turned back to the window. His eyes locked with hers and narrowed in anger.

"Who's there?" he yelled as the window opened further and he leaned out. "Alixa, is that you?"

No, no, no.

Nearly falling over in her haste, Alixa hopped the wall separating the two balconies and ran for the library door. If she could get to her room without being seen, she could convince her father she wasn't even there. That it had been all his imagination. Yanking open the library door she skidded around the corner to the hall, and straight into the arms of the waiting Dreach-Dhoun soldiers.

ALIXA BOLTED UPRIGHT from her bed and stared at the door to her room as the knob twisted with a creak. She hoped desperately it wasn't her father again. Her arm still hurt from their encounter the day before. Holding her breath in fear, she exhaled in a sigh of relief as the slight form of her maid, Ella, filled the doorway.

"I brought you food, Lady Alixa." The maid stepped past the burly guard stationed outside Alixa's chambers, giving him a wide berth. Her hands busy holding the serving platter, she tried to close the door with her foot, but the guard growled at her.

"Leave it open."

Ella bestowed him a look of pure steel, belying her tiny frame. "Whether you have been ordered to keep the Lady Alixa under lock and key or not, I'm also here to help her dress. I don't think the Duke would appreciate you watching. Now, shut the door."

The big man looked slightly taken aback by the venomous tone, but he did as asked. As soon as the door closed, Ella dropped the tray on the dressing table and the two young woman embraced.

"Oh God, I've been so worried, milady." She ran her hands over Alixa's arms. "Have they harmed you in any way?"

Alixa's resolve broke under Ella's concern and tears flooded her eyes. "Not really, but what's going to happen to me? My father is so angry and I can't handle him when he's like this. I'm scared, Ella. He knows I know. I couldn't bring his entire world down around him. Now I'm nothing more than a liability." She breathed heavily. "Why couldn't I just lie and pretend I hadn't heard anything?"

She hadn't just admitted to eavesdropping, she'd thrown the word traitor at her father. That's what he was and she wasn't one to hold back. It'd been a mistake. How could he betray the King? It shouldn't surprise her, but that didn't stop any remaining love she had for him from shattering under the weight of secrets.

So, he'd locked her away as he always did. Three days now. She'd had a guard watching her every move. No one had been allowed in. Her only visitor had been her father, wearing his anger and displeasure like armor. And instead of his anger waning, it seemed to have increased two-fold. Last night's visit had been the worst. The pungent odor of wine wafted off of him the moment he entered the room. There had been no deep sighing of regret or uncertainty from him like the first two times. It had been an out and out visit of censure. What had he done to deserve such a contemptible and surly daughter? Why had she turned out so much like her mother, the witch who had destroyed his life? Why was she so incredibly stupid she couldn't see what he was doing was all for the good of the Isenore people?

Each accusation had been accompanied by a hard shove so

by the time he'd pinned her against the dressing table, Alixa had truly been scared for her life. Her hand behind her back curled around a heavy iron candlestick, the itch to slam it into his head crawling under her skin. He stared at her, distaste evident in his face, before turning without another word and exiting her room. Not until she'd heard his footsteps fade away down the marble hall did she relax and let the weapon fall from her hand.

"That I can't answer, milady, but we have very little time. You must listen carefully." The fear in Ella's voice only intensified Alixa's own. "The Duke left early this afternoon. I have no idea when he'll be back, but Cook has overheard his discussion with the visitor who's been here these past few days. They want to take you away, milady. I'm not sure where, but I got a feeling it's not anywhere good."

Take her away? To Dreach-Dhoun? No, it can't be. He was her father. He wouldn't do this to her…would he?

"You have to go. Escape."

"Escape?" she repeated dully. Then again, but this one more forceful as the idea blossomed in her head. "Yes, escape. But where would I go?"

"What does it matter?" Ella asked. "But you must leave. I fear you're in danger here. Listen and listen well. As we speak, Edric is in the loft above with a rope to pull you up off the balcony. From there you will proceed through the servant's quarters to the lower levels. I will take you to the wine cellar. There's a hatch to the aqueducts that leads out under the wall to the river. It will get you out and away from any of the guard's notice. Edric will meet you at the river with a horse."

Alixa nodded her head in agreement even though this whole escape plan, this whole thing seemed so surreal. "Why would you and your brother help me? Why put yourself in danger? If you get caught-"

"We won't," Ella assured her with way more confidence than Alixa was feeling. Grabbing the younger girl's hand, she smiled at her. "And you need not ask why. You have always been more like a sister to me than my mistress. You know that. I would do anything to keep you safe... little sister."

Alixa's eyes filled up once again along with Ella's, but her maid shook her head. "No time for tears. You must hurry and change. I need the guard to see you still here after I leave. Your escape will be a mystery to all. Now move."

ALIXA HALF-RAN, half stumbled down the stairwell, one hand trailing along the stone wall to keep her from falling. The tiny flame from the lantern Ella carried their only source of light.

She breathed a sigh of relief as they hit the bottom of the stairs. They'd made it into the cellars without being caught. Ella didn't stop there. She ushered Alixa along the corridor and into a storeroom, the lamplight casting shadows over the barrels and crates lining the floor. Alixa was shocked to see so many supplies, especially after her father had forbidden her from handing out scraps at the back entrance to the starving children because he'd said the House of Isenore could barely provide for their own staff. Obviously, another lie, since there were enough supplies here to feed them all for a year. How many of the staff knew about this? Most of them would have no need to visit the cellars, but surely a few were in on it. Some of the people she'd known her entire life were traitors just like her father.

There wasn't time to dwell on that. Near the rear of the

room, Ella pushed a basket out of the way to reveal an iron handle resting on a wooden hatch in the floor. It took the two of them, using their whole bodies to lift it before it fell against the stone floor with a loud clang. The hole was dark and dank and a putrid odor hit her nose, but it also reeked of freedom.

"This is as far as I go, milady," Ella held the lamp high revealing the tears already flowing. "Remember, the aqueducts will take you straight to the river where Edric awaits. From there head into the woods. Ride swift and fast and don't look back."

Alixa nodded before pulling the tiny woman she'd known since she was a child into her arms. "Thank you for everything, Ella. I will miss you, my friend."

Ella gave her one more squeeze before pushing her away. "Go now. Be free, little sister."

A shout from the corridor startled them both. "Oi, who's there?"

"Guards," Alixa muttered in horror as she froze in fright. Ella was the first to react.

"Go. I'll distract them. They won't follow you."

The iron ladder down was rusty and broken in spots and Alixa feared it wouldn't hold her weight, but she didn't slow her descent, even as the hatch slammed shut overhead, cloaking her in darkness. She was more afraid of the guards catching her. Ella proved to be true to her promise of holding them off however, and Alixa hit the bottom with a loud splash. She paused to catch her breath as darkness surrounded her with a suffocating pressure and panic clawed at her throat. She blew out a series of short breaths, trying to regain control.

Having no choice but to keep moving, she turned from the stairs and laid her hand against the slimy wall, taking her first step into the unknown. No turning back now. Dampness saturated her boots and the hem of her dress, the cold seeping into her very bones. She was actually glad for the darkness since she couldn't see what she kicked about with every step, but the odors had bile rising in the back of her throat.

Dragging her hand along the damp wall to find her way, the walk seemed to take an eternity. She kept glancing back expecting at any moment a hand to fall on her shoulder. Finally, a sliver of light appeared up ahead. Alixa grinned to herself in the dark. The end of the tunnel. Hurrying now, the sliver grew bigger as the tunnel began to fill up with moonlight. Rushing water reached her ears and she knew it was the river's waterfall. Breaking into a run, Alixa fell out of the tunnel into the river, up to her knees as the stench of decay was replaced with sweet, fresh air. The water was freezing, but she didn't care. She didn't care that she was soaked to the bone or that her teeth chattered so loud she could hear them. She was out. Out of the tunnel. Out of the castle. Out of her father's reach. She was free.

"Lady Alixa," the voice called to her from the riverbank as Edric reached toward her to pull her out of the water. She grabbed his hand in thanks, grateful for his help.

"Ella," she gasped as soon as she could catch her breath. "There were guards–" She jumped as a burst of wind rustled through the leaves nearby.

"Don't worry, Milady, my sister can talk her way out of anything." Edric shifted his eyes from side to side, the nervous tic belying his assurance.

All it did was increase Alixa's dread. Her teeth clamped down on her lip as she rocked from one foot to the other.

"Your horse awaits in the trees over there." He pointed with his chin and Alixa spotted the dappled work horse laden down with sacks of precious food. He'd taken care of her, but soon she'd be on her own with no home and nowhere to go.

"I can't thank you enough, Edric," she whispered, her voice choked with tears as a crushing fear constricted her chest. "I will always be indebted." She patted the small blade hanging at her waist under her cloak, reassuring herself it was still there.

Edric nodded solemnly. "Stay safe."

"I will try, Edric. I will try."

A loud trumpet broke the night's stillness and Alixa's heart smashed against her ribcage. The alarm! They already knew she was gone.

"Hurry," Edric shoved her towards the horse.

Alixa bundled up her soaked skirts and climbed onto her horse. Without another word, she turned into the trees and dug her heels into the mare's flanks, making her jolt forward.

The trumpeting alarm joined with shouting, but the sound of her horse's pounding hooves soon drowned it out. It was Alixa's last contact with House Isenore as she galloped into the forest and toward her freedom.

7

Trystan kicked his heels against his horse as he sped through the woods standing between the palace and the town. He'd needed desperately to get out of the palace and clear his head. Images of Willow flashed through his mind. Her delicate, pale skin. Her soft blonde hair. She was small and fragile and he couldn't deny her beauty, but she was missing what he'd always imagined in a partner. She'd make a good queen, but he'd hoped for someone who could ride and hunt and help keep the kingdom safe. His hopes were unrealistic though and he knew his father had chosen well for Dreach-Sciene.

He'd always known he wouldn't get to choose and she was the daughter of a close ally, so it made sense, but she followed him around like a lost puppy. He didn't want obedience or adoration in a wife. He wanted partnership. He wanted to be challenged. He didn't need love, but he wanted a mutual respect.

Soon, his horse wasn't the only one thundering down the

path. He glanced back and pulled up on the reins with a sigh to allow his uncle to catch up. Geran Drake was a stern man. He was younger than the King and had been raised only as a pawn for the realm to move – much like Rissa with her marriage to Royce Eisner.

"Nephew," Lord Drake said when he reached him. "You shouldn't be out of the palace without your guards."

"Just exercising my horse." Trystan patted his horse's long neck, eliciting a snort from the beast.

"There are stable lads for that. I'm sure you have other duties to attend to."

He narrowed his eyes in irritation. Since he was a child, his uncle had been trying to assert his authority over him, but that was before he was Toha.

Trystan turned his horse. "Return to the palace, Lord Drake. That's an order."

A harsh laugh burst out of his uncle. "You don't give me orders, boy."

"Actually, I do. I –"

A high-pitched scream pierced the woods.

Trystan kicked his horse around and jerked his head from side to side, scanning the trees for the source of the commotion. His uncle prodded his horse forward and took off in the direction it came from.

Trystan followed close behind him, terrified at what they were about to find.

A low moaning filled the woods and they used it to lead them. He almost missed her. She was leaning up against a tree with an arrow stuck in her leg. Weak cries escaped her lips.

A second arrow whistled by, sticking into the tree right above the woman's head. Trystan jumped from his saddle and ran towards her as his uncle took off in the direction the arrows were coming from.

Lord Drake's disappearance into the trees was soon followed by the unmistakable sound of a sword fight. Trystan didn't think twice about helping the woman. Lord Drake was one of Dreach-Sciene's most celebrated swordsmen. He was quite capable of taking care of himself and didn't need his help. Trystan approached the woman slowly.

Blood seeped past the arrow, trailing down her leg into the dirt. Her head jerked up and her eyes widened in fear. White-blonde hair that was matted with grime hung around her shoulders. Her face was streaked with mud, but her icy blue eyes shone through.

He held up his hands. "I'm not going to hurt you."

The woman whimpered and Trystan crouched down in front of her, examining her leg closely.

A loud grunt of pain came from nearby and Lord Drake reappeared, still on his horse, re-sheathing his now bloody blade. "Is she alright?"

"We need to get her to the palace healer." He turned back to the woman. "My name is Trystan. I'm the Toha of Dreach-Sciene. You're safe now."

Her lips moved, but no sound escaped.

"What?" Trystan leaned closer.

"I need to see the King," she whispered.

Trystan sprang into action. She'd been attacked while on her way to the palace. He didn't know the woman's name. He didn't know why she'd come. He didn't know why she'd been attacked. None of it made sense and he was going to get to the bottom of it. The Palace woods should be safe and he took it as a direct attack on the King that anyone would dare do battle in them.

He glanced once more at the arrow in her leg.

"Don't remove it. She could bleed out," his uncle warned.

Trystan looked into the woman's eyes and she gave him a slight nod of permission. He stood and bent to lift her into his arms, careful not to bump the arrow. Blood from her wound soaked into his sleeve. His uncle helped him lift her onto his horse. He climbed on behind her and took off as if it was his own life in danger.

His uncle stayed behind to find out what he could off the body of the man he'd killed and then take care of him.

Trystan didn't slow until he reached the gates. The guards came running when he stopped and jumped from his saddle.

"What happened, Toha?" one of them asked as he helped Trystan lift the woman down.

"Trystan." Davi came running when he saw them. "Is she alive?"

"She needs the healer." Trystan hoisted her into his arms and took off in the direction of the healer. In order to get answers, she had to be okay and soon.

Davi followed and pushed open the door to the healer's quarters without knocking.

The palace healer was an older man who'd been there since long before the war. He used to tell Trystan stories of the healing that could be done when magic was present.

Well, there was no magic now. Only a woman who'd been attacked on their very own land.

"Toha," the healer said, jumping up from his seat at a wooden table in the corner. He rushed towards a bed on the other side of the room. "Lay her here."

Trystan did as he was told. "She took an arrow to the leg and now she's lost consciousness."

"I can see that. You saved her life by bringing her here." The healer rummaged through his tools and Trystan knew he was being dismissed. The old man was the only person in the palace who could even dismiss the King. He didn't like anyone getting in the way of his work.

Outside the room, Trystan started walking. "I need to see my father."

"Trystan," Davi said, keeping pace with him. "What is going on?"

"I don't know, Davi. I don't know."

The King was in the practice yard with a few of his advisers when Trystan found him. They were watching Avery show off her sword-play against a large man.

"Sire." Trystan interrupted their conversation. "I must speak with you."

The King made apologies to the men around him and joined his son. "What is it?"

"A woman was attacked in our own forests."

His father reeled back in shock.

"She was on her way here to see you. I don't know why. She's with the healer."

The King took off and Trystan and Davi followed as close as they could. When the King reached the doorway and looked inside, he stopped. His hands shook at his sides. He opened his mouth to speak and then closed it again.

Trystan glanced passed his father to the now conscious woman. Her eyes were glazed, but they sharpened as soon as she caught sight of the King.

"Sire," the healer said. "I've just finished sewing her up. She needs to rest."

The King didn't budge. He breathed out heavily. "Lorelai?"

Davi sucked in a breath. The prince looked curiously at his friend, realizing now was not the time for questions.

"My King," Lorelai wheezed, clenching her teeth against the pain. "It's good to see you once again."

The King moved further into the room. He clenched his fists at his sides and stiffened his shoulders. Trystan couldn't remember seeing his father at such a loss before.

"You disappeared," he said. "I tried to find you again."

"It became too perilous for my kind."

"Seems it still is." He gestured to her leg.

A wry smile formed on her lips. "I knew what showing myself would mean. I had to come."

"Why?"

She released a sigh and her body sagged, seemingly exhausted by his questions. The old healer intervened before she could answer.

"She'll still be here tomorrow, Sire. I really must insist she rest."

Her eyes had already begun to drift shut and they reluctantly left her to her sleep. The sun was beginning to dip below the horizon as they stood, waiting for the King to speak.

He finally did, but it was not to them. He caught the eye of a maid nearby. "Inform the kitchens I will be dining with the Toha, the Princess, and Davion in the Princess's quarters." The maid scurried away to do as she was told and the King turned back to the two young men in front of him.

"Rissa is in her rooms. She must hear this as well."

Rissa was preparing to go to the hall for dinner when they showed up at her door. The King closed the door behind them, cutting them off from the servants bustling outside.

Trystan looked into his father's serious face, feeling an impending importance in the words he was about to say. Excitement pulsed through him.

"Sit," the King ordered. "All of you. We have much to discuss."

RISSA LISTENED to her father with an open mind. She saw the skepticism on the faces of Trystan and Davi but refused to believe her father a maker of tales.

It had always been easier for her to wrap her mind around the existence of magic because she felt it, or at least felt it used to be there.

So when her father told them they had a seer in their palace, it was no great leap for her. They'd been hearing of seers their entire lives, knowing them to be real. But there was a great difference between knowing something and truly believing in it.

Theirs was the only magic that persisted in Dreach-Sciene because it wasn't earth magic – a fact none of them had truly known until the earth no longer held power, but the seers continued to see.

"Wait a moment," Trystan said. "A noble man will rise to defeat the darkness?"

"That's what she told me, yes," the King responded.

"And you believe it means me?"

"I did, yes."

"And now? Because I made a request to go, to try to fix what was broken."

A pounding sounded on the door. Before Davi opened it, the King responded to Trystan.

"Son, we don't even know where to begin – or if it can be done."

Davi grunted, pulling the door wide.

Rissa looked to him and saw a woman she assumed was Lorelai collapse through the door into Davi's arms.

"Lorelai." The King jumped to his feet as Davi carried her towards the bed.

The poor woman was out of breath and obviously in pain. She must have limped all the way here.

"I had to wait until the healer gave me a moment alone before making my escape," she wheezed.

Davi set her down and looked into her face. "You shouldn't have done that."

"Davion?" she asked, tears springing to her eyes. "Is it really you?"

He nodded.

"You remember me?"

He brushed her filthy hair out of her face and smiled. "Only bits and pieces, but I know you took care of me."

"Sire." Lorelai took her eyes off Davi to look back to the King. "It can be done." She leaned her head back against the pillows with a sigh of pain. "Because I know where to start."

The room was stunned into silence as they waited for her to explain.

"Sona. It starts on the Isle of Sona."

Trystan leaned forward. "How do you know this?"

"I doubt you know much about the power of a seer." She paused. "I can feel the use of magic. Back when everyone was able to wield it, it was an ineffective tool. But now, well, now there are only two people with the power to wield magic in Dreach-Sciene."

"The Tri-Gard," the King whispered.

"Yes, the very ones who stripped our land of magic in the first place are the only ones who can give it back. One of them is known to be a prisoner in Dreach-Dhoun, but that is a problem for another day. They've been in hiding like my kind has, but it's time they come into the light. And one of them has made their first mistake."

"They used their magic," Rissa finished the thought. The excitement was building within her and she knew she had to be a part of whatever was going to happen. She felt like the earth itself was reaching out for her help.

"Why were those men after you?" Trystan asked.

"I revealed myself. Seers aren't looked kindly upon by those who want our magic. We are the only connection left to the Tri-Gard. The last remaining remnants of a power which was once possessed by all. They can't take it so they take us instead."

All conversation was dropped as a gaggle of servants showed up with their dinner. Both Trystan and the King seemed to be lost in their thoughts. Rissa told them where to put everything and sent one with a message telling the healer Lorelai would be staying in her rooms.

Davi helped get some food into Lorelai as the rest of them barely ate.

"I have to go," Trystan finally said, breaking the heavy silence.

"No."

"Father, this is our chance. It's my duty. You said as much at my ceremony. A Toha's duty is to help his people. We need to restore our kingdom. We need to keep our people alive. I'm going. I'm sorry, but you can't stop me. I have to do this."

The King seemed to shake as he looked at his son, worry etched into every feature.

"I'm going, too," Davi said.

"And me," Rissa put in.

"Absolutely not," Trystan argued.

"No," the King agreed.

Rissa folded her arms across her chest, her lips tight with anger. They expected her to stay behind? Disbelief turned into irritation. They weren't even listening to her. Her pulse raced as she narrowed her eyes and watched her father give in to her brother as he always did.

The King looked back to Trystan with a weary sigh of resignation. "You're right, son. It's your duty to our people and I must be as brave in sending you as you are in volunteering. You will choose a contingent of men to accompany you."

"No," Lorelai interjected. "A few men can accomplish what many cannot. Speed. Stealth. I can't accompany you because of my injury, but I know of someone in Sona who will be able to trace the magic just as I could."

"Understood," Trystan said. "I'll take Davi, Avery, and one other."

Rissa huffed out a breath, unable to keep quiet any longer and looked to her brother. "This is just as much my duty as yours. They're my people, too."

"You are not the Toha."

"But I would be – if I had been born first. You don't understand." She stepped towards him pleadingly. "It's not just the people. It's everything. I feel like the earth is calling me. It isn't supposed to be devoid of magic. It isn't right. I know you've never believed in my connection, but please, Brother, believe in me now. I need to be a part of this." Her voice was clogged with unshed tears as she glanced between her father and her brother.

When her eyes traveled to Davion, he looked away.

"I'm sorry, sweetheart," her father finally said. "The best thing you can do for this realm is to remain safe so your marriage can strengthen our alliances."

Rissa stumbled backward. Her brother tried to reach out in comfort, but she jerked away from him. "That's all I'm good for? To wed and bed a man I despise?" She shook her head in disbelief and then straightened her shoulders, her voice going cold. "Your Majesty. Your Highness. Davion. I would appreciate it if you leave me to my rest. This dutiful daughter has a journey to prepare for."

"Your brother's wedding will be postponed," her father said softly. "We have no other choice. So, you don't have to travel for quite some time."

"No," she said, her voice devoid of emotion. "I will keep my schedule. I'm of no use here and am better suited to sit in Willow's sewing room than perform any duties here at the palace apparently. Now, respectfully, Sire, go."

The King looked at her with sad eyes and Rissa knew he thought he was doing what was best for her, but anger and disappointment warred within her and she turned her back on them to look out the window over the land she wanted to save.

Davi lifted Lorelai from the bed and together the four of them left to go make their own preparations. Preparations they thought had nothing to do with her.

As her eyes roamed over the darkened landscape, she knew with certain clarity if her brother was going to bring magic back to Dreach-Sciene, then she'd be by his side – no matter how hard they tried to stop her.

DISMAY CLUTCHED at Trystan's chest as he watched Rissa prepare for her journey. She left without so much as a farewell to her father, brother, or Davion. The three men stood in the courtyard with their host of servants and guards as the wagons were loaded and she climbed onto the bench of one of them. They stepped forward to speak to her, but she wouldn't meet their eyes. Refraining from even a backward glance, she gave the order to move out.

When Trystan looked to Davi, he saw the same despair mirrored back to him. Rissa felt betrayed and belittled, but he knew that would lessen as she realized they were all trying to protect her. He just hoped she'd forgive them in time.

He couldn't bear the thought of her in any kind of danger. He hated that she was traveling through the very same woods in which Lorelai had been attacked – but at least Lord Drake had taken care of the threat. What he couldn't stand even more was he was soon leaving on a dangerous task and he didn't have her blessing.

Dying frightened him less than dying with regrets.

Trystan turned away from the road to walk back in the iron gates, but Davi didn't move. His eyes remained on the woods into which Rissa had just gone. Trystan clasped a hand on his friend's shoulder and went to find some preparations to do to occupy his mind.

His sword was as sharp as it could be, yet Trystan still found himself sitting at the grinding stone. He enjoyed the steady vibrations against his blade, the loud grinding noises in the air.

There was nothing left to do. The packs were ready, the maps were received, the advice was given. As prince, he'd never undertaken much responsibility, and as Toha he was still untried. The weight of the realm pressed down on his shoulders and the grinding sounds rang in his ears.

Davi was taking their impending expedition as lightly as he took everything else, but to Trystan, it seemed an impossibility that they'd succeed. Even if they found the two missing members of the Tri-Gard, the third was locked in a dungeon guarded by the dark king.

Everything about Dreach-Dhoun terrified Trystan. He wasn't embarrassed to admit it. And he knew eventually he'd need to cross those borders.

Sweat shone on his brow and he wiped it away as he pulled his sword back and sheathed it.

"Are you prepared for what lies ahead, Toha?" Lorelai's voice came from the doorway.

He turned abruptly and saw her hobbling forward using a walking stick to stay upright.

"I am, mistress."

Lorelai was recovering. Rissa's maids had cleaned her up and Trystan was shocked by her beauty. He'd looked on in moderate horror as his father stuttered the first time he saw her after she'd bathed. It wasn't often the King grew flustered. He'd met the seer when she was little more than a child, but she was a woman now. She'd stay at the palace under the King's protection.

"Dear prince." She sat in a chair along the wall with a sigh. "I don't mean physically prepared." She gestured to his sword. "You must be prepared in here." She touched a finger to her head. "And here." She placed a palm over her heart.

His eyes met hers and all bravado seemed to fall away.

"It's a dark road ahead for you."

"You've seen what is to come?"

"Not in its entirety. I know many possibilities and only one can come to pass. But I've always seen the burden on your shoulders."

"The burden of Toha?" he asked, desperate to know more.

"The burden of which I speak has nothing to do with position. There's an ancient curse, one of death, that now falls to you."

Trystan sucked in a breath, unable to speak. Lorelai leaned her head back and dropped her walking stick with a clatter to the ground. When she spoke again, her voice sounded as if it was coming from afar.

Someone you love will die because of you.

Someone you love will sacrifice their life for yours.

Someone you love will forsake your name.

Death.

Sacrifice.

Betrayal.

A curse of kings.

She looked back at him and her shoulders shook. "I'm sorry," she stuttered, reaching for the stick she no longer held.

Trystan scrambled to hand it to her, not knowing what else to do as her words ran through his mind. Darkness closed in and he couldn't shake the feeling of impending doom.

Lorelai used her walking stick to push herself to her feet and her light words stood in contrast to those spoken only moments before. "Good luck, Toha. May you succeed where others have failed to even try."

She rushed from the room as fast as her injured leg would allow, leaving Trystan behind, staring after her in bewilderment and shock. Good luck? She'd just informed him he was cursed and that was the best piece of advice she could give?

Up until he'd met her, he'd never even seen a seer, let alone magic. How could he be cursed? A cold shiver racked his body as the full weight of her words settled in his chest.

So much death. Maybe he was doomed before his journey even began.

THEY LEFT BEFORE EVEN the birds had woken. No one was to know what they were doing, lest their enemies hear. The Toha, his second in command, and his top sword-master were all leaving, but the King assured Trystan his remaining officers were more than capable of continuing the training.

Trystan, Davion, Avery, and Rion climbed into their saddles. Rion was a young novice who was chosen because of his skill with a bow. Trystan hated bringing one so young along and was reminded again if they'd allowed Rissa to join, they'd have no need of Rion.

He shifted in his saddle and looked at each of his companions in turn, thinking of the Seer's curse. Would they be the ones to fulfill it? He tried to push those dark thoughts away.

Davion's usual jovial attitude was gone in place of stern fortitude. Avery's face was a mask of cool indifference, which was not unusual for her. Rion was the only one who showed any kind of fear, but he did his best to hide it.

"I believe in you, son," the King said. "I believe in all of you."

Belief. That's what Rissa had asked of them.

Trystan pushed the thought away and nodded to his father. "We'll find them, father. And then we'll come back and figure out a way into Dreach-Dhoun."

"Go with the power of the realm behind you." He looked at each of them and then shocked them by lowering himself to one knee in respect and honor. "Be our hope."

Trystan gave his father one last long look and then tore his eyes away and gave his horse a hard kick. He took off down the road with his companions thundering after him and as they entered the dark woods of Aldorwood, they could no longer see the palace behind them.

The first five days of their journey hadn't been the easiest of travel. The road to the port city of Whitecap in Aldorwood would have had Trystan and his party arrive much quicker, but they'd forgone that route. Instead, they'd decided to travel through the forest into Aldorwood. It would take a few days longer but it was a much less traveled route and the fewer people they met along the way, the better. Trystan's face was well known and the last thing he needed was speculation on why he was away from the castle and traveling without the royal guard. Plus, the road to Aldorwood was filled with bandits. The royal guards traveling with Rissa would deter any attack, but four horsemen traveling alone were easy targets. The only people they would probably encounter in the woods were traders and farmers.

The weather was more of a bother than anything at the moment. Every day had been colder and wetter than the one before. The bare branches of the trees provided little protection from the sleet that soaked through their cloaks, leaving them chilled to the bone. This morning was no exception. The rain finally slowed to a drizzle, but the wind sliced no less. Trystan pulled the hood of his cloak further over his face as Davi's whining reached his ears.

"Become my second in command, he said. It's an honor, he said. We'll have grand adventures, he said. This? This, Toha, is not a grand adventure."

Trystan merely glanced over his shoulder in amusement. "I don't recall saying any of that, actually."

Davi met the Prince's amused glance with a frown. "Well not in so many words, but it was implied. And I was foolish enough to believe you. Now, look at me. Stuck in the middle of the forest, cold, wet and looking as attractive as a drowned rat in a water barrel." He let loose a dramatic sigh. "What I wouldn't give to be curled up in front of the warm fire in my room right now with a mug of ale in my hand and the new maid rubbing my feet."

Rion, riding alongside Trystan, perked up in his saddle at the comment. "Ooooh, you mean the redheaded girl? She's a looker, alright. She kind of reminds me of the Princess." He swerved his head in Trystan's direction at realizing what he'd let slip. "No disrespect, Toha. I didn't mean anything by it."

Trystan bristled, but sensed the boy's unease and let it go.

Davi, however, did not. He snorted in indignation. "What? She does not. Are you blind, boy? She looks nothing like the Princess. She doesn't even begin to compare."

This had Trystan laughing out loud. "Back down, Davi. The boy meant no harm. Thou doth protest too much, methinks."

"Protesting? I'm not protesting. I'm merely suggesting the boy has poor vision."

"No, you were saying the new maid can't hold a candle to

Rissa's beauty. At least that's what I heard. How about you, Avery?" Trystan glanced over his other shoulder at the sword-master following along. The woman hadn't bothered with a hood and the cold rain had plastered her hair to her head like a helmet, but she didn't appear to be the least discomforted by it. Then again, she never appeared to let anything bother her. Her typical no-nonsense look stayed in place at Trystan's question, not a trace of a smile to be seen.

"I gather that as well, Toha," she responded.

"Hmph, of course, you do," Davi scoffed at Avery's answer. "Trust you to side with the Prince, Avery. You always did believe he was capable of no wrongdoing, even when he was the one behind most of our boyhood escapades. I was just the innocent bystander."

"Innocent," was all Avery said, but the way she said it had Trystan shaking with laughter. The word said quite clearly bull was afoot.

"Ouch. That stung a little, Mistress Payne. Not gonna lie." Davi, always the dramatic, gave her an overblown huff of false exasperation, much to Trystan and Rion's amusement, but Avery chose not to respond. She stared ahead in stoic silence as always.

They continued for a few more hours in relative calm, each lost in their own thoughts. Even Davi had fallen quiet. Trystan let himself be lulled by the calm and muffled trot of his horse. Just a few more hours of riding then they would find a suitable place to camp for the night. Hopefully, they'd be able to find some firewood that was still dry enough to burn, otherwise, they would be in for a very cold night.

The scream that pierced the forest spooked Trystan's stallion so much he had to rein him in with a strong hand to keep him from bolting.

The scream died off only to be followed by the unmistakable sound of clanging swords and colorful cussing.

"This way," Trystan bellowed, and as one they turned into the thicket of trees to their right.

The sight that met their eyes as they advanced into a clearing on the other side of the copse was not something they were expecting. A hooded figure in a muddy, torn cloak was surrounded by a circle of five uniformed men. Although two of the tunics were unfamiliar, the three others identified them as Isenore soldiers just as the long dark curls peeking out of the hood confirmed their target was a woman. She was trying to hold them off with her rapier, but as skillfully as she handled the weapon, she was no match for their heavier blades. She thrust and parried with admirable form, but the circle was closing in.

"You fool, we have to take her alive," one of the soldiers growled as another of his brothers swung at her a little too enthusiastically and she cried out as the blade grazed her shoulder. She rewarded her attacker with a thrust to his arm in return and he screamed as the thin blade pierced his skin.

"Five against one. Hardly fair odds, what do you think, men?" Trystan's voice echoed around the glade, startling all blades still. Six pairs of eyes turned their way in disbelief.

"This is no concern of yours," the soldier who had admonished the other earlier spat at the newcomers. "She is but a mere prisoner escaped from our lord's keep. Be off with you, peasants."

"No concern?" Davi asked in calm surprise as he leaped nimbly from his horse. "Five Isenore soldiers chasing down one female prisoner? She must be dangerous to the realm indeed and that, my friend, does concern us."

"They lie," the woman screamed. "They're under orders from Dreach-Dhoun."

Dreach-Dhoun? Trystan didn't have time to wonder the validity of the accusation before the soldiers turned their attack on them. What was going on? Why would Isenore soldiers attack?

Sliding from his horse and landing lightly on his feet, he pulled his sword just in time to block the sharp blade aimed for his chest. The steel hit him with a bone jarring clang. His attacker was a burly man and all of his weight fell behind his weapon as it tried to make Trystan succumb. Instead, Trystan slid his blade down to the other man's hilt and flicked it away easily.

The prince swerved and tried a low attack, but his opponent was just as practiced and deflected the stroke. Metal clanged against metal as Trystan parried blow after blow. Out of the corner of his eye, he saw a second Dreach-Dhoun soldier approach. His blade glinted in the sliver of sunlight poking through the clouds and trees as it sliced down and Trystan, sword still occupied with the first attacker, tried in vain to shift away before the blade made contact with any of his body parts. He slipped on the wet grass and stumbled, tensing as he expected any moment to feel the steel rip through his skin. Instead, the attacker's broadsword dropped onto the ground and he screamed in agony as a fourth blade joined the fight and severed the thumb of his right hand.

The look of surprise in the soldier's eyes as he pulled his bloody hand to his chest was almost funny in its indignation. It was enough to distract Trystan's first opponent and the prince took advantage. With an angry cry, he smashed the Isenore soldier's sword out of his grasp. The man stumbled back, his gaze darting to the blade at his feet, but Trystan growled,

"Leave it and leave now before I change my mind about letting you live." He didn't need to be warned twice.

"Retreat," the Isenore man yelled as he swiveled and ran, leaving the sword where it lay.

The prince averted his gaze from the departing soldier, ready to thank his unknown savior for saving his neck. Instead, he fell mute as he came face to face with a familiar someone he couldn't quite place at first. The hood had fallen away in battle and the light hazel eyes and dark curls sparked his memory. He breathed in disbelief, "Lady Alixa?"

She stared back, wild-eyed, covered in grime and the crimson splattered rapier held above her head adding to her barbaric look. But the amber-flecked eyes flashed in shocked recognition. "Prince Trystan?"

A silence descended over the group as the last soldier vanished from their sight. A sword battle was not what any of them had expected to find today, but find it they did. They waited in anticipation, making sure every last living soldier had left, but none appeared. The soldiers were gone. Davi finally sheathed his sword and headed toward Trystan with a cheeky grin. "Well, that was some excitement to an otherwise dreadfully boring morn- Lady Alixa?"

Spooked, Alixa turned in Davi's direction and brandished the sword his way, halting his approach. Hands up in the air, he backed away. "Whoa, watch where you're pointing that thing." He glanced Trystan's way and whispered, "What the hell is she doing here?"

"She can hear you," Alixa responded, hiding the rapier under her long cloak. She smoothed her hair and straightened her shoulders as she faced Trystan once again. The sight of her standing as stately as she could even though she resembled a gutter rat right about now had Trystan struggling to hide a grin. "Thank you for your help, Your Highness. I didn't realize I was so close to the castle. I must have gotten turned around on my journey. If you could be so kind to help me find my horse, I'll be on my way."

Trystan couldn't help it as a snort of disbelief escaped his lips. "Be on your way? I think an explanation is in order before you are 'on your way' anywhere. Why were your own men attacking you, and why would you say it was under Dreach-Dhoun's orders? And most importantly, why are you here, all alone and in the middle of Aldorwood?"

He didn't mean for his voice to be as sharp or demanding, but it only succeeded in Alixa shaking her head and clamping her lips tight.

"Fine," Trystan conceded. "If you don't wish to share your information, then we will take you back to Isenore and speak with the Duke himself."

"No!" Alixa grabbed his arm and Trystan glanced down in surprise at the claw-like grip. "You can't take me back there. I can't go back there."

The pleading in her voice was matched by the despair in her eyes and the prince found himself drawn in by her misery.

"Why not, my lady?" he questioned softly.

A range of emotions flitted across her face; pride, fear, shame. The pride won out. Taking a deep breath, she held her chin high as she gritted through her teeth. "I can't go back there, Your Highness, because my life would be in danger since I just found out my father is a traitor."

"AND YOU ARE POSITIVE?" Trystan asked for the third time after hearing of Alixa's escape. The girl's eyes flashed with irritation.

"I know I'm but a mere woman, Your Highness, and must appear easily confused, but I'm not mistaken." She paused. "My father, the Duke of Isenore has betrayed our kingdom to Dreach-Dhoun. The presence of his soldiers here should be proof enough."

Trystan failed to respond to the girl's comment, but Davi muttered, "Goodbye damsel in distress, hello ice-queen," earned him a glacial glare.

"The King must be told." Trystan crossed his arms as he considered what this meant. His father would be furious. Isenore would feel his anger as well they should. Loyalty was important to Trystan. A thought crept into his mind and he silently chastised himself for thinking it. When one of the realms three kingdoms was choosing their enemy, a part of him was happy Rissa would not have to marry Royce.

Davi pulled himself up straighter, still on the matter of informing the King. "Agreed, Toha. It would be a disaster if he didn't know immediately. We have no choice but to return."

"No." Trystan's gaze moved to the youngest member of their party. "Rion, return to the castle at once. You must deliver the news of the Duke's betrayal to the King. Tell him everything that has transpired here. We will continue on our mission, we can't afford to lose any time. It's important we complete our quest now more than ever. Between you and Lady Alixa, I trust the message will be delivered."

Alixa peered up at him from her position on the tree stump where she sat. "Wouldn't I have to travel to the castle as well to deliver the message? That is something I don't foresee in my future."

Trystan's eyebrows drew together and he frowned. "But Dreach-Sciene castle is the safest place for you to be right now. My father will protect you. Keep you safe from any Dreach-

Dhoun or Isenore soldiers that may be searching for you. Surely, you must know your father or King Calis will not stop looking for you with the knowledge you possess."

"I'm well aware. Just as I know the castle is the first place he'll look for me. They expect me to run to the King. No, I won't be going to the castle."

She was being unreasonable. Trystan pinned her with an exasperated look. "Then where will you go, my lady? Or do you plan on setting up a straw hut here in the middle of the forest and living like a commoner?"

"You make that sound like it's a fate worse than death. Trust me, Prince Trystan, there are far worse ways to live." Her voice was sharp with disdain.

"That isn't what I meant...enough of this arguing. I would very much like you to accompany Rion. I'm only trying to keep you safe." Trystan turned his back on Alixa, expecting her to follow his orders. He understood her fear, but he was certain the palace was the only safe place for her. He approached his young messenger and laid both hands on the boy's shoulders. "Rion, you must ride swift and stealthy and away from prying eyes. Can you do this?"

"I will, Your Highness," the boy replied with a curt nod.

"Er, Toha?" Davi's voice had a peculiar lilt to it, almost as if he were laughing but trying to keep it hidden. What about this situation warranted laughter? Trystan turned in annoyance only to follow Davi's pointing blade. Alixa's back was all he could see as she retreated from them and into the trees.

"Lady Alixa, where are you going?"

"To find my horse and continue on my way," she threw back over her shoulder as she kept walking.

"Continue where?" he asked.

"Anywhere but where you have asked me to go."

"Surely you jest. Alixa, stop." She kept walking. "As your prince, I command you to stop." Trystan's voice rose in irritation and finally, Alixa did as he asked.

Sighing for all to hear, she turned back around and placed her hands on her hips. "Yes, my Prince?" she drawled.

The heated flush of anger stained Trystan's cheeks. "I think you have mistaken me, my lady. I didn't ask, I ordered you to accompany Rion to the castle. I can't in good conscience leave you out here in the wilderness on your own with Isenore and Dreach-Dhoun soldiers nipping at your heels. My help is in your best interest."

Alixa rolled her eyes. "Forgive me, Your Highness, but I don't recall asking for your help. And I will not bow to obeying orders as easily anymore. I've already survived on my own these past few days, I will endure."

Trystan threw a side glance at Davi, questioning if he was hearing the same thing. Davi merely shrugged and grinned at his friend's annoyance.

Alixa began moving again, not waiting for anyone.

"Alixa, wait." Trystan went after her. "You can't do this on your own. If you won't go with Rion to the castle, then at least accompany us. We can take you to Whitecap and help find you a safe haven."

This seemed to interest the girl. She paused and turned around again. "Whitecap? Yes, that may be the answer. Or Sona. You did say you were traveling to Sona. That's on the other side of Dreach-Sciene and as far away from Isenore as I can go. Maybe that's the answer." Her voice was low as if she was speaking to herself, but then giving a little nod, she raised her strange gold-flecked eyes Trystan's way. "Okay. I will go with you. But first, I need to find my horse."

Trystan heaved a sigh of relief at her answer and a small

smile tugged at the corner of his mouth. Good. At least she was starting to see some sense. He much preferred her to be with them than on her own.

But then Davi's worried, "Are you sure about this, Toha? Having her with us may complicate things. Are you sure this is the right decision?"

Trystan sighed and rubbed the back of his neck, now doubting his rash offer. "I sure as hell hope so, Davi."

King Marcus Renauld was not a contemplative man. He was a man of action, decision. Some would call him hard; his children would say he was unfair. But they would understand one day. When he was no longer there to guide the kingdom and the weight fell on Trystan's shoulders, they would know what it meant to place realm above self.

As he stood atop the walls of the palace that had always been his home and looked out over the land that had once held so much hope, he didn't take in the desolate state. He didn't wonder what the future held. When his eyes roamed from left to right, they had a purpose, they always did. He looked for movement, for attack. It was a habit left from the years of the war. Twenty years later and some things never go away.

He closed his eyes for the briefest of moments, imagining he could see all the way to the sea. His son would be close by now. It would be a long time before he had news of their quest so he shut off those thoughts in his mind. Worry did no one any good.

He turned back towards the guards nearby. They were no longer under his direct command – even when their Toha was far away. The King preferred it that way.

The day Trystan became Toha, his twentieth birthday, was also the twentieth anniversary of the darkest day in their history. He remembered it well. The day the magic was leeched from their land. That night had been the longest and coldest he'd ever experienced. He'd been sure the sun would refuse to rise the next day.

But it did. And they persisted.

The guards bowed their heads to their king as he passed by. They were young men, newly trained. They most likely only chose to join his household to be fed. It saddened him that it had come to that in Dreach-Sciene, but sadness was another useless feeling.

A sad king was no good. If his son succeeded in his mission, their kingdom could once again flourish and most importantly – eat.

Trystan's success would also bring war. There was no avoiding the fact. Twenty years ago, the war hadn't been finished and the time was coming for it to resume once again.

Across the courtyard, Lorelai pivoted on one leg, trying to bend down to lift something she'd dropped on the stones.

The King rushed forward as she started to fall. His large hands grabbed hold of her thin waist as he steadied her.

"Your Majesty." She let out a breathy laugh.

"Lorelai." He hadn't released her. "Are you okay?"

She turned clear blue eyes up to look at him and smiled brilliantly. "Yes. Thanks to your gallantry."

The King was struck by how beautiful she'd become. When

he first met her as a girl, she'd had an eerie quality about her that now intrigued him. Her almost white hair hung down her back, brushing against his fingers as he still held on tight. Most of the women at court wore their hair in extravagant designs. Hers was simple, plain, and he remembered she didn't come from a noble background – even though she spoke as if she did.

"Your Majesty," she said, looking at him quizzically.

He then realized it'd been a few moments since he spoke. He released her, made sure she wouldn't fall again, and then bent down to pick up the item she'd dropped.

It was a knife – one from his armory by the looks of it.

Her eyes widened in alarm. "I'm sorry. I just …"

"Do you not feel safe in these walls?" His tone wasn't accusatory, more worried. He had a strong urge to protect the seer.

A tear appeared at the corner of her eye. "I just … I've been in hiding for a long time. I can't remember the last time I had someone protecting me."

She winced but tried to cover it up.

"You're in pain," the King said, his eyes flitting to where her injured leg was hidden beneath her skirts.

"Yes." She stumbled back, trying to use her walking stick to steady herself.

The King waved down a servant and handed him the knife before reaching out and lifting the slight woman easily into his arms. "You need to rest," he said, walking briskly up the steps and into the palace.

She let out a single whimper as her leg was jostled but then clamped her lips shut despite the pain he knew she was in. He couldn't imagine the life she'd lived since that first night he met her. She'd had to hide from those who didn't trust her magic because they didn't have theirs.

The strength in her was beautiful and he found himself enjoying the weight of her in his arms.

A servant scurried ahead and opened the door to her rooms before they arrived. He stepped through and kicked the door shut behind him in anticipation of the servant's inevitable questions about what he could do for them next.

Lorelai sighed as the King put her down on her bed. She sat up with her back against her pillows and motioned for him to sit next to her.

It was improper. It wasn't right. But the King –used to giving orders, not taking them – couldn't make himself walk away.

He removed his sword from his belt and set it aside. The bed dipped as he sat. He considered her for a long moment before removing his own knife from its sheath at his waist. The hilt was adorned with jewels from the royal treasury. They didn't hold much value in a world where food was the greatest commodity, but they were beautiful.

He extended the hilt towards her. "You wanted a knife with which to protect yourself. This is much more serviceable than the blade you chose."

She hesitated before taking it from his grasp.

"But I swear to you that you will have no need to use it," he said as he watched her examine the blade. "For I will protect you."

A small smile tilted her lips and she set the knife on the table beside the bed with a nod.

The King moved to get up from the bed, but Lorelai's delicate hand landed on his arm. "I believe you, Sire," she whispered. "I trust you to at least try."

He looked into the once icy eyes that now held a fire that lit his very soul. Her grip on his arm tightened and their gazes did battle to see who would make the move both of them wanted.

Lorelai leaned in closer to him and he met her halfway in a searing kiss. Her arms came up around his neck and he moved to pull her in closer before remembering her injured leg.

He laid her back delicately and kissed a line across her porcelain skin as his hands fiddled with the laces on the front of her dress.

When she was finally laid bare beneath him, his eyes traveled the length of her, marveling at her perfection.

It'd been seventeen years since his wife died giving birth to their daughter. She was the love of the King's life. It was a love born of turmoil and despair, but nothing would ever compare to it.

He'd had many mistresses in the years since. That was nothing new. But as he held Lorelai against him, he knew with complete certainty she was important. *They* were important.

A LOUD POUNDING woke the King from his restful sleep. He and Lorelai hadn't gone down to dinner the night before, opting to have it brought to them instead, knowing that by morning, the entire palace would know the King slept in her rooms.

That didn't bother him, but the pounding was a reminder he must return to his duties. He rolled Lorelai onto her side away from him, kissed her soft cheek, and covered her with a blanket. On the way to the door, he quickly pulled on his clothes.

He pulled open the door to find two guards standing there with worried expressions on their faces.

"Sire," the one the King knew to be named Garret started. "You need to come with us."

"Has something happened?" The King stepped out into the hall and shut the door.

"Rion has returned."

"Rion?" Alarm bells rang in his head. "But I sent him with my son."

"He says he has an urgent message from the Toha for your ears only. He's in your office."

The King all but sprinted down the hallway with the guards trying to keep up. He turned the corner and marched across the palace as fast as he could. Trystan's mission was delicate and if something had already gone wrong, it didn't bode well.

All thoughts of the night before had drifted from his mind as soon as he had to be the king again. That was the price.

The King's brother, Lord Drake, was waiting outside his office.

"I saw Rion return," he said. "He was riding his horse as hard as he could. He refused to tell me anything until you arrived."

"That's because I'm the king." He put a hand on his brother's shoulder. He hated constantly having to remind the younger man of that fact, but it was necessary when he constantly tried to help him rule.

Lord Drake looked away to hide his scowl as the King entered his office. He nodded to his brother that he could follow.

The young Rion was pacing nervously and didn't hear the other men enter. Lord Drake cleared his throat and the boy turned abruptly, red stretching from his cheeks to the tips of his ears.

"Your Majesty," he croaked out, bowing abruptly.

"Why have you returned?" Lord Drake asked.

The King shot his brother a harsh look and then sighed. "Have a seat, young man, and tell us what is going on."

All three men took their seats and waited in suffocating silence before Rion began speaking.

"The Duke of Isenore has betrayed you," he blurted.

The King's brow furrowed in confusion.

Lord Drake growled. "If you're going to start accusing our allies of treachery, boy, you best start showing us your proof."

"The Lady Alixa," he stammered. "We found her fighting off her father's men in the woods. They were trying to drag her home."

"If she disobeyed her father than they're within their right," Lord Drake said.

"Geran." The King held up a hand to stop his brother. "Let us get the rest of the story."

"She found her father meeting with agents from Dreach-Dhoun about an alliance. They've been sending supplies to Isenore. They have whole storerooms of food and other necessities. As soon as she saw this, she ran. Not only were the Duke's soldiers sent after her, but they had Dreach-Dhoun soldiers with them, Sire."

"How are we to trust the word of a girl who betrays her father?" Lord Drake asked.

The King's calm demeanor began to slip as anger seeped into his very bones. He jumped from his chair, startling both the other men. "I was going to give them my daughter," he yelled. "My little girl. The best part of me." He kicked at the chair he'd been sitting in, sending it crashing against the wall with a loud crack.

"A fool. That's what I am. Eisner has always been a slimy little slug, but even I didn't think he'd go this far. Ahhh." He pounded his fist into the wall, thinking of the deal he'd made for Rissa. She'd sat in this very office and cried, begged, pleaded because she knew before he did. The Eisners weren't to be trusted. And now everything could fall apart. They were a powerful ally and would now be a powerful enemy. "Has he been betraying us all these years? We've been scouring the palace for a spy, but was it one of our own nobles?"

"We don't know it's true," Lord Drake said calmly.

"Don't be an idiot, Geran. Of course, we do." He was still yelling. "My son would not send Rion back unless he believed it. And if Trystan says Isenore has betrayed us, then they surely have."

The King looked to Rion who was gripping the arms of his chair, afraid of his very own king.

The sight made the king's burst of anger fizzle and fade. There was no time for anger, only action. "First things first," he said, more in control now. "Rion, rest up tonight because tomorrow I'm sending you out to some of the minor nobles. We need to keep a lid on this until the time is right, but there are those who need to know – especially ones whose land borders Isenore. You can go."

Rion hurried from the room and the King turned to Lord Drake. "I'm sending you into Isenore. Eisner betrayed us, but it doesn't mean his nobles have. I need you to find out how many of them have succumbed to Dreach-Dhoun's persuasion. I'll have personalized letters drawn up saying you're performing inspections. Those that resist will be put under suspicion. You leave tomorrow. This is a dangerous mission. We don't know who is in league with him."

"I can handle it."

"I know you can." The King opened the door. "Garret," he called.

Garret entered the room.

"We're cutting off supplies to Isenore until we know who we can trust," the King said. "Even though it doesn't seem like they need our supplies. Garret, I need you to ride as fast as you can to cut off the supply wagons that left two days ago. Leave immediately."

Garret nodded and went to prepare.

The King turned to his brother. "It's more important than ever that Trystan succeeds because now it looks like there will be war either way."

This journey couldn't get any more complicated. Davi scratched the side of his head and squinted out at the dark horizon. The waves crashed against each other as they churned in the strong winds. Even the seagulls had abandoned the docks today, the sky empty of life except for the threatening clouds blotting out the sun.

"There won't be any ships setting out for Sona for at least a week, maybe two," the captain told him as he wound a rope neatly around his large hand.

"We'll pay handsomely." Davi untied the pouch at his waist and shook it. The gold coins inside made an enticing sound.

The thick-necked captain leaned forward as if called by the coins then shook himself. "No. Those coins won't spend at the bottom of the sea and that's where we're likely to end up if we set out today."

Davi pulled the pouch away and sighed as he turned to walk further up the dock. He'd been the fifth captain to turn him down. They all said the same thing – the crossing was too dangerous in these conditions.

The weather wasn't expected to let up any time soon, but it was hard to tell. It was too unpredictable without magic to keep it in balance. But they didn't have a week or two to sit around Whitecap scratching their asses. With the new information about Dreach-Dhoun and Isenore, it was more important than ever they accomplish what they set out to do and do it before it was too late.

Trystan was waiting further along the docks. He looked towards his friend hopefully, but Davi just shook his head.

"Everyone I talked to said it was too treacherous," Trystan said.

"Ever wonder if we should listen to them? Maybe they're saving our lives."

"We have to risk it."

"Well, unless you'd like to swim … That might be hard for the Lady Alixa in those skirts of hers." Davi smiled wryly. "I still don't see why we've allowed her to come."

"She believes Sona is the safest place for her."

"Not if we drown trying to get there. Besides, you were so adamant your sister stay behind. What makes Alixa different?"

A grimace passed over Trystan's face. "This mission is not for Ri."

"She's capable of anything Alixa is. Hell, she's probably a match for you or me." Davi paused. "I hate what we did to her."

"If you're so desperate for her company, she's here in Whitecap," Trystan snapped. "But I will not put her in danger."

"I don't see how that is your call. She's not one of your soldiers under the Toha's command."

Trystan pulled his cloak tighter across his shoulders as the wind whipped around the pair and Davi watched the man he considered a brother. He'd do anything for him and that included telling him he was wrong. As Toha and eventually as King, there would be very few people who would speak honestly.

The two men walked shoulder to shoulder back to the inn where they were staying. Avery was already sitting in the inn's tavern with a mug of ale in front of her. She wasn't alone. An older man wearing the green and gold of the house of Lord Coille sat in front of her.

When Trystan and Davi entered, he stood.

"Toha." The man bowed.

"The Duke knows we're here, I'm assuming," Trystan said in reply. They hadn't planned a visit to the Duke because they were anxious to be on their way and wanted as much secrecy as they could manage. The prince visiting the Duke would be anything but secret.

"He does. Noblemen asking around the docks to charter a ship into a storm raises suspicion. I've been sent to fetch you."

So much for secrecy.

"We don't have time for a royal visit." Trystan's irritation stemmed not from the request, but from their failure to accomplish their task.

"Then, sir, it's a good thing there will not be one. I'm not taking you to the estate. I'm to bring you to a ship that departs for the Isle of Sona in only a few hours' time."

Trystan snapped to action. "Davi, gather our belongings from our rooms. Avery, I need you to make arrangements with the inn about stabling our horses until we return. I will find Alixa."

Davi returned with their packs only moments before the rest of the group joined him outside the inn. Excitement fought with nerves inside of him. He'd never been on a ship.

The King had taken his children on many state visits to Sona, but never the orphan boy in their household.

He shook those feelings and followed Lord Coille's servant through the narrow streets of Whitecap. It was a coastal town down to its core. The smell of fish sat heavy in the air. Vendors sold anything and everything ships brought in from the sea – fish, shrimp, crabs, oysters, shells. It all had a worth. But alas, even the sea's offerings were dwindling with no magic to bolster it.

The docks had seen better days. Raging storms and surging seas had warped the wooden planks. The only industry in town was the sea so boats, large and small, lined the docks. They were all in for the duration of the storm and jostled for position at the overcrowded mooring.

They were led to the far end of the berth where a small vessel rose and fell in time with the waves beneath it. Any paint that had been applied when it was new had long since peeled away; leaving the planks blistered and bubbled like they carried some disease. The sail attached to the mast was multi-colored swatches, attesting to the numerous repairs it must have undergone over the years. Even the figurehead, possibly a mermaid at one time, had eroded away to an unrecognizable lump with a tail.

"We're going in that?" Davi asked. "I think I'd rather swim."

"Then go ahead," someone said, stepping up on deck. "No one is stopping you. Idiot." The last word was spoken under her breath, but Davi still heard the unmistakable disdain that meant Rissa was there. A smile spread across his face as quickly as he'd come to expect when he saw that girl. No matter what, she could always make him smile.

"Ri?" Trystan asked. "What are you doing here? What's going on?"

"I found you a boat, brother. A simple thank you would suffice."

His look of disbelief escalated to annoyance. "You're still not coming."

"I didn't ask to come."

"Good."

"Let me finish. I didn't ask because that would mean you have the option to say no. You don't."

Davi swung his head back and forth between brother and sister like he was watching a chess match. A grin spread across his face. Rissa had always been better at chess.

"Father said you were not to come."

"I don't see him, do you? Besides, I know you've been having trouble finding a ship. The fact of the matter is without me, you don't get this one. Lord Coille seemed to think it was a good idea – once I convinced him."

"You would jeopardize the mission?" Trystan stared at her incredulously.

"The way I see it is if you say no, it's you who's putting it into question."

Rissa was well-versed in twisting words to suit her needs and it caused Davi to laugh. Trystan glared at him, Rissa shot him a grin.

"Why should she not have the same opportunity to do whatever you're going to do in Sona?" Alixa jumped in. "Do you have something against women?"

Trystan sputtered. "I let you come."

"Only to protect me. When we got to Sona, I was going to demand to help you even though you were planning to leave me with the Duchess. You don't think we can actually help."

"What about Avery?"

"She's the exception, not the rule."

Trystan looked at the still grinning Davi. "I'm not going to win this one, am I?"

"Sorry, Toha. You are only a pawn in this and they are the queens."

Davi stepped on board the boat and had to catch himself as it swayed beneath him. He walked towards Rissa and a warmth took over from the cold that had been in his bones since leaving the palace. "It's good to see you."

Rissa threw her arms around him and he stumbled in surprise.

"I'm happy to see you both," she whispered, pressing her face into his shoulder. "I'm glad you're okay. But I must admit, I'm truly curious as to how Alixa Eisner has ended up accompanying you. There had better be a darn good explanation."

Davi grinned. "There's an excellent reason. I will tell you shortly, I promise." He breathed her in, smelling the salty sea air on her skin, and closed his eyes, enjoying the warmth that pulsed through him when she was in his arms. Footsteps sounded behind them as the rest of their group came on board and they reluctantly broke apart. Davi watched the warmth in Rissa's eyes turn to ice as she looked at her brother. A huff left her lips and she turned towards the new man who'd just appeared.

He was a middle-aged man - short in stature, but broad in the chest. His sun-browned, wrinkled skin spoke of the many hours spent staring into salt-sprayed horizons.

"This is Captain Andric," she explained.

"Toha," the captain said. "It's an honor to have you aboard my vessel."

"Can I ask why you're sailing when everyone else refused?" Trystan shook his hand as he waited for an answer.

"I don't have a choice, sir. I've been ordered by the Duke to obey your every command. The Duke says your mission is important and I am to help you to the best of my ability. Plus, the fiery redhead over there who paid my fee can be very persuasive. I don't know what I fear more, her or the storm."

"Are we going to drown?" Davi asked.

Rissa laughed.

The captain kept his expression serious. "If we do, I promise it will be quick in these waves."

"Not making it any better."

HUMILIATION STABBED at Davi as he laid against the solid wood of the ship.

"Just let it all out." Rissa patted his back and he hung his head over the side of the ship and heaved for the third time since their departure hours before.

"I'm not a child," he grumbled as his stomach rolled once more.

"Of course not." Her tone was indulgent and Davi would have scowled at her if he didn't feel the contents of his stomach coming up once again. At this point, it was only water and acid, but it hurt just the same. He heaved once more, finally running a shaky hand across his lips.

"I think I'm done."

Rissa helped him sit up and when he almost fell sideways, she made him lay on the ground. Sitting beside him, she pulled his head into her lap and stroked his hair, trying to ignore the chill from the constant sea-spray.

He hummed deep in his throat. "Now I know why I never got to take ship as a child. It was the fates saving me from this."

Rissa laughed and Davi closed his eyes to savor the sound,

letting it soothe his aching head.

"You wanted to go on a ship?" she asked. "I always hated having to leave the palace for dull royal visits."

"I was jealous of you and your brother – getting to see the realm while I was left in a home that was never really mine."

He knew these were things he shouldn't admit, but his foggy brain couldn't seem to stop them from crossing his lips. When he opened his eyes and saw the pity on Rissa's face, regret stabbed at him. He didn't want her to feel bad for him.

Her next words surprised him because they were filled with more hurt than pity. "You didn't feel like it was your home?"

"I'm sorry, Princess. I don't know what I'm saying. I'm just so dizzy."

"You do too know what you're saying and I want you to hear me when I say this, Davion." She put a hand on each side of his face. "The palace is your home. It may not have always seemed like it as a child, but we are your family. The next time you say differently, I'll kick your ass."

"You wish," he murmured weakly.

She leaned over him, smoothing the sweat-soaked hair back from his forehead. "Don't think me taking care of you means I'm not still mad. I am. I'm so mad at you, Davi."

"I know." He coughed and wheezed.

"You didn't stand up for me." Her voice grew quieter. "You left me behind."

She stopped speaking when the first drops of rain landed on the deck around them. Davion would do anything to hear her voice again, but a chill raced through him. Water crashed over the side of the boat, drenching both him and the Princess as more rain came.

He pushed himself away from Rissa who was scrambling to her feet. Her fiery hair hung limp about her face and her dress was not in much better shape. When he noticed the blue tinge to her lips, he forced himself to his feet.

"We need to get below deck," he called over the now thunderous rain.

Before she could respond, the boat rocked as it rose on the crest of a wave. Water crashed over the side and Rissa was thrown forward. Her shoulder collided with the wooden rail and her scream was cut off as her mouth filled with water from another crashing wave.

The boat rocked again and she was thrown to her knees.

Fear surged through him as he watched her knock about, giving him the strength to stand and dart towards her. He wrapped strong arms around her waist and hauled her to her feet.

She let out a scared whimper, her feet frozen to the spot.

"I got you," Davi said, his voice rumbling right by her ear.

He didn't know where he got the moment of strength after being so sick, but he kept a firm hold on her as they stumbled their way toward the cabin.

He yanked the door open and pushed her in before shutting it behind him.

With the rain shut away from them and the storm raging out on the sea, her words came back to him. She was right. He hadn't stood up for her.

"How was I supposed to disobey my king? Your father? Not to mention your brother? Even if I had stood up for you, it would've made no difference."

Someone coughed to his right and for the first time, he noticed the others in the room. Trystan, Alixa, and Avery huddled nearby, wrapped in blankets. All eyes were on Rissa and Davi.

Rissa didn't seem to notice their gazes. Her only focus was

the man in front of her. She stepped closer. Close enough to touch. Close enough to kiss. And also, close enough to attack him.

She only looked like she wanted to do one of those things. Rissa had a way of staring straight through him, searing her disappointment into his skin. She could hurt him, torture him, using only her eyes.

Her lip quivered and she clamped her teeth down on it to force it to stop. "It would have mattered to me."

She looked around at the others in the room and scowled when she stopped on her brother. She flicked her eyes between him and Davi. "You two are unbelievable."

TRYSTAN HATED that his sister was with them on such a dangerous mission, but a part of him had also been relieved to see her. Ever since Alixa brought them the information about Isenore, guilt had been building up inside of him. He should have tried to convince his father Royce Eisner was not good enough for the Princess. Because he'd known. Maybe not the complete truth. But something had always been off about Eisner. Rissa had seen it. There was such fear in her when she found out the news.

As disappointed as he'd been about his impending marriage to Willow, he couldn't imagine what Rissa had been feeling. Willow might not have been his first choice, but she was sweet and her family was loyal.

None of that could be said for Royce and his family. They'd betrayed the realm once twenty years before in the war and it seemed like they were doing it again.

Nearby, Davi dry-heaved into a bucket. Rissa didn't move

to help him. She sat in the corner of the room with her back up against the wall. She'd stripped off her soaking dress and replaced it with a pair of simple trousers and tunic from her pack – not clothes suitable for a princess, but good for what they would have to do. A blanket was spread across her legs, but she didn't huddle beneath it as the rest of them did.

Her arm sat across her chest as her fingers clasped the simple gold pendant their father had given her. He didn't think she'd taken it from around her neck since it was first placed there. Rissa looked up as if she too had been thinking about him. Her lips pressed together in a thin line and she dropped the pendant against her skin.

Trystan rose and walked towards her. It was their second day at sea and they were all ready to be done with this part of the journey. He glanced at Davi with a smirk.

"We won't be able to get him on another ship." He forced out a laugh.

"That's fine," she said, loud enough for him to hear. "He can stay in Sona. Oh wait, it's only your sister you forbid to accompany you."

"Ri." He sighed, rubbing the back of his neck. "I'm sorry."

"For what?" She narrowed her eyes.

"Leaving you out of this."

"You think that's why I'm mad? Because I was left out?" She rose to face him. "Trystan, you didn't believe in me. You still don't. Admit it, you don't think I'm capable of helping you."

He was silent.

"Admit it," she growled. "To you, I'm just a princess, nothing more. I'm meant to just marry that jerk in Isenore and start popping out heirs."

Alixa let out a chuckle. "Not happening now."

"What?" Rissa glared at her then turned to her brother.

"What does she mean? And for that matter, you still haven't told me what the hell she's even doing with you."

"You should be thankful, Princess," Alixa said. "My father has betrayed the realm and your marriage will never take place. Royce is a lout, anyways. My father's treachery has saved you quite a fate."

Rissa stumbled back as the boat lurched and clapped a hand across her lips. "You waited two days to tell me this?"

"If it makes you feel any better, they don't want me here either."

"Alixa," Trystan growled. "You're not helping."

Trystan reached out and gripped Rissa's shoulder. She flinched and he gripped her harder. "You're with us now. There's no turning back. Can we put this behind us?" He extended his other hand to touch her necklace, but she pushed him away.

Davi mumbled something unintelligible and lunged for the bucket once again. Rissa rushed to kneel at his side. As desperate as Trystan was to make things right, he didn't stop her. He shook his head, a small smile coming to his lips as he watched the two of them together. They cared about each other and he knew Davi would protect her if ever he could not.

A crack of thunder shook the cabin and Trystan turned when he heard Alixa yelp. She was shaking. He dropped down beside her. "You okay?"

The floor tilted and she didn't speak until she could force the words past the lump in her throat.

"Fine." Her voice faltered.

"Have you ever been to Sona?" he asked, trying to recall all of the council meetings that had taken place in Sona when he was a child. Most of the dukes and other nobles brought their children, but he couldn't remember Alixa being at any of them.

"I'd never been out of Isenore until your ceremony," she admitted.

"How is that possible?" He hadn't meant for his question to be as offensive as it sounded.

"Do you think I lie?" she snapped. "Not all of us were royal princes who could travel the realm at a whim just for the pure pleasure of it."

"You presume to know me, Lady Alixa, when in fact, your ignorance is plain."

Red spread across her cheeks. "And you presume to know your people when you are nothing but a fool."

"What is that supposed to mean?"

"My father's treachery shouldn't have come as such a great surprise to you. It didn't to me. Did you know Isenore is closer to Dreach-Dhoun castle than it is to the palace of Dreach-Sciene by half? Did you know our mines have been failing for years just as your crops have? I've been down in those mines many times for inspections. How often do you visit your farmers?"

When he was quiet, she nodded. "That's what I thought. Your people are starving, Trystan. While you throw balls and train an army that has no chance without magic, real people are struggling. And you know what happens when people hurt, when they hunger? They are vulnerable to treachery. Dreach-Dhoun has been supplying many of the nobles in Dreach-Sciene. So, this mission of yours – whatever it is – probably won't even make a difference."

He started to speak, but she wasn't done yet.

"I don't know exactly what it is you're planning to do in Sona, but your sister deserves as much of a chance at helping her people as you do. You don't have the only claim on caring or on bravery."

"You're right," Trystan finally said. "I don't know everything as well as I should. I only found the extent of the realms troubles weeks ago. I don't even know if I believe in this magic stuff."

"Oh, it's real. I've seen it used across the border in Dreach-Dhoun."

"Maybe you're right about my sister, too. I just can't see straight when it comes to her. It's my job to protect her."

"Someone who loves her would be able to recognize she can protect herself."

"How do you know she can?"

"Haven't you seen the fight in her eyes?" Alixa stared at him and he knew what she said was true. He sighed loudly, trying to push away the protective instincts he'd had since the day his sister was born. His mother had died that day and at three-years-old, Trystan had known he had to take care of that baby.

She wasn't a baby anymore.

He went to where Rissa was still kneeling beside Davion and pulled her to her feet. The boat rocked and he wrapped her in his arms. "If anything happens to you … I'm so sorry."

"Do you believe in me, Trystan?"

"Always."

She squeezed him back. "Then we can do this."

That night was one of the worst of Trystan's young life. The storm grew until he was sure it would break apart the boat and their mission would fail right there in the raging waters between Aldorwood and Sona. It would serve as a tragic ending to something that never truly began.

Trystan, Alixa, Avery, Rissa, and Davi huddled together for warmth. None of them slept as they listened to the creaking of the ship, the cracking of the wooden planks. The single window in the cabin shattered as a plank broke free and slammed through it, spraying glass inward. After that, the howling wind tunneled through the now open window, sounding as if a cyclone had entered the space. It blew their belongings about and brought with it spraying rain.

They were drenched and freezing, convinced they were going to die.

Davi sat up and scooted back next to Rissa. They were both shaking as he gathered her into his arms. Trystan watched them. The scene was the only thing keeping his mind occupied.

"You have to forgive me," Davi yelled over the wind. "I can't die with you mad at me."

"We aren't going to die, you idiot." She curled into him.

"Then I can't live with you mad."

"Fine. You're forgiven. Happy?"

He rested his chin on her shoulder and nudged her face with his nose.

A smile curved her lips.

He pressed his lips to the side of her face and lingered. "At least if I die, I get to do it with a pretty girl in my arms."

"We aren't going to die."

"If you say so."

Trystan glanced at Alixa who was watching the scene in fascination as the only respite from their fear. She leaned close to his ear. "Are they allowed to be in love?"

He knew what she meant. The Princess and the King's ward. "No," Trystan said back quietly as if they were conspiring. "But I'm not sure they know they're in love. At least, Davi doesn't."

"Hmmm. Interesting. You people might not be as boring as I expected."

He knew it was meant to be offensive, but he laughed. It

was cut short by a loud crack followed by the sounds of wood splitting in half. A large pole flashed by the window before crashing into the water.

Captain Andric started barking out orders to his men who ran out onto the treacherous deck. He then turned to his passengers. "No need to panic. That was just the mast."

"The mast," Trystan yelled. "Don't we need that to sail?"

Captain Andric closed his eyes for a brief moment. "Yep." Then he walked away without further explanation.

"Like I said," Davion groaned. "We're all going to die."

The rest of the night passed in a state between panic and disbelief. Morning brought an end to the rain and with it came calmer waters.

Trystan was too exhausted to be happy. They'd been warned by the other captains what going out in such a storm could mean.

The deck was trashed. Water still stood in some places and other areas were cracked and broken. The mast had long since sunk, leaving behind a broken off pole.

As Trystan looked out on the water, he saw the best thing he'd ever seen in his life. Land. They'd made it to Sona intact and alive. It was cause for celebration and all he could feel was relief and a realization of how close they'd come to being fish food.

Their journey would only get tougher from here, but they were all in it together. He just had to trust. Trust that what they were doing was possible. Trust that it would make a difference. Trust that his companions could take care of themselves.

The captain's men brought out long oars and began rowing them stroke by stroke towards shore.

The arrival at this dock was worlds away from the one they'd left in Aldorwood since the sun was shining, and with the warmth came a promise of hope. Or maybe the hope was more relief they were still alive and standing on solid ground. Either way, four travelers stood on the docks soaking up the scenery in contentment while waiting for Avery to acquire them a wagon that would be willing to take them to the Duchess of Sona's estate.

Sails of every color flapped in the wind against the brilliant canvas of blue sky. The ships that sat docked along the pier were in much better shape than the one they had made their crossing on. These ships were not all fishing vessels. Trading was also a huge part of the livelihood on Sona and every one of those ships were decorated to try and outdo the other.

A web of netting and ropes held sailors high up in the air like flies caught in a spider's trap and they called out to one another in jest as they worked. Even though these people were suffering the hardships of every other realm in Dreach-Sciene, the air still vibrated with the promise of today being a better day.

The mid-morning sun was relentless and Rissa removed her cloak in response to the heat. It didn't take long for the sailors to notice. Their good-natured comradery turned to wolf-whistling and cat-calling. Something they surely wouldn't have done to any well-bred lady, but Rissa, dressed in the tight britches and silk shirt with her red mane of hair flowing freely down her back, looked nothing like a princess. Trystan glanced over at his sister in irritation. "Rissa, if you insist on wearing that ridiculous get-up, at least cover yourself with your cloak."

"I think not, brother. It's hot and I prefer not to sweat."

"Good idea," Alixa removed her cloak as well and the whistling increased two-fold since she was dressed similarly. Gone was the torn, soggy dress she'd worn for the past two days. Someone, most likely Rissa, had provided her with a white cotton tunic and britches, tied tight at the waist with a red sash. Mid-calf boots and her rapier hanging at her side, there should have been nothing ladylike or appealing about Alixa's appearance, but Trystan found himself shocked at how the clothing hugged the curves he didn't realize her thin frame possessed. Heat rushed to his cheeks as his appraising gaze met her mocking stare, one brow raised high in question.

"For the love of God, both of you cover up right now before you cause those sailors to fall from their perches in shock." He growled the order but to his dismay was totally ignored.

Alixa glanced at Rissa. "Is he always this uptight?"

Rissa nodded, her green eyes sparkling with laughter. "Unfortunately, yes. Most days that stick up his butt is shoved in sideways. But I'll tell you a secret. Ignore him long enough and he'll go away. Now, I don't know about you, but I'm dying of thirst. Shall we see if we can find an open tavern?"

Trystan sighed as he watched the two women make their way down the dock, chatting and leaving the boys to carry their belongings. Rubbing the back of his neck in frustration, he threw a question Davi's way. "When did I lose control?"

A deep chuckled emanated from his second in command. "Oh, Toha. I find it hilarious you thought you were ever in control of those two." He bent down and hefted three bags over his broad shoulder. "The thought of a drink appeals very much right now. An ale may even settle my stomach."

Trust Davi to think of ale as a cure for an ailment.

The tavern was easy enough to find. It was the second building on the pier, next to the trader's guild and it was open for business despite the early day. The gloomy interior was quite the contrast from the sunshine outside and it took a moment for their eyes to adjust. Trystan wondered idly why it was so dark in here considering it was mid-morning outside, but then he realized every window had been painted black to keep out the day. Obviously, the owner preferred to keep his patrons losing track of time when drowning their sorrows.

The place was comparable to any other tavern he'd ever been in. Stained, wooden tables placed at random around the large room, back dropped by a hefty stone hearth, cold at the moment. A few fire-blackened lanterns shed dim light over the already few patrons that occupied a shadowed corner. Behind the bar stood a pot-bellied, surly man, the glower on his face directed at the four entering his domain. You think he'd be a bit happier to see paying customers.

A table in the far corner, away from the curious eyes of the others in the room, was their target. They no sooner sat before a buxom young thing, used to peddling her natural wares as well as the ale no doubt, sidled up to the table. "What can I get you?" she asked, pushing her chest out, her words and actions meant for Davi alone. The other three may as well have been invisible. Davi smiled brightly back. "What are you offering, darlin'?"

"Four ales," Rissa interjected, throwing a sharp look Davi's way. "Nothing more."

The serving girl shrugged and smiled at Rissa in amusement before sashaying away with enough swagger to throw a hip out of joint. Davi watched in appreciation before Rissa's irritated kick to his shin underneath the table pulled him back to attention.

"Ow, what was that for?" he threw her way as she sighed in exasperation at his stupidity.

A companionable silence settled over the four as they sipped the bitter brew supplied to them. Alixa was the first to break the calm.

"So, why are we here?"

Trystan looked up at her soft-spoken question. "You tell me. It was your and Rissa's idea to find a tavern. We just followed along."

"No, I mean why are we in Sona? You risked all of our lives on the crossing by insisting we leave amidst a storm. Plus, traveling incognito as you were raises suspicion. A prince does not travel without being accompanied by Royal guards unless he doesn't want anyone knowing what he's up to. There's a reason we're in Sona, so what is this mysterious mission you all speak of?"

Her hazel eyes studied Trystan with a shrewd intelligence and he knew she wouldn't fall for any vague explanation, but he tried anyway. "We're here to see the Duchess on an important matter pertaining to the realm. We will deliver you to her household as promised and she'll provide for your safety. That's all you need to know."

"Very magnanimous of you." Her lips twisted distastefully. "Too bad it's all bull." She ignored Davi's snort at her crudeness and Rissa's quiet laughter. "Something of utmost importance has occurred for the Prince to leave his kingdom and his life of privilege. Something has brought you to Sona with a vengeance. I demand you tell me what it is."

"You demand?" Trystan raised a sandy brow in astonishment. "You are in no position to demand anything. What we are doing here is really none of your concern."

Alixa's jaw dropped in surprise as she regarded Trystan across the top of her ale mug. "None of my concern? I've left my home. I've betrayed my father with my admittance of his betrayal to you. I've ruined my family name for the good of the kingdom. I've paid my dues to the realm, so it is my concern."

"You weren't even planning to inform the King of your father's treachery until we found you. You were just running away."

"Screw you," she spat.

"She deserves to know why we're here," Rissa interjected quietly.

Trystan whirled on his sister in annoyance. "What if she's a spy? Have you even thought of that? What if she set herself up for us to rescue her? What if this 'poor damsel in distress' is all an act? And you want to just hand over the most powerful piece of information the kingdom has had in a long time?"

"Oh right. Like that statement isn't going to make me ask more questions." Alixa rolled her eyes. "And seriously? You actually think I set the whole thing up? Like I somehow knew the Prince would be traveling through Aldorwood and I conveniently had Dreach-Dhoun soldiers just waiting at my beck and call to intercept you? You think I placed myself in danger to get you to rescue me? That has to be one of the stupidest ideas I've heard in a very long time. And if I remember correctly, it was you who demanded I come along."

"She has a point there, Toha," Davi muttered, only to promptly fall mute at Trystan's glare.

"Okay, I admit it does sound a bit inconceivable when portrayed that way," Trystan said grudgingly. "But to what do you attribute your miraculously timed rescue? Coincidence? Happenstance?"

"I think it's destiny." Rissa's voice was soft as she switched her gaze from Alixa to her brother. "I have a feeling Alixa is supposed to be with us. Call it intuition or a sixth sense, but I feel she has a part to play."

"A feeling?" Trystan mocked. "You'll have to do better than that to convince me, Ri. A feeling does not an ally make. No, we will drop her with the Duchess as promised, then be on our way. We have much more important things to worry about than Lady Alixa's loyalty. And there will be no more talk on that matter." He held up his hand silencing the undoubtedly scathing remark about to fall from Alixa's lips.

Her eyes darkened in anger, but Avery's arrival with news of a wagon saved the prince a tongue lashing. Trystan would never have admitted it, but Avery's timely interruption was most welcomed. He may have stopped her for the moment, but Alixa was not the type of girl to stay quiet for long, of that he had no doubt. He watched as she and Rissa walked away, leaving him and Davi to carry the bags once again. He placed his unfinished ale back on the table with a scowl and got to his feet, feeling Davi's gaze on him the whole time. "What?" he shot at his friend in irritation.

"Maybe you're wrong on this one, Toha. Maybe we should trust her. If Rissa feels she's to play a role…"

"Rissa believes far too easily in her so-called intuitions and twinges of magic. She's always spouted stuff like that since we were children. I didn't believe in superstitious stuff back then and I'm not going to fall for it now." His voice rose with his irritation and curious eyes shifted their way once again. Sighing, he ran a hand through his golden hair as he got himself under control.

"I agree Rissa had more than her share of imagination as a young girl, but I'd trust her with my life." The serious look on Davi's face matched his tone. "She's wise beyond her years, my Prince. There's something about her. Something I can't quite put my finger on, but I've seen her in the garden. She has a kinship with the earth that I've only heard spoken of in old tales. Maybe you should trust her instincts on Alixa."

"I'm sorry, Davi but I can't. I just don't trust that girl. I know I insisted she come with us, but she goes as far as the Duchess' estate, no further. She can't ever know the reason we are here. My gut feeling is she'll cause far more trouble than she'll be worth."

Hoisting the bags over his shoulder, he huffed after Avery and the girls, oblivious to the amused grin spreading on Davi's face. It's not that he didn't believe his prince, for he did. Alixa would indeed cause trouble, but not in the way Trystan imagined.

The wagon Avery had procured had seen better days. So had the driver. A little old lady with clothes that were barely more than tatters and a head with clumps of matted gray hair that peeked out from under a dirty wool cap. And the fishy smell hanging in the air like a cloud didn't come from the wagon alone. But her face held a wide smile, oblivious to the show of missing teeth and black gums.

"Ello me lovelies. Well don't be shy, 'op in the back." She jerked her thumb over her shoulder before her wrinkled eyes settled on Davi with interest. "Exceptin' for you, dearie. You ride up front with me."

A fleeting look of disgust passed over Davi's face before he covered it with his typical charming smile. "I appreciate the offer, good mistress, but I'm quite okay with riding back here, thank you."

"Well, I'm not. We've a long ways to travel and I like to talk to 'elp pass the time. Ride up 'ere or no ride." She patted the empty seat beside her with far too much enthusiasm. Her movement only increased the foul stench.

Davi's eyes held a plea as his gaze moved over the group. Trystan hid his smile behind a cough and shrugged at his second in command before pulling the bags from Davi's shoulder and tossing them into the back of the wagon. The girls were giggling uproariously and trying to pretend not to. Even Avery had a smile on her face that looked totally out of place.

"Awww come on, you guys. Help me out here," he whispered in panic.

Trystan dropped a hand on his friend's shoulder in fake sympathy. "We all have to make sacrifices, Davi. For the good of the kingdom."

Davi sighed as he pulled himself up to full height and ran his hands through his long hair, resigning himself to being the old lady's company. "Why is it so hard being the beautiful one?" He muttered to no one in particular as he hoisted himself up to the front seat.

It hadn't been an easy task getting inside the estate to see the Duchess of Sona. The guards barely glanced at the fishmonger wagon before ordering them away from the estate entrance. Their disbelief at Trystan's insistence he was the Prince of Dreach-Sciene here to see the Duchess had escalated into ridicule which only served to infuriate Trystan. Upon closer inspection of the Toha sword pointed at their necks, however, they soon changed their opinion. One had scurried off to inform the Duchess of their arrival and they'd been ushered inside. Avery stayed behind to watch over Alixa while Trystan, Davi, and Rissa were escorted into Lady Destan's private study.

If the Duchess was surprised by their unexpected arrival, she hid it well. Her face was impassive as she studied the dirty trio of travelers from her wingback chair beside the fire. Their ruined clothes and unkempt appearance was totally at odds with the clean lines of perfection in the elegant room. Their muddy boots left prints on the spotless rug underneath their feet, but the Duchess paid little notice. Her only indication of dismay, a slight wrinkling of her nose, letting them know the stench of the fish wagon had permeated their clothing. Being the true lady she was however, she said nothing of the foul odor.

"Prince Trystan, Princess Rissa," she spoke, her voice betraying her concern. "I would say it was an unexpected pleasure to see you, but I fear greatly your presence here is a bad omen. Please tell me something grave hasn't happened to the King?"

"No, my lady, fear not. Our father is well." Rissa was the one to answer and the Duchess' shoulders relaxed in relief.

"We've come on other matters." She glanced sideways at Trystan and he picked up the conversation.

"Much has happened since our last meeting, Duchess. We've learned from a trusted source that Duke Eisner has been collaborating with King Calis in Dreach-Dhoun."

The Duchess ejected from the chair as if a spring had been placed underneath. "You speak the truth?"

Trystan nodded solemnly.

"Does King Marcus know?"

"We have sent word, yes."

The noblewoman crossed her arms across her chest as she let the information digest. "Sadly, it doesn't surprise me. I long suspected Eisner of hiding supplies. He appeared far too well fed for someone living in lean times. But I never suspected he'd be in cahoots with Calis. I just imagined him holding rations back from his people – which is still bad." She eyed the travelers with her shrewd stare. "As shocking as the bit of news is, you didn't travel all this way to tell me that. There's more?"

"Yes. A seer has made herself known to us and the King and she brings with her an unbelievable story. She claims one of the fabled Tri-Gard is here on Sona and has used magic. She's felt the disturbance."

"Impossible." Lady Destan's face was a mixture of disbelief and scorn. "A seer claims a Tri-Gard is here? But it can't possibly be, otherwise, I would have been told by…" She trailed off as she glanced back at Trystan with a guarded shame in her admission.

"I find it interesting, Duchess, that you are shocked by the claims of this rumor more than the thought of an actual seer who is not supposed to still exist." Trystan's words were spoken softly, the tic above his left eye the only outward sign of the anger brewing in his stomach. It didn't go unnoticed.

"Don't play me for a fool, Your Highness. If you're here, then you already know I as well keep a seer in my employ. I'm sure your own Oracle would have told you that." The Duchess' voice was laced with steel, letting them know she was not about to play this game. "Ciarra has been my advisor for years. I've never told anyone of her existence, not even your father, since I feared - and still fear - for her life. She's like a daughter to me and I'm not ashamed of my secret. I would do anything to protect her."

"Even keep her presence unknown from your king? A fine line between omission and betrayal, is it not?" Trystan's question was harsh, causing the Duchess to take a sharp breath.

"We aren't here to judge you, Lady Destan," Rissa interjected, always trying to keep the peace. "We understand your fear for your seer, especially if she means as much to you as you say. We know the dangers they endure. The one who came to see us was attacked on her journey and badly injured. You are right to fear for her life. But if what she says is true, then your duty to the kingdom must overcome that fear. If your seer can lead us to the Tri-Gard, it will surely turn the tides of this war. The Prince knows this as well as I."

Trystan acknowledged his sister's hard glare his way with an abrupt nod. "Rissa is correct. I apologize, Lady Destan. Why you have chosen to keep this piece of knowledge away from my father is for you to know. But we are here now asking for your help. According to Lorelai, your seer must have felt the magic just as she did. She can trace this magic and lead us to the Tri-Gard member. If we have any hope of keeping our kingdom alive and out of Dreach-Dhoun's hands, then we need to find this person."

"Are you positive of this?" Lady Destan paced nervously back and forth in front of her visitors. "Ciarra has never steered me wrong in the past. If there was a Tri-Gard member performing magic on my island, why would she not have told me?"

"Why don't you ask her, my lady?" Rissa gently inquired.

The internal struggle on Lady Destan's face was evident for all to see. Finally, she closed her eyes for a brief moment and her shoulders slumped in resignation. "You're right. If there's a way to end this and if Ciarra can help, then we need her to do so. I will send someone to fetch her." Striding to the ornate door, she pulled it open to fetch a servant. Instead, a dark haired, familiar figure fell through at the unexpected void and crumpled into a heap on the floor. In an instant Trystan was at her side, yanking Alixa to her feet.

"What the hell are you doing?" he yelled as he shook her so hard she nearly fell again.

Pulling her arm from his grasp, she snarled his way, "What does it look like? Since you wouldn't tell me anything, I thought I'd eavesdrop and find out for myself."

Trystan's lips flapped a couple of times before settling into a thin line. "You were listening to our conversation?"

"Huh, yeah. That's what eavesdropping means, dumbass."

"Alixa, how could you break our trust?" Rissa stared at the other girl in disbelief.

"I didn't break anything," she scowled Rissa's way. "I just needed to know what was happening. And you should all be thanking me. This is how I found out about my father's treachery. If I hadn't been eavesdropping, I wouldn't have known to warn you and he would know that a member of the Tri-Gard was here on Sona, ergo so would King Calis."

Davi placed his hands on his hips and blew a stray piece of hair out of his eyes. "Well played, Lady Alixa. Not even the Prince can fault that logic."

"Wait. You mean to tell me you've been traveling with the traitor's daughter? And she just overheard our whole conversation?" Lady Destan stared at Alixa in growing horror.

"I am not my father," Alixa shot back. "So don't...."

"I'm sorry, Your Highness," a flustered Avery interrupted as she ran into the study and slid to a stop. "I turned my back for one moment and she disappeared." The sword-master yanked Alixa's arm toward her in a tight grip. "You. Leave with me right now."

"What's the point?" Alixa protested as she dragged her feet, fighting against Avery's pull. "I already know...what's happening...let me go, you big ape."

"Prince Trystan," The Duchess yelled over the now colorful cussing being hurled Avery's way. "What is the meaning of all this?"

"Get her out of here, Avery," Trystan demanded, his face flushed with anger.

"All of you be quiet." Rissa's voice echoed around the room, stunning them all into silence. Even Alixa stopped her cussing to stare at the Princess in shock. "This is ridiculous. Avery, let her go right now."

The sword-master obeyed and Alixa yanked her arm to her chest, rubbing at it and glaring Avery's way.

"Everyone, calm down. This behavior is helping no one. Trystan, Alixa stays. She already knows the big secret and I'm telling you she can be trusted." Rissa chose to ignore Trystan's glower and Alixa's snort of triumph. "Lady Destan, could you please fetch Ciarra. We need to find out if she can help us. And maybe Avery could stock up on our supplies from your kitchens?"

"Of...of course," the Duchess agreed. "I'll send someone to find her now."

"Good." Rissa nodded her head as the Duchess exited the room. Glancing sideways at her brother, she exhaled in exasperation. "Oh, stop your sulking, Trystan. Someone had to take control of this fiasco."

"That's my girl." Davi threw a dimpled grin her way.

"Oh, stuff it, Davi."

Alixa cursed under her breath as she stumbled for about the tenth time that day and struggled to keep up with the shadows ahead of her. A swamp. Of course, this Tri-Gard member would be hiding in a darn swamp. Like really? Couldn't they have found a nice cave in the mountains or a hut on the sunny coast? No. They decided to make their home in a gator infested, breeding ground for disaster.

The murky swampland underfoot wasn't the only hindrance to their travel. An ever encompassing, white mist clung to them, beading on their skin and soaking their clothing. The mist made it impossible to see more than four feet ahead and even to judge time. They had already been walking for hours and it must have been the middle of the day, yet only a pale imitation of sunlight made its way through the thick canopy of intertwined branches and vine webbing hanging above them. Even the light from the lanterns they carried barely broke the gloom. Alixa had stifled a few screams at what she first believed to be spiders trailing over her arms and cheeks, only to realize it was nothing more harmless than the hanging vines. The absence of light was making her imagination work overtime.

But still, she trudged on. Slogging through the pools of stagnant water and ankle-deep mud flats. Through darkness and damp that seeped through her clothes to leave a constant chill on her skin. The past week traveling outside the flatlands of the marsh had been bad enough. But in here? In here the air that permeated the mist was cold and wet and stank of decay and death. Even the inner swamps of Dreach-Sciene hadn't escaped the loss of magic.

She questioned her decision more than once as she struggled to lift her mud-laden boots. Why hadn't she accepted the Duchess' invitation and stayed behind? She was quite aware of the Prince's reservations about having her with them. Even after all she'd been through, he still didn't trust her. And really, she couldn't quite place her finger on the reason why she wanted to go with them so badly. Maybe it was the guilt at knowing her father was a traitor to the kingdom that these other four were trying so desperately to help.

Maybe it was the shock of having Rissa defend her so emphatically. The other girl truly felt that Alixa was to play a part. Not that Alixa believed in prophecy or intuition, but it was a nice feeling knowing someone actually wanted her around. Or maybe she just liked the idea of rebelling against her father. Maybe after all this time, it was the only revenge she could carry out for her mother. Whatever her reason, she should have known it wouldn't be easy. Just the way her luck had always gone. Nothing in her life was ever easy.

The inability to see was uncannily eerie, the silence even more so. Alixa had thought the swamp would be full of life, as

slimy and gross as that life would be. Frogs croaking, mosqui-
toes buzzing; anything but this silence and hollowness that felt
wrong and added to her unease.

"Are we heading the right way, Ciarra?" Trystan's voice
broke the silence, causing Alixa to jump. "Can you feel the
magic?"

"I have no idea, My Prince," the young woman answered
back, her voice timid and unsure. Unlike Alixa who had forced
her way along, the young seer had to be dragged every step of
the way. She'd practically gone into hysterics when confronted
by Lady Destan on the subject of the magic disturbance felt by
Lorelai. She hadn't gone so far as to lie, but she'd cried her way
through the whole questioning. Yes, she'd felt the same as
Lorelai. Yes, someone on Sona had used magic...and it had
terrified her to no end. She knew what it meant to bring attention to it. She knew it would mean people would come looking
for her to force her to lead them to the disturbance, and she
wanted nothing to do with that. So she hadn't told anyone, not
even the Duchess. Lady Destan had covered her disappointment with Ciarra well enough, but it was there, along with the
distress that she would have to order the girl to go with them.
The Duchess was loyal to her King and whether or not she
wanted Ciarra to go on the quest didn't matter. It had to be
done. The Tri-Gard had to be found. Ciarra had followed her
orders without question, but the order did nothing to stop the
girl from whimpering the whole time they had been on the
move. This crying had annoyed Alixa for days and was most
certainly the reason for her sharp tongue right now.

"What do you mean, you have no idea? You're the one with
the ability to find this person, yes? So do it already."

"I'm trying," the girl shot back. "But it's not that simple. The
magic was used just once and the effects are like a ripple in a

pond. The more time passes, the wider the ripple becomes so that the originating point becomes harder to find."

The lantern of the person beside her pointed her way and Alixa squinted at the flaxen haired girl ahead of her. "Take it easy on the poor girl, Alixa." The smooth tone could only belong to Davi. "She's trying her best, no doubt. I'm sure it's not easy being a seer, now is it, darlin'?"

The girl nodded and threw a smile of adoration Davi's way. "It so isn't. Thank you for understanding, Sir Davion."

Oh please. Could the girl be any more nauseatingly sweet? Alixa had had enough of her simpering and fawning over the Toha's second in command. And why did all women respond to Davi like that? Even Rissa? Oh sure he was handsome enough, with his swarthy looks, but take away the face and the muscles and she was pretty sure all that would be left would be a shallow shell. Honestly, she didn't see the appeal. He and Trystan couldn't be any different. She didn't understand how they even stayed friends; Davi with his flippant nature and Trystan with his straight-laced seriousness.

"In case you haven't noticed, we don't exactly have all the time in the world here." Alixa glared his way. "If it's this dark during the middle of the day, imagine how dark it will be at night. And I for one don't want to be traveling in this swamp at night."

"Why, you scared, my lady?" Davi teased. "Any creature still alive in this swamp will be around during the day as well as the dark. Night time makes no difference."

"Uh yeah it does, moron. Do you not realize what lives in swamps? Alligators. And alligators are primarily nocturnal. Let me break that down for you. Nocturnal means they like to do their hunting at night."

Anyone else would probably have taken offense to Alixa's

condescending barb, but not Davi. Instead of being angry or embarrassed, his laughter echoed in the mist. "Really? I wasn't aware of that." His white teeth gleamed at her through the haze. "You're not just a pretty face, are you?"

She smiled sweetly back even though the remark annoyed her to no end. "Unlike you, no." This only made him laugh even harder. His laughter brought the bobbing lanterns of the others as they doubled back.

"Did we miss something funny?" Rissa asked in annoyance as the other three entered the small circle of light. Alixa knew the irritation grew from jealousy. She hadn't been the only one to notice Ciarra's falling over Davi. It must be extremely hard for the Princess watching the man she loved to flirt with anything in a skirt.

"Just a lesson on alligators," Davi teased, oblivious to Rissa's jealousy and Trystan's scowl. "Seems that our Alixa here…"

"Isn't quite the useless traitor the prince makes her out to be," Alixa finished for him as Trystan's grimace turned her way.

"I never said you were useless, Alixa."

"No, just a traitor and a manipulative witch who set up a whole attack by Dreach-Dhoun soldiers to integrate herself into your group."

"Until you prove otherwise, I'm entitled to my opinion." Trystan didn't wait for Alixa's outraged response. Instead, he threw a question Davi's way. "Why have you stopped moving? I didn't say we were resting up. We keep moving until I say it's time to stop." He ignored Davi's smart-ass salute as he turned to Ciarra. "It's time you earn your title, seer. Tell us which way we must go."

"I… I feel we are close, Your Highness."

"Good," Davi sighed and flicked his wet hair back out of his eyes. "And hopefully this Tri-Gard has a nice roaring fire we can lounge beside and a keg of ale. Oh, and a leg of lamb roasting over that fire would be appreciated."

Rissa snorted. "Really, Davi? How can you think about eating at a time like this?"

He threw a dimpled grin her way. "Well, Princess, I could think of other things we could do besides a nice roaring fire, but I'm afraid your brother would not approve."

"Quiet. All of you." Avery's whisper chilled Alixa more than any shout from her would have done. Nothing seemed to bother the woman, which made her unease now all the more terrifying. Her companions obeyed without question, pulling their weapons as the sound that spooked Avery met their ears.

"What is that?" Alixa whispered, grasping her blade tightly as the stealthy slithering mixed with quiet splashing. Something else was moving about in the swamp waters and it wasn't them.

No one answered. Six sets of eyes tried to pinpoint the intruding sounds that seemed to be all around them. Whether it was numerous 'others' moving or just echoes of one, it was hard to tell in the vastness of the mist.

"Don't move." Alixa barely heard Trystan's whisper over the loud thrumming of her pounding heart. She couldn't move even if she wanted too. The mud mired her down with its sticky grasp and refused to let go.

Alixa's eyes darted over her shoulder as a splash sounded behind her. Was there a shadow moving in the mist, or were her eyes playing tricks on her? The remains of the splash faded away and an eerie silence fell once again.

Minutes passed as not one of them dared to make a move or even breathe as they strained to hear any more movement. But there was nothing.

"I think whatever it was has passed on...." Trystan's comment was cut short by Davi's yell of terror as he was yanked backward and disappeared into the swirling mists.

"Davi!" Rissa screamed as she lunged for the spot where only moments ago he stood, but all that remained was his lantern wobbling on the ground where he dropped it.

"Davion," Trystan's voice was filled with panic as he swung his lantern through the mist, trying to catch sight of his friend. Sounds of splashing and scuffling met their ears and Alixa swore she could hear a muffled 'help' but of Davi, there was no sign.

"Davi, answer us," she yelled, holding her blade in front of her and slicing at the fog like it was filled with unseen enemies. A scream fell from her lips as a shadow too small to be Davi, loomed abruptly in the glow of her lantern. She jumped back and held her forearm up over her head in defense as a withered, old man materialized out of the gloom and hurled a heavy stick at her head. She closed her eyes, waiting for the painful moment of contact. Instead, the stick collided with something behind her with a loud thunk.

"No, Guy. Back away."

Alixa turned on her heel and watched in disbelief as the little man smacked the snout of the long creature practically on top of her. She hadn't even heard it approach. The alligator opened its mouth, displaying rows of spiked teeth and Alixa's gut clenched with fear. The man showed no such fear. Instead, he smacked its snout once again.

"Go on with ya, Guy. Stop the snarling. And where's Gert? What's she done with the boy?"

The alligator snapped its mouth shut and turned almost casually as it sauntered into the mist.

"Well, what you waiting for, girl?" The odd little man yelled at her. "Bring the light, we can't lose him."

"Trystan, this way," Alixa yelled over her shoulder as she made the split-second decision to follow the stranger. She heard the splashing as the others ran in her direction.

Running at top speed, she almost bowled the little man over as he stopped abruptly in front of her. Skidding to a stop beside him she had to bite back the scream at the sight that met her eyes. The mist wasn't as thick here, broken in spots by the grove of trees. The gator they'd been pursuing had come to a stop on a little mound of dirt canopied by a snarl of dead branches. It wasn't alone on its perch. It was joined by a bigger one, and this huge monster was crouching over a huddled shape that was undeniably Davi.

"What the hell is going on?" Trystan demanded over Ciarra's crying as the rest of the group caught up.

"Davi," Rissa cried in horror as she too saw what Alixa had seen. Raising her bow she nocked an arrow, but the little man pushed it away from targeting its intended victim.

"Don't shoot it. You'll only antagonize it." His next words were aimed at the gator. "Gertie girl, what are you doing?" The creature actually looked over at the stranger as if knowing it was being spoken to. "You know better than that. People make you ill. Let the boy go and I'll bring you back a nice fat turtle."

The creature opened its mouth in a wide yawn, showing the impressive teeth. "Yeah, yeah, I've seen those chompers many times. They don't scare me. Don't make me use the stick. Let the boy go."

As if the thing understood, it appeared to reluctantly move off of the prone Davi, giving him room to roll over. His movements were sluggish as if he feared moving too fast would cause the creature to pounce.

"If I were you, boy, I'd move quicker and get out of there before she changes her mind."

Davi didn't need to be told twice. Alixa exhaled in relief as Davi lunged and rolled down the slight incline. He barely hit the water before he was on his feet and scurrying toward the rest of them, straight into Rissa's open arms.

"We should go," the little man said and he stepped into the mist as if he knew exactly where he was headed. When none of the others moved to follow, he turned back with a raised brow. "Or you could all stay here and wait for Gert to decide she's too hungry to wait for her turtle?"

It was all the incentive they needed. Davi grabbed Rissa's hand and they all hurried after the odd little man.

"Davi?" Trystan questioned as he sprinted alongside his friend and sister.

"I'm fine, Toha. The thing barely broke skin. It mostly just got my shirt. Although, I'm calling bull on your nocturnal gator theory, Alixa."

Alixa snorted in relieved laughter. Unbelievable. "You're an idiot, Davi."

Trystan nodded in agreement before catching up to the stranger and grabbing his arm. "Wait. Stop. We need to talk."

"We do, Toha. But not here. The swamp has ears."

"You know who I am?"

The little man finally stopped hurrying to study Trystan in the glow of Avery's lantern.

"Of course. I know who you are just as I knew you would come." He furrowed his brow. "Although I didn't see the part about Gert trying to eat your friend. That part eluded me."

"Your pets tried to eat me?" Davi questioned weakly as if the whole thing was finally starting to sink in.

"Oh, dear me, no." The odd little man gave an even odder

laugh, "No, no, no. They aren't my pets. In fact, I'm surprised Gert even agreed to let you live. Usually, she doesn't listen to anything I say. But that's typical of any female I've ever encountered. Guess this was your lucky day, boyo. Now let's get inside before she realizes I lied about the turtle."

THE STRANGER DIDN'T HAVE to introduce himself. Unless there was a whole village of people living in the swamp away from civilization, then he was the one they were looking for. The Tri-Gard elder.

The door to his home as he called it was nothing more than a crevasse in a rock formation that rose up from the mist like some hulking monster. If you didn't know it was there, you'd pass on without notice. It was narrow, so narrow Alixa held her breath as she squeezed her way through. It didn't take long for a light to appear up ahead and the passage soon gave way to a large opening cut in the middle of the mountain. For someone who supposedly had lived here for so long, the old man didn't have much in the way of creature comforts. A small cot sat propped against one wall. A mismatched table and chair lined another. A large fire pit in the center of the room served as light and heat for the space, but it was the piles that sat randomly around the room that caught Alixa's attention. Piles of books, every size, shape, and color imaginable. The books dominated the space, some threatening to fall over they were piled so haphazardly. It made sense. If you were a hermit hiding from the world, what else would you do to pass the time?

"Come in. Come in," the old man said as he pushed a pile

out of the way to make room. "Sorry about the mess. Careful where you step. What did you say?"

His sharp question startled Alixa. She hadn't heard anyone else speak. To whom was his question directed?

"Of course, they know I'm not used to company anymore. Do they look stupid to you?" The next question was directed to the far wall and Alixa peered into the shadow expecting to see another body, but there was no one there. She glanced uneasily at Trystan whose brow furrowed in puzzlement.

"Who are you talking to, good sir?" he asked and the old man turned back, a slight look of confusion crossing his face before it disappeared.

"No one of importance. Allow me to introduce myself. I am Briggs Villard, gatekeeper of magic and the one you seek. And you are?"

Alixa glanced around at the others in confusion. "I thought you foresaw our arrival? Didn't you say you knew who we were?"

"I am a legendary keeper of magic, not a mind reader. If you wish me to know who you are, you will have to tell me." He crossed his arms and huffed their way like they were the ones being difficult.

"I am Trystan Renauld, Prince and Toha of Dreach-Sciene." Trystan stepped forward.

"Yes, yes, I knew that one." Brigg's barked out a laugh.

He moved on, pointing to the next in line. "This is Davion, my second in command, Avery my sword-master, Ciarra, the seer who brought us to you, Alixa Eisner, daughter of the Duke of Isenore and my sister, Rissa---"

"Princess of Dreach-Sciene and daughter of Marissa." The old man finished for him.

"You mean Marissa Renauld," Trystan said.

"In the end, yes, but beginnings matter too, and in the beginning, she was someone else." The old man stepped forward and peered into Rissa's face with his bright, beady eyes. He came so close his tufts of gray hair brushed her cheek and she stepped back in alarm. "Yes, I would have recognized you anywhere. You look very much like your mother." He glanced back over his shoulder at the wall again and snapped at the empty air, "Of course I see it. I'm not blind."

"He's stark raving mad," Davi muttered and for once Alixa tended to agree. The old man pulled his attention back to them once more, a grin splitting his wrinkled cheeks.

"I assure you, Davion second in command, I am quite sane. Sane enough to know I made a mistake when I let my magic slip out and allowed you to find me. Sane enough to know the reason you've traveled all this way to seek me out. And sane enough to know that you're all wasting your time. There is nothing I can or will do to help you."

Of all the things Alixa had imagined could possibly go wrong, this was not one of them. She thought maybe they wouldn't find the Tri-Gard member, or worse that he or she had already passed on. Refusing to help them was not something she believed would happen.

"But you are a guardian of Dreach-Sciene," Alixa countered. "Sworn to protect the realm and its people. You've already betrayed the position once by taking the magic away. You owe it to the kingdom and to us to help bring it back. Our lands and our people will not survive much longer without it."

The little man's mouth gaped at Alixa's words like this was the first time he'd heard such a thing. "The magic is gone? How can that be? Who would do such an unspeakable thing?"

What exactly was going on here? Alixa met Trystan's gaze and was relieved to see he was just as confused.

"You did, Briggs. You and the other Tri-Gard members. You betrayed Dreach-Sciene and the people for King Calis," Trystan's voice was soothing as if speaking to a child.

"I did?" The old man stared at Trystan but his gaze was vacant, unfocused as if his attention was turned inwards searching for a reluctant memory. "Yes. I remember. Lonara and I....we did something. I miss her. It would be nice to see her again. But the last time we met, we did something.... something we were forced to do. Ummmm," his fingertips rubbed at his temples as if willing the memory to the surface. His smile dropped away and he snarled over his shoulder at the unseen presence on the far wall. "Yes, I know what we did. It was Ramsey. He can rot in that hell of a dungeon for all I care. Of course, I'll help them. Of course---didn't I just say I would?"

Davi took a step closer to Trystan and whispered out of the corner of his mouth. "Toha, I think we have a problem. I think our Tri-Gard guardian has way too many bats flapping around the old belfry, know what I mean?" He twirled a finger at his temple in emphasis. "I think he's a lost cause."

"No." Trystan shook his head in denial. Taking a step toward the snarling old man, he placed a comforting hand on Brigg's shoulder. "So, you will accompany us on our mission, Master Briggs? You will help us bring magic back to Dreach-Sciene?"

The man's snarl dropped away so quickly Alixa thought for a moment she must have imagined it. The wrinkled cheeks stretched into a smile once more as he spread his hands wide, encompassing his guests.

"I most certainly will accompany you. It will be a grand adventure indeed. We must find Lonara. She'll know what to do." He clapped his hands once. "Just give me a moment to pack my things."

He walked over to the table and grabbed a faded red silk bag sitting there. Opening the bag, he removed a white crystal attached to a leather thong. He turned back to them as he placed the leather strap around his neck and the crystal reflected the glow from the lanterns with a thousand tiny prisms of light.

"The Tri-Gard crystal," Rissa whispered as her eyes sparkled with excitement.

"What?" Davi asked.

"It's how he still has magic in Dreach-Sciene. The crystals were used to strip the realm of magic."

"Oh, dearie." Briggs grinned as he glanced her way. "There is so much more to it than that. Our crystals were also the reason the land had magic in the first place. They kept the balance. Now, no more chatter. Let's be off."

"Be off?" Alixa was starting to agree with Davi. This man was nuttier than a bowl of pecans. "Didn't you want to pack your things? All you've taken is that crystal."

"Ah, yes. Right you are, my dear. There is something I'm forgetting. Now, what is it?" He tapped a dirty finger against his chin, deep in thought. As if suddenly remembering, he straightened his back and pointed Davi's way. "Yes, of course. I do believe we first need to find a turtle else I'm afraid Gert won't let you, my boy, leave the swamp alive." Oblivious to Davi's gasp of horror, his smile encompassed them all. "Now, who's up for a turtle hunt?"

13

"Your Majesty." Lorelai rose from the bed to wrap her arms around him from behind. The King's chest was broad and firm from the hours he still spent practicing with his sword. She didn't know why he persisted in those skills. When it came to war, she doubted very much he would be on the front lines this time. That would fall to his son, the Toha of Dreach-Sciene. "What has your mind so occupied?"

He looked back over his shoulder to meet her eyes, but she was right. His mind was elsewhere.

"That is nothing you need concern yourself with." He turned to take her into his arms and kissed her solidly.

The frustration began to melt away as he led her back to the bed. The King was a virile man, she'd come to realize. She was many years younger than him, but it didn't seem to matter so much. She knew what he wanted. His heart would always be with the wife he'd lost, but she wasn't looking for his heart.

She let her sleeping gown fall to the ground before he

pushed her onto the bed once again.

No one said she couldn't derive pleasure from this mission she'd been tasked with as she awaited her final orders.

They were all soldiers, whether they wanted to be or not. Every single person in both Dreach-Sciene and Dreach-Dhoun would be caught up in the war. It would come at a cost. What separated the true warriors from the weak was the ability to accept that cost.

She'd been accepting it her entire life. And she would do what needed to be done – no matter what that was.

The King's strong hands moved up her sides and over her shoulders until they were cupping her face. He was such a gentle man and she almost hated betraying him. Almost. She knew the price if she didn't.

"Marcus," she groaned.

He stilled for the briefest of moments. She'd never been so informal with him even though they'd been involved in the most personal of relationships for weeks.

"Say it again," he growled. A plea, not a command.

Interesting, she thought.

"Marcus," she whispered, stretching up to take his bottom lip between her teeth.

A smile lit up his stern face and she realized how unusual it must be for him to hear his name without the title of King in front of it. Power was a lonely pursuit.

He rolled her over so she was straddling him and her blonde hair fell wildly about her shoulders. He reached up to tug on an errant strand, still smiling in a way she hadn't seen before. He looked almost … happy.

It looked good on him. He was handsome, but always so severe. When his face softened, he could be any man, not just a king.

She sucked in a breath at the joy that brought her. Getting close to the King was not supposed to mean caring for his well-being, especially when it would only make her final task that much harder.

A tear fell from her eye and confusion clouded his face.

"Lorelai," he whispered. "Why do you cry?"

Her lips quivered as she forced them to smile. "No reason, Sire."

His eyes shuttered at her returned formality and Marcus was replaced with the King.

She rolled off of him and he got up, keeping his back to her. "I must be off. I have some duties to perform this morning."

He got dressed and combed his hair before rushing from the room without a backward glance. Lorelai sighed as she too prepared for the day.

She was still at the castle for her own supposed protection, but her days were long with little to do. Much of her time was spent wandering, taking note of everything she passed in case it proved useful later on.

The stables were one of her favorite destinations. The constant noise was a comfort to her aching conscience. Horses didn't judge, but sometimes it felt like their large eyes could see right through a lie. One couldn't hide their true selves from the gentle beasts.

A chestnut mare in the first stall snorted and stamped her foot as Lorelai ran her palm against the curved back.

She looked into the horse's eyes. "Don't look at me like that." She patted the long neck. "It's not like I have a choice." The horse jerked her head away and Lorelai sighed. "I know. But loyalty to one's family means something, too."

She turned when she heard a horse gallop into the court-yard and went out to see who it was. A girl sat bareback atop her horse. She slid down and asked a nearby stable boy to take the horse. She swiped the hat from her head and a dark braid fell out. "I must see the King."

When none of the servants responded, Lorelai stepped forward. "I believe he's in the training yard. I can take you."

The girl tilted her head in thanks and Lorelai led her to the King. He was sparring with one of his officers. Sweat dripped from his determined face as he stepped forward to deliver what would be a killing move against a real attacker. In practice, it only served to knock the other man on his backside and steal the breath from his lungs. He panted and wheezed until he could finally speak.

"Well fought, Sire."

The King helped him to his feet and then caught sight of Lorelai. He smiled wide and she thought everyone in attendance must know what she was to him.

"Your Majesty," she said. "A messenger has arrived for you."

The dark-haired woman stepped up and bowed. "Sire, I have urgent news."

"Come," the King beckoned, accepting his shirt from a nearby servant. "You as well, Lorelai."

They followed him into the palace to his office. Lord Drake was absent and Lorelai was happy for the reprieve. There was something about the King's brother that made her skin crawl. He couldn't be trusted. But then, neither could she.

The King turned back to the Messenger. "Now, what is the urgent matter? Does it have to do with my son? My daughter?"

Lorelai knew the King had been anxious to hear of his children. She thought it endearing how much he loved his children. He truly was a good man. Kind. Loyal. He loved his people. He was the kind of king people followed willingly and that was why she'd been sent.

"In part, Sire." The Messenger took a breath. "The Duchess of Sona has entrusted me with a simple message for your ears only." She glanced at Lorelai nervously.

"Speak your message," the King commanded.

She swallowed hard and met his gaze. "The Toha and princess have completed his mission on Sona successfully."

A loud breath released from the King and his face relaxed. "Thank the earth." Then, as if replaying the message in his mind, his back straightened. "Wait ... the Princess?"

"Yes, Sire. Princess Rissa was with the Toha when they spoke to the Duchess."

He closed his eyes for a brief moment. "I should have known." He sat down, slumping back as resignation washed over him. "You said your message was only in part due to them?"

"I'm a trader, Sire. I travel between the Sona and the villages of Aldorwood and Isenore quite a bit, distributing goods and also ..." she stopped speaking.

"Gathering intel for the Duchess." The King leaned forward. "I understand your role, go on."

"Usually, we must take the roads because of the size of our wagons rather than the shorter path through the woods to get to the palace. Two days ago, the group I was with was attacked."

The King pressed his lips together, allowing her to continue.

"They were soldiers wearing the colors of the Duke of Isenore. At first, they came to us saying they were looking for the Lady Alixa. We all know she is rumored to have been kidnapped. We allowed the soldiers to travel with us and make camp with us. In the night, there was a slaughter."

Lorelai gasped even though she wasn't all that surprised.

Average citizens always took the worst of it in times like these.

The King's face was an emotionless mask. "How did you get away?"

"I …" She sucked in a breath. "I had set up my things on the edges of our camp. I'm good with a blade and they use me as a lookout for bandits or wild animals. We didn't expect the attack to come from within the camp. One of the older men yelled to me that I must reach the King seconds before he was cut down. I had my own horse so I took off. I didn't even have time to saddle him."

"You were very brave."

"Bravery has nothing to do with it, Sire. I had to get here to deliver my message, but also to relay what I've seen. We weren't the only ones. I rode along the road for a day and a half after." She paused and closed her eyes for the briefest of moments. "There were others. Traders. Entertainers. Travelers. Even a few soldiers in the Aldorwood colors. All dead. Sire, the realm's roads have always been home to bandits, but this is different. You must get out the word that they are no longer safe to travel. What it means for moving supplies to the villages, I don't know and that frightens me."

The King sat motionless for a moment. "The forest roads will have to do between here and Whitecap. There are other less known roads through Aldorwood. The villages of Isenore are no longer our problem and we have to hope those people are being supplied by the Duke with what he gets from Dreach-Dhoun." He puckered his lips as if his own words left a sour taste. "You may go and get a warm meal in the hall."

The Messenger bowed swiftly and left.

The King rose from his chair and went into the hall to search for one of his officers – a man named Grant. He explained the situation. "Send our swiftest messengers to the villages to post notices about keeping away from the trade roads. Find a scout who can make haste to Isenore in search of Lord Drake. I need him back at the palace and out of that realm. And tell our captains to ready a small force to take care of these invaders. Isenore is now an enemy. Anyone in Aldorwood or Sona wearing their colors will be seen as such."

Lord Grant left to carry out the King's orders.

The King marched back into his office, sat down, and lowered his head into his hands.

Lorelai moved behind him and kneaded his neck with her hands.

"This kingdom could really use its Toha right now," he said.

"It has a king," she responded.

"One of the greatest lessons I've ever learned is that a king is not everything to the people, nor should he be. This realm needs both of us." He breathed heavily. "I only hope I have not sent him on a fool's errand because Dreach-Sciene is falling apart and we could all use a little bit of hope right now."

She bent to kiss the top of his head and he turned to look at her. The pain swirled in his eyes. He cared about every single one of his people.

And that, she thought, *is why he will lose this war.*

Lorelai left him to his tasks and went directly to her room. She hadn't slept in there in a while since the King took comfort in having her in his bed. She pulled out the small stack of parchment she'd procured and a feathered pen.

She began to write.

The Princess Rissa has joined the prince on his quest. They are on schedule. We received word they succeeded in Sona, but nothing since then. I hope you're still tracking them.

The King has responded to the attacks on the roads as you wished. His messengers are going out now. I will await my final orders.

Forever your loyal subject.

She didn't sign her name in case the letter was to be intercepted. Rushing towards the stables, she found the man she was looking for. Thom was one of the messengers, but also a part of her uncle's extensive network in the realm. He would pass the letter off to the next person in the chain.

She pressed the letter into his fingers. "Why did my uncle wish for the people of Dreach-Sciene to stop using the main trade routes?"

Thom considered her for a moment. He'd been a favorite of her uncles and he saw his mission in Dreach-Sciene as a step down.

Her blood boiled at the way his eyes scanned her from head to toe. She pulled her arms in to cover her chest and he snapped his eyes back to her face. He seemed to be considering if she was worth the information, but she was his master's niece so her questions must be answered.

"With the trade roads treacherous, no trader will venture into Isenore. The paths that cut across Aldorwood don't reach the border."

Lorelai understood immediately. "He's trying to starve Isenore into supporting their Duke. Of course. The nobles are still loyal to Dreach-Sciene."

"For now." He led his horse out into the courtyard and she followed. "Eventually they will either submit to Eisner or die." Hauling himself into his saddle, he gave her one more look. "I'll be back in a week."

She didn't say a word as she turned to walk back into the palace as if there wasn't a hand squeezing her heart, reminding her that she was betraying every person she passed. And worst of all, she was a traitor to a king she knew she could have respected, could have followed, could have loved.

Rissa was glad to be out of the swamp and back in the forests of Aldorwood. Their crossing had been much calmer the second time and upon reaching Whitecap, they'd secured another horse for Briggs and gotten out of town as quickly as possible. Everyone had been anxious to get on the road after two days aboard another boat.

It had been three days since leaving the civilization of Whitecap behind and they'd ridden hard and rested little.

Rissa curled her fingers in, crushing the dead leaf in her grasp. It flaked apart and she let the pieces lift in the breeze. Even in their sad state, the trees calmed her.

She'd shed many of her clothes as the sun beat down on them from above. Anyone who saw her now would not see their princess in pretty dresses. They'd see a tired young woman dressed almost as a man. The trousers she now wore were large on her and she'd pushed the sleeves of her tunic up to her elbows. Her fiery hair was swept off her neck in a simple tail.

Her father had been right. Her brother had been right. A journey such as this was no place for a princess – so she wouldn't be a princess.

"Weren't we shivering around our fire only nights ago?" Davi asked, kicking his horse to move up beside her.

She glanced at him as he wiped the sweat from his brow. "It's nothing new for Dreach-Sciene to have such fast-changing weather."

"No, but I'm usually curled up in my palace barely noticing."

She grinned. He probably hadn't realized he said, "my palace". She always wanted him to think of it as his home. He wasn't officially a member of the royal family, but he still mattered.

"Something wrong, Ri?" he asked, a single dimple appearing in his cheek.

She looked away, realizing she'd been caught staring. Nothing new.

His grin widened and she wanted to punch him.

"Just exhausted," she mumbled the excuse.

His smile dropped. "Dammit, me too." He swiped a hand across his face and looked back at the rest of their group. Alixa was hunched over in her saddle only half-awake. Trystan wasn't faring much better than her. Avery sat upright, her back straight, but her eyes had large dark circles beneath them. The only one who looked unaffected by their journey was old Briggs. His white hair stuck up every which way making him look crazed, but his eyes were bright and he talked constantly, not seeming to notice that no one was listening.

The old man fascinated Rissa. He was a member of the Tri-Gard, the mythical guardians of magic. He could be powerful, but that power was limited without his two counterparts. The man had eyes that seemed to see everything. If Rissa didn't know better, she'd think he was a seer. She knew he'd seen a lot, done a lot, and assumed he knew how this would all play out.

There was a power in being sure of the future – even when it was far from set in stone.

He looked up as if he knew she'd been watching him. She looked for any sign of remorse in his eyes. The Tri-Gard were the ones who destroyed the future of Dreach-Sciene. Coerced or not, they still drained the land of magic. But all she saw in him was an intense curiosity. He cocked his head to the side, challenging her to ask him her questions.

She turned in her saddle, still feeling his eyes on the back of her head. "Come on," she said, snapping her heels against the sides of her horse and trotting down the path that led out into the open land. Before long, the forest was at their backs.

"We should stop and rest the horses," Trystan said, looking sideways at Alixa. The horses didn't need to rest quite yet, but maybe she did. Maybe they all did.

"No," Briggs said simply. "I don't think they know where we are." He directed that at the invisible person who always seemed to be in his head then turned to Trystan. "Do you know where we are?"

"There's a village nearby," Avery said.

"Correct." He looked to the sky. "Why isn't she the leader of this group? She's much smarter than the rest." Briggs moved into the lead. "I don't know about the rest of you, but a bed sounds better than another night on the ground."

"You think there'll be an inn?" Davi asked. He clutched at

his chest. "Or a tavern? I would kill for some ale warming my belly right about now."

"There used to be an inn here. I think. Maybe not. No, I'm sure of it. I haven't been there in quite some time. If not, we'll just have to find some lovely ones who are more than happy to share their beds."

Alixa started coughing and Rissa's jaw dropped.

"Ha, maybe he isn't so insane after all – despite his 'pets' trying to kill me." Davi laughed.

"Did he just say he's going to find a whore?" Rissa whispered to Alixa.

"Not a whore, my dear," Briggs chastised. "I prefer to call them creatures of kindness."

Trystan and Davi were still laughing as they rode down into a valley dotted with farms. Rissa pulled back from the others and slowed her horse to take in the scenery. At first glance, there was a beauty in it, a simplicity that seemed very much appealing. She'd always wondered about those who grew their food, worked hard, raised families, and lived as normally as they could.

These people were the backbone of the realm. They sustained Dreach-Sciene and in return, the crown tried to take care of them.

As she peered closer, however, she started to see the cracks in the beautiful façade. The fields they passed were sparse as if the life had been drained from them. She guessed it had. That was why the realm faced tough rations. Extreme weather swings and a lack of nourishing magic meant that food was not so easy to grow these days.

The village came into view and Rissa immediately knew there would be no inn – probably no 'creatures of kindness' either, by the looks of things. Thin faces peeked out of doors as their horses trod on the cracked and broken road.

Many of the small homes looked ready to fall, but it was the eyes Rissa met that gutted her. Her horse slowed and her eyes connected with an older woman's gaze, dull and defeated. There was fear too and she wondered what these people had been through to fear strangers in such a way.

They didn't recognize their prince and princess, but she hadn't expected them to.

Trystan stopped his horse and slid off. The rest of them followed suit. Rissa stood next to her horse, holding the reins tightly as hungry gazes landed on the beast. A revulsion coiled low in her belly and it was all she could do to stay where she was and not jump on her horse and ride away as fast as she could.

These were their people.

She stepped up next to her brother and put a comforting hand on his arm. Their family was charged with the welfare of the realm and they were failing.

Briggs hung back, but Rissa caught sight of him out of the corner of her eye and scowled. She'd never forgive him for what the Tri-Gard did to them and this was just a reminder of that.

"Who are you?" a gruff voice said, stepping forward. He was a tall man, but thin, and each of his hands was clamped on the shoulder of a scrawny child. "We don't have anything to give you. No food. No shelter. You should keep riding."

His voice was calm, even, but there was an underlying threat in it. Rissa glanced at the bow hanging from her saddle. She'd feel much better with her fingers curled around the smooth wood, but that wouldn't help the situation.

Trystan drew himself up even as Davi shot him a warning glance. "I am Trystan Renauld, your prince and Toha."

The man's eyes widened before narrowing to slits. Rissa was worried he wouldn't believe them.

"Toro," he said, looking down at his children. "Tara. Run along now to your mother." His eyes scanned the crowd that had gathered. He let out a sigh. "Like I said, we have nothing for you."

"Go back to your palace," someone in the crowd yelled.

"You've already taken enough!"

The first man who spoke scratched his chin. "I'm sorry, Your Highness. You already have everything that holds value to us. My own daughter is on her way to join your father's army. When the war comes, it will crush us, but you can't break what is already broken. Please, just leave us be."

He turned sadly and went after his children.

Rissa's hand found its way into her brother's as a tear fell down her cheek. A quiver ran through Trystan before he gave her hand a squeeze and released her, turning to the rest of the group.

"Looks like we'll be sleeping on the ground again."

Without another word, he mounted his horse and gave it a small kick. They decided to head back into the woods to camp for the night, but as they left the village behind, Rissa couldn't get those people off her mind. The desperation of their lives nearly killed her. Silent tears tracked down her face.

Trystan was trying to be strong, but she knew her brother. She knew the villager's words would not soon be forgotten. The Toha would carry them with him until he could do something to change their meaning until he could prevent the people of Dreach-Sciene from being crushed even further than they were.

Camp was set up in silence and Rissa walked off to take a moment to calm her shaking hands. Once the rest of them were out of sight, she sat against a twisted tree and leaned her head back. An instant calm filled her. She placed one hand on the ground and the other rubbed the necklace at her throat.

The soothing hum began and she closed her eyes to lose herself in the connection. The night was unusually warm, but it was different than the warmth that flowed into her.

A sigh escaped her lips.

She didn't know how long she'd been there when the crunch of dried leaves alerted her to someone's approach.

Cracking open an eye, she groaned when Brigg's face came into view. He was the last person she wanted to speak to. She blamed him for that village – for everything really. She'd never had magic, but she knew deep in her soul she was meant to; that they were all meant to. But it was stolen.

"What do you want?" she asked.

He held up his palms to show he meant no harm and then sat down across from her unwelcome.

She snatched her hand away from the ground and the hum stopped abruptly. When she met Brigg's eyes, she realized he'd been watching her. His eyes widened and he smiled.

"I knew it," he said, his voice hushed. "From the moment I met you, I knew. Oh, this makes so much sense. She had it too so it would only stand to reason that her daughter would follow in her footsteps." He looked to the side. "Didn't I tell you she was special?"

Rissa sat forward abruptly. "Who are you talking to? What are you talking about?" she snapped. "What about my mother? What did she have?"

Joy lit up his face and for a moment, she forgot to hate him.

"The Tenelach," he whispered as if it was some big secret.

"What the hell is that?"

He looked like he wanted to chastise her but shook his head instead, too eager to share his knowledge. "What do you hear when you touch the ground?"

She considered him for a moment. She'd never told anyone about it because, with the loss of magic, anything out of the ordinary was treated with suspicion.

But she so desperately wanted to know what it was and he'd mentioned her mom. Maybe he was just crazy enough to believe her.

"It sings to me," she admitted, waiting for the disbelief to cross his face.

It never came. Instead, an excited laugh burst from his lips. "Tenelach is a connection to the earth that can still exist outside of magic. Without magic, you feel comforted and whole." He leaned forward. "But with it, with Tenelach and magic combined, the things you can do are ..."

As he searched for a word, she waited to hear "strong" or "powerful."

Instead, a smile broke out on his weathered face. "Magnificent. Like my crystal, it changes the way your magic shows itself. It magnifies it."

"You mentioned my mother. Did you know her?"

His look turned wistful and he nodded. "Very well. She was the only person I've known personally to have Tenelach. It's a very rare gift that is passed down from mother to daughter."

Her fingers brushed the necklace that had been her mothers and Brigg's eyes widened. He leaned closer to examine it.

"This was hers?" he asked.

Rissa nodded.

As he reached for it, his shirt sleeve pushed up and she

caught sight of a tattoo on his wrist. Without thinking, she reached forward to push his sleeve up further. It was a triangle inside of a circle with symbols surrounding it.

Briggs turned his wrist so she could get a better look. "This marks me as Tri-Gard, we each have a different one," he explained as he began to point to each of the four symbols. "Magic. Light. Harmony. Fate. All things that must exist for the earth to thrive."

Rissa snatched her hand back, remembering how she was supposed to feel about the man. She stood abruptly. "And yet you drained the land of magic."

"I didn't have a choice." His voice was so low she almost didn't hear him. "No, I've told you a million times that's the truth." He wasn't speaking to Rissa. "I couldn't very well turn on another member of the Tri-Gard." He cocked his head, listening. "No, Ramsey didn't turn on us. Fine! Maybe he did. Go away."

Rissa watched with guarded eyes as he seemed to wait for a moment, before nodding in satisfaction.

"There is always a choice," she said.

He stood to face her. "Not when you're a member of a sacred trinity. Not when the only other option is destruction. That's what would have happened. One of the Tri-Gard was fully prepared to use all of his power to help Dreach-Dhoun wipe Dreach-Sciene off the map. We weren't supposed to involve ourselves in the affairs of the realm. I will wait for the day when you children realize that you're only here because we made that choice."

He stalked back towards the camp and Rissa looked after him, amazed that his mind could shift from insanity to that of a wise old man so fluidly.

THE FIRE CRACKED and sprayed sparks into the air. They'd found a spot in the woods that was sheltered from the wind and the rain that started to pound down. The trees above them provided their home for the night.

Trystan leaned against his pack and watched the flames dance before him. Dinner had consisted of some dried meat and bread – courtesy of the Duchess of Sona after they had returned Ciarra none the worse for wear. Now the exhaustion settled around their group. They'd been going non-stop since leaving the palace of Dreach-Sciene. Some of them had been through more than others.

His eyes found Alixa who was asleep nearby. She'd crashed as soon as camp was set up. Rissa was next to her. She crossed her arms over her chest as she sighed deeply, fighting sleep. Trystan could tell there was a lot on his sister's mind – because those same things were also on his mind.

Many would call him stiff, formal almost to the point of uncaring. He didn't wear his emotions out for everyone to see like his sister did. Instead, he let them tangle him up on the inside.

Davi sat down with a grunt and leaned forward against his knees. Trystan wanted someone to say something, anything to distract them.

Davion was always good for meaningless talk, but his words that came out weren't meaningless at all. "Do you think we even have a chance at success?"

"Of course, we do."

"Don't give me the Toha response. It's me, Trystan. I know how hopeless this is. Even if we find this second Tri-Gard

178

member in the mountains, how the hell are we supposed to get to the third? He's in the dungeons across the border."

"I don't know, Davi. Sometimes I think I shouldn't have left the palace. I'm the Toha. My place is there. My generals are having to do my rightful job. But then other times, I realize that none of that matters without us succeeding in this mission. It won't matter how prepared the army is if they starve to death. So, yeah, it seems hopeless when we know we'll have to cross the border, but it's also hopeless if we don't."

It wasn't what he'd been expecting, but it was all Trystan had.

They hadn't realized Avery was still awake until she spoke. "Even if we can get to the third Tri-Gard member, we shouldn't expect much from him after twenty years in those dungeons."

"What do you mean?" Davi asked.

Avery sat up and faced them. "King Calis is a cruel man. I've been to the border many times, and once I met this man. He'd somehow escaped from the dungeons and made it into Dreach-Sciene. He told me that King Calis has never had a prisoner he hasn't tortured. He wants to kill his enemies, but he loves doing it in the most painful way possible. He's kidnapped the sons and daughters of some of the Isenore nobles. After using them to get what he wants, he delivers them in a bloody heap to their families. They're never returned alive. He strips away dignity, self, and family. The only hope a prisoner has when taken by King Calis is to die swiftly. If I'm ever captured, I am willing to slice my own throat rather than suffer the humiliation of a death at Calis' hands."

Her words trailed off and nothing more was said as her breathing became more even and she drifted to sleep.

"Typical Avery," Davi muttered as he stared at the sword-master. "Full of nothing but rainbows and sunshine."

Trystan squeezed his eyes shut. He didn't fear many things in this life, but Dreach-Dhoun instilled a terror in him.

"She's right. I can't imagine what they'd do to the prince of Dreach-Sciene if they ever captured me."

Davi bristled. "Or me. They'd try to use me against you."

"It would work. I'd give him anything to prevent you or Ri from being his prisoner. I'd do what I had to do to save you from that pain."

"Do you mean that?" Davi turned to face him.

"Of course, I do."

"Then we can never fall into his hands. I don't want him to have anything over you or the realm." He looked into Trystan's eyes. "Do you get what I mean?"

"Davi – "

"No, don't argue. I know we're going into Dreach-Dhoun and you're going to say something about how a rescue attempt is possible, but Trystan, we only get one chance at getting to the third Tri-Gard member. One chance. We can't waste that on other rescue attempts. Make me a promise."

"Anything."

"If there's a possibility of me being taken prisoner and you're somehow free, I need you to kill me. If it's possible. Only then. Don't risk yourself or the kingdom for me."

Trystan jerked even as he knew the meaning behind his words. Dreach-Dhoun would never have Davion under their power and Trystan realized having the Toha would be even worse. No rescue. Just a good death.

Trystan pushed a breath past his lips. "Only if you do the same for me."

"A pact?" Davi held out his hand. "We don't let either of us go to that fate."

Trystan clasped it. "Truwa, Brathair."

"Trust, Brother."

As they continued to clasp hands, the enormity of the situation washed down upon them. Death was better than capture, but would they be able to do it?

A loud pop broke them apart as a log shifted and fell in their fire that didn't seem to be throwing off as much warmth as before.

Trystan closed his eyes as a drop of water leaked through the tree cover and landed on his face. The exhaustion took over and he allowed his body to relax into a dreamless sleep.

DAVI WOKE LATER than the others, but his body didn't feel any more rested than the night before. After spending most of his life behind the high walls of the palace of Dreach-Sciene, he found constant traveling to be a pain in the ass, literally.

He grimaced as he sat up, his muscles screaming at him to stop. He turned his head from side to side, stretching his sore neck, and his eyes landed on Alixa. She looked to be sleeping still, but a moan left her and her body shook.

"Uh, guys," he said, getting to his feet and walking over to crouch down near Alixa.

Her hair and dress were soaked with sweat and her chest rose and fell rapidly. He reached out to grasp her arm and shook it. She didn't wake.

"Trystan," Davi called.

The prince appeared at his side in a matter of seconds.

"What's wrong with her?" He lowered himself to the ground on the other side of Alixa.

"I don't know. She won't wake up."

Trystan placed a hand against her face and her eyes sprang open.

"What's going on?" she asked, her voice no more than a whisper. She groaned as she tried to sit up. "I feel like I've been trampled by a horse."

Trystan placed a hand on her shoulder to keep her from rising further. "Are you okay?"

"Yes." She laid her head back. "No."

One moment, she was looking up at them and the next, she was scrambling to her feet and rushing away. They heard the unmistakable sounds of someone vomiting. When she rejoined them, she scowled.

"Shouldn't we be getting on the road?" she asked as she sat down once again. Her movements were sluggish.

"Absolutely not." Briggs walked up to them. "Look at you."

"I can't very well look at myself now, can I?"

"What's wrong with her?" Trystan looked to the old man like he had all the answers.

Briggs pushed Trystan and Davi out of the way and knelt down. He pressed a hand to Alixa's forehead and waited a moment. "No fever, yet she sweats. Vomiting. Pain." He looked her in the eyes. "I'm sorry to inform you, my dear, but you are dying."

She inhaled sharply and squeaked, "What?" as Trystan gripped her hand. Davi was even too stunned to speak.

Briggs shook beside them and Davi shot him a glare. That only made it worse. A laugh burst from Briggs' mouth.

"I'm sorry." He mimed wiping a tear from his eye. "An old man has to find his entertainment somewhere. You aren't at death's door quite yet, Lady Alixa." He got to his feet. "Exhaustion. That's all it is. You've been through so much in the last few weeks and your body needs time to rest."

He ignored the, "Not funny, asshole," she threw in his direction.

"We don't have time." Trystan stood to face him. "We must get on the road. Do something to help her."

"I know what it is you ask me to do, my prince. But were I to use my crystal, every seer in the realm would know of our presence. Even then, the body isn't something that can be fixed by magic. I could make it so she could ride her horse and finish this journey, but it wouldn't cure what's in here." He touched his head. "Or here." His hand pressed against his chest. "Let her rest. Our journey will not fail because it took one day more. But it might fail if we are not at our best."

Brigg's started laughing and mumbling to himself about a 'good joke' as he ambled away.

Alixa's eyes had drifted shut in the middle of their conversation and Davi stood.

"Guess we're staying here for the day."

"We should try to hunt to increase our food supply." Trystan sighed, anxious to resume their journey.

"I'll find Ri."

"What for?"

"Trystan." Davi put a hand on his shoulder. "Have we seen any animals besides the occasional bird on our way?"

Trystan shook his head.

"It won't be easy to find any. The sooner you realize your sister is better at some things than us, the sooner you realize she belongs on this mission, the better off we'll all be. Plus, I'll bet she could use the distraction after yesterday."

"We all could."

Davi squeezed his shoulder and left him behind to walk further into the woods. "Ri, Ri," he called. "Show your pretty little face."

Women's voices sounded nearby and it only took him a moment to recognize them as Rissa and Avery. They were laughing about something. Davi couldn't remember hearing Avery laugh. She was always so serious and formal, but if there was anyone who could get her to open up, it was the Princess.

Davi smiled when he caught sight of them. If they didn't already know, no one would guess that girl was a princess at the moment. She was walking next to Avery, covered in dirt stains.

A small animal hung on a rope at her waist, staining her shirt with blood. Avery carried another in one of her hands.

Rissa had her bow in one hand and her quiver of arrows attached to her back. When she saw Davi, her face lit up.

He sucked in a breath. Even with smudges on her face, and leaves stuck in her bright hair, she was beautiful. Being away from the palace could almost make him forget who she was. She was just a beautiful girl and he was an average guy who would do anything to protect her.

Avery's smile dropped, but Rissa's widened as they got closer.

"Look." She pointed to the animals at her waist. "We're going to have fresh meat."

"Trystan was just saying we needed to hunt." He laughed.

"Didn't you know? I've always been one step ahead of him." She joined in his laughter.

He stepped closer and peered at the animal she held. "Rat? You're going to make me eat rat?"

"If your delicate belly can't handle it, feel free to let us have your portion," she challenged.

He narrowed his eyes. "You couldn't find anything better?"

"A thank you would suffice, Davi. Or an 'I'm eternally grateful that you spent hours looking for anything we could eat so we don't starve to death'. How about 'Rissa, Avery, you and your rats are the best things I've seen all day because when my stomach is empty, I get cranky'?" She reached him and patted the side of his face. "Pouting isn't attractive."

They walked by him and he grumbled. "No one has ever told me I'm not attractive."

Rissa burst out laughing and then spun to face him again, a smile still on her face. "Oh, and more good news. We found the river."

"How is that good news? Crossing won't be fun."

"Oh, don't be such a worrier." She nudged his arm. "There's a bridge. The point–" She poked his chest. "Is that now you won't have to smell so bad."

He grabbed her finger and leaned close. "I'm not the one with blood dripping from my belt."

She looked down and shrugged, making him laugh again.

"What happened to the prissy little princess I've known most of my life?"

She stepped away quickly. "I've never been that girl."

Without another word, she walked by him. Avery stared at him curiously.

"Davion." She sighed. "I was there the night the King brought you home. I know you've always been treated as family by them. They've treated me as such since I came into their service. It's the way of the Renaulds. But I've always had to remind myself that I am not family. I am not royalty. That is why it's easier to keep the formalities in place. It keeps the boundaries firm in my mind. You would be smart to do the same."

The sword-master's words weren't anything he hadn't heard before, but the longer they stayed away from the palace, the harder it was for him to see the truth behind them.

Avery followed Rissa and the two women dropped their rats at Trystan's feet. Rissa put her hands on her hips in smug satisfaction.

It looked like she was just glad to show her brother up, but Davi knew the truth. Everything Rissa did was for her brother's approval, his acceptance. She wanted him to see her as capable, strong. Trystan said something to her that Davi couldn't hear and then she walked away, passing him once again.

Avery watched him as he turned and followed Rissa away from the others. He stayed back, but she knew he was there. Before long, they entered a clearing that had a narrow stream running through it.

"It only stays narrow for a short time," Rissa said, not turning to face him. "Avery and I followed it knowing there'd be more animals close by. It widens to the East of here and I'm assuming goes all the way to the sea."

"I don't remember you going on many hunts. How did you learn?"

"All it takes is skill with a bow." She finally turned to face him. "I used to go on the hunts every time we visited the Duke of Aldorwood. He was the only noble who didn't mind a woman coming along." She shrugged as if that was nothing.

To her, it didn't hold meaning, but for him, it was another reminder he wasn't one of them. He remembered how lonely the palace always felt when they went on their royal visits and he was left behind. As a child, he hadn't understood. As he grew older, it became clear.

"I want to bathe," she stated. "I don't care if you stay, but if you look, Davi, I'll – "

"I won't, although I'm curious as to what you'd do to me."

She smiled sweetly. "Trust me, you don't want to know."

He laughed.

She broke eye contact as a faint blush rose in her cheeks and her fingers toyed with the edge of her shirt. She walked to the edge of the water. He did the same and turned his back to her. He pulled his shirt over his head and his sore muscles pulled and strained. Riding for days and sleeping on the ground had left him aching all over.

The slow-moving water was cold, and the air held a chill, but he didn't know when the next time he'd get a chance to bathe would be. He washed as quickly as he could and then submerged his shirt to scrub it. He had a dry one back at camp.

Davi could feel Rissa's presence behind him and when he turned, he found her watching him. She'd been smart enough to bring a new shirt and had finished before him.

"Ohhhh, so you're allowed to watch me?" Davi grinned.

Rissa didn't return the smile. Her eyes grew heated for just a moment and then she scrambled away from the edge of the water.

Something was on her mind and Davi wasn't going to let her get away that easily. He went after her. "Ri, wait."

He ran to catch up to her and when he grabbed her arm, she spun. "What do you want from me, Davion?"

"I just want to know what's wrong."

"Besides the fact that we're on this journey that is basically impossible? Or the fact that if we fail, our realm is doomed?"

"I know what's wrong with this mission, but that's not what's eating you." He sighed. "I know you, Ri."

"Obviously not if you think I was a prissy little princess. I'm not a child, Davion."

"I know that."

"Do you? Okay, then I'll change that. I'm not a prissy little girl like …"

"Like what?"

She narrowed her eyes, trying to decide if she should say what she wanted to say. "Like those girls you chased after at the palace."

He broke away from her gaze and looked to the side. "I don't want you to be like them."

Her face told him she didn't believe him, but she didn't press it. She stepped back, threw her bow and wet clothes on the ground, and put her hands on her head. "I feel more like myself out here than I ever did behind those walls. How sad is that? This mission is horrible and I've never felt better. We saw a village yesterday that was slowly starving to death. They hate us and they probably should, and all I could think this morning is that this is where I'm meant to be."

"That's not sad."

"Did you know I can hear the earth sing?" She spun around once. "That sounds crazy, right? My whole life, I've thought I was a little crazy. But I'm not – at least according to Briggs, although he might not be the best judge of crazy. My mom could hear it too. I've never told anyone because they wouldn't believe me. I barely believed myself."

"Then why are you telling me?" It sounded far-fetched to Davi, but Rissa believed it and that was enough for him. The color had risen in her pale cheeks and she'd never looked more beautiful, more passionate.

She ran her hands through her wet hair. "Because I love

you." Her eyes widened as if she couldn't believe what she'd just said.

Davi sucked in a breath, unable to force it out past his lips again.

"I know you don't feel the same way," she said quickly. "And that's okay. I'm a big girl. I guess I'm just in an over-share mood and you don't need to hear all of my ramblings. But Davion, last night I found out that I got something from my mother – something more than a simple trinket. I got a part of her and it made me see things so differently. I've always thought I was only special because of my birth status, but now I know I'm special because she was. I have something to give to this mission. I can help more than just shooting a few arrows. I know I can. Okay, you can stop my talking at any moment. Just please don't hate me over something I can't control because I can't. I've tried so hard not to feel like this."

When she stopped talking, her chest heaved as she breathed heavily.

Davi couldn't take his eyes off her as everything inside of him screamed to walk away, but his feet stayed firmly in place.

She opened her mouth to speak again, but her words were cut off as Davi leaned forward and pressed his lips to hers. She stilled for a moment, stunned, before yanking him closer and kissing him back. Her lips were soft and warm and they invited him in.

He dropped the wet shirt he'd been gripping to the ground and wrapped his arms around her small waist, pressing her into his bare chest. She whimpered into his mouth and opened for him. Her hands explored his chest, leaving heat everywhere they roamed. They moved up until her arms wound around the back of his neck and she buried her fingers in his thick hair.

It was as if the world spun around them until everything else was a blur. They were the only things that mattered. Kissing Rissa felt like putting the final piece of a puzzle into place. It felt right. It felt like something he hadn't even thought to dream of.

His whole life, he'd treated her like a little sister who tagged along after him and Trystan. He'd cared for her and felt connected to her, maybe even had a crush as she got older. But in that moment, it clicked. He was completely and hopelessly in love with the princess of Dreach-Sciene.

She melted against him, allowing him complete control, giving him her full trust.

"Ri," he whispered, pulling away to catch a breath. Her eyes found his and in them, he saw the depth of her feelings. It sucked the air from his lungs.

"Davi." She put a finger to his lips. "Don't say something stupid right now."

His laugh vibrated against her fingers and he rested his forehead against hers. "I don't know if this mission will succeed or what will happen if it does, but …" A lump formed in his throat. He'd never cared about anyone enough to say the words. Ri looked at him without expectation in her eyes and he knew none of those other women mattered.

It was always her.

It would always be her.

Only he would be stupid enough to fall in love with the Princess.

The Princess and the orphan ward. It was ridiculous.

She traced the curve of his lips in wonder. "I never thought you could feel the same way."

He couldn't believe what he was hearing and the vulnerability of her gaze nearly killed him. He'd put it there. With all the years of making fun of her crush with her brother. With the comments about her being his sister. With the countless women he'd paraded in front of her.

She'd been right to be hurt.

And she loved him still.

He realized he needed to say something as no words came to his lips. She sensed his nervousness and rose on her toes to press her lips to his once again.

This kiss was different. The first had been full of a fiery passion, intense. Now, as his lips moved in sync with hers, the kiss held a promise, a spark that ignited something inside of him.

He pulled back and looked at her. "God, I love you."

A brilliant grin appeared on her face and she pushed his dark hair out of his eyes. A laugh bubbled out of her and he pulled her to him once again.

She's the princess. The thought was only fleeting and for the first time, he pushed it away. It didn't matter what else she was. This was Rissa. His Rissa. And he'd do anything to keep her, even if it meant defying the man who'd raised him. His respect for the King wasn't half as powerful as what he was feeling now.

"I don't think we should tell Trystan just yet," she whispered against his lips.

"I do like my head and would prefer to keep it on my shoulders for a bit longer." He laughed. "Just don't go making eyes at me in front of him."

"Me!"

"You're right, he'd just assume you were acting normal since you always look at me like that."

She punched him in the stomach and he barely even moved. "For that, I'm taking these lips and walking away."

She tried to turn, but he grabbed her arm and pulled her back in. Her yelp was cut off by a searing kiss that left her breathless and dizzy.

"Ok," she said. "Now I really should go." She put a hand over her heart and breathed deeply to calm her frantic pulse as she stumbled back to camp.

Davi watched her go and ran a hand through his hair. *Well, that was not how I was expecting this day to go.*

A grin stretched across his face as he rejoined the group.

15

He didn't scream anymore. In fact, it had been years since Ramsey Kane screamed. He still looked like a young man, maybe in his forties, but King Calis knew his looks were a lie. Ramsey had seen many more winters than most.

He may have looked young, but the way his body moved was like that of an old man. Years of torment did that to a person.

King Calis Beirne looked on as his old friend took a heavy boot to the stomach in silence. The thud of contact echoed around the stone chamber, but Ramsey only closed his eyes and curled his legs up as best he could. He'd learned quickly – protect your weakest points.

Calis liked a fast learner.

The King held up a hand, his fingers curled into a fist. The man delivering crushing blows to the Tri-Gard member stopped immediately and stepped back.

Ramsey slowly uncurled himself as the King walked

towards him. His eyes opened as much as they could. The day before, he'd taken a blow to the face and the area around his right eye was swollen and bruised.

Calis glanced down at his bruised knuckles. When he decided to issue punishments himself, he usually only used his magic, but Ramsey had looked at him with those familiar eyes and he'd lost it.

He'd had the man in his dungeon for twenty years and his rage still burned hot from the betrayal. Ramsey's family had once been loyal. It had been because of him that the Tri-Gard obeyed the King's commands. He'd convinced them to strip Dreach-Sciene of magic.

And in repayment, the King had imprisoned him, tormented him.

After performing the rite that drained the magic, the other two members of the Tri-Gard fled, destroying his dream of complete control. Without them, he couldn't finish off Dreach-Sciene for good. He could only keep them at bay since the moment he stepped into that realm, he wouldn't have magic at his disposal. The best he could do was keep Ramsey until he found the others once again.

"I hope you're having a pleasant day, Ramsey," Calis drawled.

Ramsey tried to push himself into a seated position, but Calis flicked his hand, sending a rush of power towards the weakened man, and he was flattened to the ground, gasping for air.

He used to ask daily why the King – who was once his friend and ally – was doing this to him. Those questions stopped many years ago, and it was partially because the answers were plain.

A smile curved up the corners of the King's thin lips and he nodded at his men to leave them alone. Once the heavy iron door shut behind them, Calis walked forward and crouched down.

"I do this for your own good, my friend."

Ramsey looked up at him, his face barely visible through the thick, unkempt beard and long reddish-brown hair. Calis remembered him as a handsome man, one who prized cleanliness and good dress above much else. He'd been a vain man.

The King chuckled to himself as he scanned Ramsey's stained and torn tunic.

It was all he could do not to wrench himself away from the horrid stench.

Ramsey spat at Calis' feet, but he lacked the saliva to have it make much of a statement.

"That wasn't very nice." The King took a handkerchief out of his pocket and wiped off his shoe. "It seems, Ramsey, that the time has finally come for you to be of use to me."

A low growl sounded in Ramsey's throat.

Calis chuckled again as he reached forward and turned his hand palm up. Ramsey's body stiffened and he was lifted into a standing position, Calis' strong magic holding him up.

The King released him to stand of his own accord and pulled a knife from his belt, angling the tip to press just under Ramsey's ribs. He loved the power rushing through his veins, but sometimes it just felt good to do things the old-fashioned way.

The Sorcerer stilled.

"Your Tri-Gard is allying with my enemies. I'm releasing you from these dungeons, but only because I need you. Feel the tip of my knife and remember that you are under my power. One false step and your death will not be quick. I will have my men batter you with magic until you no longer remember your own name and then string you up and bleed you dry ... slowly."

He pulled his knife away and returned it to its sheath as he marched to the door and pulled it open to speak with his men outside. "Clean him up. I don't want to smell his stench when he's brought to the throne room."

The King walked away with two of his guards in tow as the others took charge of Ramsey. He should have felt remorse. Ramsey was only one of those who betrayed him all those years ago.

If he was honest with himself, they weren't the real reason he'd spent so many years tormenting Ramsey. That fault belonged to the man's daughter, the woman who fled Dreach-Dhoun when all he wanted was her. He'd been a prince at the time and his father told him to forget her, to use what he was feeling to fuel his actions.

Then his father was killed in the battles and the young prince became king. He'd never forgotten his father's words and the hate he'd harbored became the backbone of his rule. Then there was the revenge. One day, he'd take down the man who took everything from him. The plan was already in motion. Marcus Renauld would die.

Dark thoughts swirled in his mind as he sat on his cold throne and waited. He ran a hand over his long, dark hair that was plaited back.

"Sire," a mousy looking man rushed into the room and dropped into a low bow.

"What is it?" the King snapped, annoyed at the interruption to his thoughts.

"I've just come from the border. The defenses you have ordered are complete and Isenore is waiting for instruction on their next move."

Calis waved a hand and a blast of power took hold of the Messenger, pushing him across the room and out the door. Isenore and that dolt of a duke were not his concern at the moment. They could wait until he was ready. He stood and began to pace, his heavy steps sounding about the room. Most of his messengers knew not to disturb him when he was in such a mood.

It seemed an eternity passed before two men appeared with a much better looking Ramsey between them. He'd been bathed and given new clothes. Calis almost let his scrutiny end there, but Ramsey's face – even in its battered state – held such a familiarity.

Calis closed his eyes for the briefest of moments and when he opened them, it was almost as if the woman he'd love stared back at him. White hot anger tore through his chest.

"Get out," he screamed. Ramsey turned to follow the guards, but Calis called him back. "Not you, you fool."

He flicked a finger and the heavy doors slammed shut after the guards' retreat.

When they were alone again, Calis allowed his eyes to scan over Ramsey. It was the first time in years he looked almost like the man he'd known before, but the differences stood out as well. He'd never been a big man, but now he was frail. He walked forward, half stumbling. There was a limp to his steps from broken bones that hadn't healed properly. Calis had taken his crystal, leaving Ramsey with no magic to heal himself.

"There's my old friend." The King infused a false joy into his voice. "I thought we'd never see you again under all that hair." He rushed forward and opened his arms to embrace the man.

Ramsey stiffened and when Calis pulled back, he saw the hesitancy in his eyes.

Not fear. Never fear.

Ramsey Kane had been the only prisoner Calis could never truly break; the only one who retained a part of himself, even after twenty years.

"Come in, come in." Calis slapped him on the back and Ramsey winced in pain. "Make yourself comfortable. We have much to discuss."

"I have nothing to say to you." Ramsey's voice was rough from disuse. He cleared his throat.

"Oh my, you need a drink." Calis ushered him towards the large table along the far wall.

"Poisoning is below even you, Calis."

The King pushed down the urge to lash out at the lack of formality. Ramsey used to call him Calis when they were friends.

"Oh, Ramsey." Calis grinned. "When I kill you, I assure you it will not be with mere poison." He poured a glass of wine and held it out.

Ramsey took it and tilted it against his lips, all hesitancy gone. As soon as he drank the first drop, he began to gulp it down, only lowering the glass when it was empty.

Calis refilled it with a laugh. "You never change, my friend."

"And you are forever changing."

When Ramsey looked at him, it was as if he saw straight through him. He'd always had an eerie way about him. The entire Tri-Gard had.

"You grow darker, Calis," he said.

"You can thank your daughter for that."

A pained look crossed Ramsey's face and Calis was brought back to the day he'd told the man about his daughter's death.

He thought the Sorcerer was going to die of grief just as he wanted to.

"Twenty years is a long time to nurse a broken heart."

It happened so fast. Calis flung his arm out and the glass went flying from Ramsey's grasp. Dark wine sprayed out across the table and the glass shattered as it slammed into the table's edge. Calis struck again, this time not bothering with his magic. His fist connected to Ramsey's jaw.

In his weakened state, Ramsey crumpled to the floor immediately.

"End of conversation," Calis grunted. "We have more important matters to discuss."

Ramsey gripped the edge of a chair and pulled himself into it, his breath wheezing in his chest.

"Someone is attempting to reunite the Tri-Gard."

Ramsey's eyes snapped up. "Who?"

"That is of no matter. They now travel with Briggs Villard."

Ramsey scrubbed a hand over his face. Calis backhanded him and he barely managed to stay in his seat.

"Where is Lonara Stone?" the King roared.

Ramsey shrank away from him. "Even if I were inclined to tell you, I can only feel her presence. I cannot pinpoint her exact location."

Calis raised his hand again and then thought better of it. "We'll know soon enough." He walked to the other end of the table where a golden bowl filled with water sat. Lifting it carefully, he carried it over and set it in front of Ramsey.

A gust of wind whipped through the room despite them being deep inside the castle. Calis raised his arms and Ramsey looked on in shock.

Magic came from the earth. One needed to be in contact with it in order to draw upon it. It could be stored in one's body in small amounts - it always was – but never the amount of power Calis had been showing. Then he saw the crystal in one of the King's hands. His crystal. The sacred crystal of the Tri-Gard.

It wouldn't provide the kind of power to Calis that it did to the Tri-Gard, but it did hold some.

The king threw his head back and laughed as the magic swirled around him. His dark hair blew out behind him until he finally lowered his arms. The wind died out, leaving behind a deafening silence. The King placed the crystal in the water and took a knife from his belt.

Ramsey waited for Calis to lunge for him. He waited to feel the blade's sharp edge. It didn't come. Instead, Calis held his hand out over the water and drew the blade across his palm, leaving a red line in its wake. Bright red dots created ripples as they landed in the water and began to swirl in a circular motion as Calis mumbled through a few short words under his breath.

"The crystal of the Tri-Gard," the King said. "The blood of the family."

Confusion clouded in Ramsey's eyes, but Calis was in no mood for lengthy explanations. He ignored the sorcerer as an image appeared in the water.

A sneer curved his lips as he took in the scene. The orphan ward of the King of Dreach-Sciene followed a girl through the woods. The girl turned back to smile at him and Calis recognized the look in her eyes. He sucked in a breath as that look ripped another shred from his shriveled heart. She looked so like her mother.

"Who is that?" Ramsey gasped.

"The princess of Dreach-Sciene."

Ramsey's eyes widened. "You mean she's …"

"Yes, my dear friend. That is your granddaughter." Calis took pleasure in the pain that flashed in Ramsey's eyes.

"She's trying to unite the Tri-Gard?"

"Along with her brother, yes. As I'm assuming you're just now realizing, she won't survive her quest. To unite the Tri-Gard, they must come to retrieve you. Actually, I probably won't kill her. She'd make a nice prize for my dungeons. I can finally do all of the things I wanted to do to her mother after her betrayal."

For the first time in twenty years, Ramsey was truly afraid. Terror shone in his eyes as they drifted back to the image of Rissa. "You're tracking them? How?"

"You're slipping, old friend. Don't you recognize blood magic?"

"But blood magic only works if …"

"Yes, I know very well how it works."

Calis refocused on the image. He couldn't hear what was being said, but he was able to track where they were and who was there. The Princess and the Ward rejoined the others around a fire.

"They've convinced Briggs to join them?" Ramsey covered his mouth with his hand.

"I already told you they had."

"One never knows when your words are lies, Calis. But that's impossible. He'd only go if …" Ramsey turned to Calis. "You're scared. That's why you've brought me from the dungeons. It terrifies you what this young prince and princess can do. You fear Briggs and if they find Lonara …"

"Then we will take them and have all three members of the Tri-Gard for our dungeons. But don't worry, my friend. They will not find Lonara for she does not wish to be found, not by them. Briggs will be joining you soon in your cozy dungeon.

Then you won't be so lonely and I will have another crystal. Not even Lonara will be able to resist the call of two."

"Where are they now?"

Calis closed his eyes, giving in to the magic to get a location. "Near the border of Isenore."

Ramsey leaned back in his chair, his movements stiff with pain, and crossed his arms over his chest. "Looks like those kids inherited quite a bit from their mother."

It was the wrong thing to say and before he knew what was happening, Ramsey was flying across the floor. Calis stomped towards him, his knife hovering in the air beside him.

Ramsey saw Calis struggle to keep it floating. His magic was draining and he needed to be recharged. The King shook as he pushed the knife towards Ramsey. The tip plunged into his leg, right below the hip.

He wanted him to scream. He wanted him to writhe in pain.

Instead, Ramsey went limp. The only indication of his pain was a slight wheeze to his breaths. It wasn't enough to quell the need for blood inside of Calis, but he needed to get outside to gather more power from the earth.

"Guard," Calis screamed. A troop of guards appeared instantly. "Get this man out of my sight. Patch him up and throw him in one of the rooms in the west wing."

They lifted Ramsey and hauled him away. Calis snatched the crystal from the water and dried his hands on the table-cloth, leaving a smear of blood.

Ramsey had been right about one thing. Much of what Calis said was lies. The Tri-Gard was being reunited and he had a plan. It wasn't fear that kept him watching, it was cold calculation. They were following every step he'd laid out perfectly.

"Hinton," he called.

His advisor hurried in. "Sire." He bowed then caught sight of the King's bloody hand. "Do you need that taken care of?"

"No." He held the crystal against his palm and the skin stitched itself together until it looked as it did before. Hinton watched in horror.

Calis, ignoring his advisor's open-mothed stare, strode towards the door.

"Send a messenger to our agent inside the Dreach-Sciene Palace. Tell her to complete her mission and return to Dreach-Dhoun. You know the code phrase?"

"Yes, Your Majesty."

The King left abruptly and didn't stop until he pushed through the doors into the back garden. He breathed a sigh of relief as he lowered himself to the ground and the power stirred and whipped up around him. A warmth rushed through his limbs and he closed his eyes in contentment, thinking of the order he'd just given.

In only a few short weeks, his revenge would be complete, and Dreach-Sciene would never be the same.

16

Nights under the stars were becoming more of an annoyance than an adventure. Being forced to rise with the sun was downright torture. Davi groaned as he slowly opened one eye and then slammed it shut again as the blast of light made him wince.

It was another chilly morning, but by late afternoon, he knew it would seem as if the seasons had changed as heat would beat down upon them.

A rustling noise jolted him from his waking fog and he jumped up, lunging for his sword, only to find a raccoon rummaging through his packs.

"Oh, save me, Davion," Rissa mocked from where she sat with her back up against a tree. Her bow rested lazily on her bent knee and an arrow twirled between her fingers. "It's such a scary beast."

Davi straightened out of his fighting stance and shot her a scowl before taking a step forward. Raccoon would be a nice change of pace for breakfast. The animal's head snapped up, ringed in black, and started to bolt. Before it got too far, an arrow struck its side and it collapsed.

Davi turned to glare at Rissa, but his annoyance didn't last long as she looked up at him with wide, innocent eyes.

"You couldn't let me get that?" He laughed.

She shrugged. "The arrow slipped."

Pacing towards the downed raccoon, Davi crouched and examined the arrow. Straight through the head, protecting any meat. "Some slip."

Looking behind him, he took in the still sleeping forms of the rest of their group and then straightened up and stepped towards Trystan. He nudged him with his foot. "Oi, Trystan, wake up."

Trystan jerked awake. "Did I oversleep? Is it time to saddle the horses?"

"It's still quite early. I killed a raccoon for breakfast."

"Yeah," Rissa scoffed. "The great Davion killed it. Don't mind the arrow sticking from its head."

Davi sent her a wink before turning his attention back to her brother. "Ri and I are going to look for water. You get some meat from that thing."

Without waiting for agreement, he went to Rissa and pulled her to her feet. Leaning close, he spoke lowly. "I need your assistance, princess."

A smile formed on her perfect lips; lips Davi couldn't wait to kiss.

She followed him away from the others. "Is this the way to the river?"

"We have plenty of water still in our packs." He laughed. "Something it will probably only take your brother minutes to realize."

"Davi." She slugged him in the shoulder.

"I like when you fight with me." He spun and gripped her waist with both his hands.

Her breath stuttered on release.

He loved the effect he had on her. Everything else about her was so familiar. Every laugh. Every movement. Every scent. Everything that was Rissa was engraved in his heart and had been since he was a child. He hadn't realized it then, but now he couldn't imagine it any other way.

When he kissed her, all the uncertainty that had always existed in his life fell away. His past was steeped in mystery, but she made him believe the past wasn't worth dwelling upon. It didn't have to be a part of him. He could choose to be better than his origins, whatever they were. He didn't have a lick of information about his parents, but they'd left him orphaned.

It was the girl right in front of him and her father and brother that mattered. They were his family.

Davi found a soft place on the ground for them to sit and just be together. Rissa shifted closer and pressed her body against his desperately. He knew the feeling. He was just as desperate for her. He brushed her red locks away from her neck and followed his fingers with his lips, teasing and tasting her skin.

Her fingers clung to the fabric of his shirt, pressing into the muscles beneath.

When his lips met hers again, he found her waiting. She'd always been waiting for him. An insane desire to erase the last few years rose up in him. If she'd told him how she felt sooner, would he have felt the same?

No. The answer was like a barrier rising up between them, forcing them apart. He'd always loved Rissa, but he hadn't been in love with her. Not until …

That night stayed frozen in his mind. The night of the ball. She'd been shrouded in a cloak of darkness underneath the dead tree in the desolate garden. Tears streamed down her face and when she told him she was to be married, regret sliced through his heart, sharper than any sword.

Only she had the power to mend it.

She loved him.

There were very few times in his life where he'd felt love, but it radiated from her. A beacon. How had he not seen it?

"Davi," she said.

"Huh?" He looked down into her confused face.

"I didn't give you permission to stop kissing me."

His lip quirked up. "Princess, I don't ever want to stop kissing you."

"Promise?"

His mouth tried to form the words, but he knew what her promise meant. What it meant to all of them. The closer they got to Isenore, the more fear radiated from their group.

That's what made him make the promise with her brother.

In that moment, he'd known. Even if they got into Dreach-Dhoun, there was very little hope of getting out.

He wanted more than anything to tell her what he and Trystan promised each other. He wanted to make the same pact with her. But she wasn't her brother. She had unending hope, unwavering belief in them, in Dreach-Sciene. It was what made her so special. She radiated light when all anyone else felt was darkness.

"I love you." He pressed his lips to her forehead. "That is the only promise I can make."

Alixa felt guilty for delaying their journey, but a part of her knew the rest of them needed the rest just as much. By the time they'd gotten back in their saddles, they were all faring better after the much-needed food and sleep.

Over the next few days of constant travel, her mind drifted to Ella and Edric. The brother and sister had been her only friends. She didn't know what had happened to them after her escape, but there was no use thinking about that. She had to believe they were okay.

And now they were headed into Isenore for the first time since she'd left. Just the thought sent a chill through her and her chest tightened.

A shaking breath escaped her lips, but it was only audible to her.

That night she had to force her eyes shut, hoping sleep could close out their dire mission for a few hours.

When they opened again, light streamed through the tree

canopy, blocked only by Rissa standing over her with the offer of food.

Alixa gnawed on the leftover meat as she laced up her boots. As they took off at a slow trot, they finally left the woods behind.

Open land stretched out before them and they made care to veer out far from the nearby village and the lands that surrounded it. She had to enjoy the openness now because soon they'd have the mountains closing in around them – the mountains that had always served as her prison.

The border into Isenore was unmarked and a few days after leaving the forests, they rode across it unknowingly. They'd seen the mountains for the past two days and as they rode closer, a foreboding feeling tightened Alixa's chest.

In that moment, she didn't know why she'd insisted on accompanying the prince and princess on their journey.

Then she did.

It was for that moment. The moment she could look into the traitorous faces of her father and brother and prove to them that she was worth something in this world; that she would be the one to take them down.

Dreach-Dhoun was an enemy. They'd killed her mother. They'd caused untold havoc. Anyone allied with them was also an enemy.

She'd had a lot of time to think on their ride. There was not an ounce of love left in her heart for the man who called himself her father. Part of her worried there wasn't any love at all inside of her. She was growing colder by the day, steeling herself for the confrontation that was to come.

Shaking her head, she tapped her foot to her horse's flanks and sped up to ride beside Avery. The sword-master wasn't one for talking and that was exactly what Alixa needed. She acknowledged her presence with an abrupt nod, not taking her eyes from the horizon and the mountains that rose up before them.

They were on the main trade roads now. There was no helping that. Gone were the less-traveled paths that meandered through Aldorwood. Isenore was laid out to avoid roads that let the enemy move unseen.

They'd only met a few passing traders – all leaving Isenore. No trade was traveling the other way. They hadn't stopped at any of the noble's estates or villages they saw, despite their desire for a warm supper and a soft bed.

Nothing and no one in Isenore could be trusted any longer.

They made camp for the night near the base of the mountains, just off the road. As Rissa and Davi cooked some of their limited remaining supplies, Alixa stood looking up into the mountains. They were only a few days' ride from her father's estate.

They would do everything they could to avoid it.

It wasn't the first time she wondered why a member of the Tri-Gard would hide so close to the enemy. Then she remembered that only twenty-years ago, the Tri-Gard had helped the enemy. They couldn't be trusted. Was this Lonara working with her father?

If she was, they were all doomed.

With a sigh, she made her way back over to the fire and sat down beside Trystan.

Huffing out a breath, she leaned forward against her knees. Her dark hair had broken free of its tie and hung forward to cover her face.

"Alixa …" Trystan started.

She laid down and turned away from him to avoid his worried gaze.

Silence descended around the fire as the world around them grew darker. Alixa finished eating and laid back, throwing an arm across her eyes.

Alixa would do anything to fall asleep, but the aches in her very bones and the dread in her heart kept her mind from easing into unconsciousness.

The boys didn't seem to have quite the same problem.

Someone snored in their sleep and Alixa looked across the fire to see Rissa laughing silently at Davi. Seemed she wasn't the only one with a restless mind.

The sound of a snapping stick reached her ears before the soft clops of a horse's hooves. She was up in an instant. Trystan shifted next to her but didn't wake.

Rissa was the only one who'd heard it too. She'd already retrieved her bow. Alixa crouched down next to where she'd laid her thin sword. It scraped against its sheath as she pulled it free.

Rissa hurried to her side and nocked an arrow.

A horse neighed as it came into view.

"Stop right there," Rissa yelled, aiming for the rider that was still cloaked in darkness.

"Don't come any closer," Alixa said sternly. The horse stopped and they waited.

Alixa took a step forward and tried to make out the person in the saddle. It was a man and he was slumped forward.

Alixa gripped her sword tighter as he slid weakly from the saddle and stumbled forward.

"Alixa?"

She knew that voice.

"Edric," she gasped, dropping her sword.

"Milady." His shoulders slumped in relief and he lurched forward, stumbling to his knees.

Alixa ran forward. "It's okay, Rissa. Drop your bow."

Rissa lowered it reluctantly, a crease between her brows, as Alixa knelt down to look at the man before them.

"It's really you," he cried, reaching a hand out slowly to touch her face. "You're alive. When I'd heard in one of the villages that you'd passed through, I didn't allow myself to hope." His shoulders heaved. "I didn't think you'd made it."

"Oh, Edric, but I did. Thanks to you and your sister."

"Ella ..." He stopped when a fit of sobs overtook him.

Alixa looked at him more closely, realizing how thin he was.

"Edric," she said softly. "When was the last time you ate."

He looked at her like he couldn't remember, but didn't get the chance to respond.

"Who are you?" Trystan's voice shook them. He'd awoken and was now regarding the newcomer in distrust, his sword in his hand.

Alixa stood and turned to shoot Trystan a scowl for his tone. "Edric is a friend and he needs help."

Ignoring the Prince's hostile suspicion, she helped Edric to his feet and led him to the fire. Davi, Brigg's, and Avery were still sleeping.

Rissa retrieved some bread, meat, and a skin of water from her saddle bag.

Edric ate with a single-mindedness that shocked them and Alixa sat next to him, watching his every move. His once hand-some face now had a dark scar running down the right side. His nose looked like it had been broken and left to heal on its own.

His already lithe frame was thin, almost gaunt.

The arms that used to show her every move of a sword,

now shook as he ate. When he was finished, he leaned his head in his hands.

"Edric," Alixa said softly. "What happened to you?"

A shiver ran through his body before he angled himself to look at her. Rissa and Trystan watched them, the latter with suspicion still bright in his eyes.

"You father knew we helped you escape." He blew out a breath. "I was out of the estate because I'd met you with the horse, but they caught Ella in the cellar." Tears appeared in his eyes and he shuddered. "They ... they ..." He couldn't say it.

"No," Alixa breathed. "No. No. No. My father had her executed, didn't he?" She knew how her father dealt with people who betrayed him. He was a cruel man. Ella was only a young woman – not much older than she was. She was punished for her loyalty to Alixa.

Edric started sobbing and Alixa pulled him into her arms as tears fell from her eyes. They clung to each other and rocked for a while before Edric spoke again.

"When I returned to the palace, a friend of mine who was also a guard told me to run. Ella had been killed within minutes of being caught. She was already dead by the time I returned. So I ran. The soldiers....they caught me but I managed to fight them off and escape with my life. I've been hiding in the mountains since then, but it's been so hard." He wiped his face and looked at her. "Thank you for the food."

She smiled sadly and buried her face in his shoulder.

"I've spent some time in the villages," he said. "I've heard things."

"Tell me."

"Your father is making examples of his nobles. Most of them are still loyal to the King but keeping quiet about it. There was one who sent his son to join King Marcus' army. The Duke had him dragged through the streets of the village near his estate. His feet were tied to a horse. By the time the horse reached the doors to the man's estate house where his wife waited, he was dead."

Alixa gasped.

"The son he sent was a friend of mine. Wren." His face hardened. "He's one of the best fighters I've seen. He'll make them pay once the war starts."

"So Isenore is still loyal?" Trystan asked. "Except for the Duke, the people will fight for my father?"

Edric looked up as if realizing for the first time that they weren't alone.

"Edric," Alixa said. "Meet the Princess and Toha of Dreach-Sciene."

Stunned, Edric scrambled to his feet so he could drop into a bow.

Amusement lit in Rissa's eyes, but Trystan just waved him down impatiently.

"Toha," Edric said, taking his seat once again. "I am sorry I did not know you."

Alixa pushed away her irritation, but she felt too broken to deal with Trystan.

And she was the reason the girl was dead. As if reading her mind, Edric wrapped an arm around her shoulders and squeezed. She didn't miss the flash in Trystan's eyes, but she also didn't care.

Edric reported on everything in Isenore, but Alixa didn't hear anything he said. The only thought that filled her mind was that her father was going to pay.

She didn't know when she fell asleep, but she woke to the sound of Davi's voice. He stood over the sleeping Edric, his hands on his hips.

"Why Trystan," he said. "You've changed your looks."

Alixa sat up and looked around, realizing Trystan wasn't with them.

Davi laughed at his own joke without a hint of suspicion in his voice. He wasn't as naturally suspicious as the prince. Since getting to know him, Alixa marveled at his ability to trust people.

She envied it.

Davi tapped Edric with his foot. "Oi, you. I'm assuming you aren't just Trystan in disguise. Our esteemed Toha has much bigger ears than you."

Edric sat and rubbed his eyes before looking up at Davi.

"Thanks a lot, asshole," Trystan said, appearing nearby. "My ears are just fine."

"Where were you?" Davi grinned.

"Taking a piss. That a problem?"

"Why do we have a stranger in our camp? I mean, he's much too handsome. Makes me feel a bit inferior around the ladies." He winked at Rissa who blushed furiously.

"You have never once felt inferior around women."

"True." He flashed his dimples.

"This is Edric," Alixa finally said. "And he's coming with us."

Everyone stopped what they were doing and stared at her. Trystan looked like he wanted to argue. He sighed, running a hand through his hair and shrugging.

"Fine," he said.

Alixa turned to Edric. "When I decided I wanted to come, he tried to leave me behind."

"That's because you're just a poor woman," Rissa put in.

Alixa nodded. "Trystan doesn't like women."

"You mean …" Edric looked a bit surprised.

Davi was laughing hysterically.

"I don't hate women." Trystan crossed his arms over his chest.

"Oh right." Rissa winked. "He likes them in his bed."

"Just not fighting alongside him," Alixa finished.

Davi was still grinning. "Welcome to this little band of misfits."

"Can you call a group that includes the prince and princess misfits?" Rissa asked.

"Okay." Davi gave Rissa a quick kiss on the cheek. "I'm the only misfit. And maybe Briggs."

"I probably qualify." Alixa raised her hand, glad for the lightness of the morning. Ella still weighed heavily on her mind and she wanted to think of anything else. "Edric too, since he's now basically an exile." She looked at him apologetically.

He shrugged sadly.

"So," Davi began, thinking way too hard. "If the majority of us are misfits, then does that mean the misfits are the normal ones and the prince and princess are truly the misfits?"

"My brain hurts." Rissa rubbed her head.

Even Trystan cracked a smile before grumbling something about going to get the horses ready and they all laughed at his retreating back. They were on the road an hour later. By the time the sun hung high in the sky, the road angled up, leading them into the mountains of Isenore.

18

Dread wracked Lorelai's body as images flashed before her mind.

When seers spoke of the sight, they called it a gift.

Lorelai only knew it as a curse. Since she was young, her uncle had been forcing her to twist her prophecies to suit his needs. He'd wanted her to only tell him of his continued success and to others, she was supposed to say what her uncle wanted them to believe.

She couldn't deny him. He'd practically raised her as his own child and given her everything she'd asked for, including a mission.

All she saw was darkness as if she'd gone blind. An eternal night rose in her mind.

"A noble man will rise," she murmured, jerking her head from side to side. "A noble man."

A figure appeared in the darkness of her mind. He was

cloaked in shadow, but his presence set off warning bells in her head.

"A noble man." Her body shook.

When she'd given the very same prophecy to King Marcus all those years ago, she was naught but a child and she'd thought she understood it. She'd thought she was twisting it just as her uncle wanted. With the devotion of a woman of sixteen, she'd been sure her uncle was the noblest man. It was about him.

An orange glow began to brighten the image. Something was burning. It was as if she hung above the ground, looking down on the destruction. The fog began to clear and she realized it was a village that was engulfed in the flames.

The man she'd seen before was gone now and her mind started to flash between images. The Dreach-Dhoun castle appeared and it too was burning. Another village – one she recognized as the village near the palace of Dreach-Sciene – had fighting in the streets.

A blackness overcame her mind again and her eyes snapped open as sweat and tears mingled on her face.

She realized now that the prophecy she'd given about the noble man had hidden it's deeper meaning from her. The King took it as a prophecy of hope. He thought they would all be saved, that someone would lead them to regain their magic.

But the cost would be everything else and now she saw it for what it truly was.

A prophecy of darkness.

A prophecy of death.

Rolling over, she crawled out from under the King's arm, surprised she hadn't woken him in the midst of her vision. The man slept like a rock. He was as stubborn as one too.

Looking down into his face, she tried to smile, but the

weight of her visions was too much. She released a sigh and crawled from the bed to get dressed.

The palace was quiet in the middle of the night. As she walked along the cold halls, she took in the cracked stone and meager decorations. It was a reminder of the scarce times in Dreach-Sciene. How long would the realm survive in a war?

Her uncle's army would be well-fed and well-equipped.

Two guards that looked like nothing more than farm lads stood near the door that led out into the courtyard. She looked into their youthful faces as they nodded to her and wondered if they would survive this war.

All she saw for their future was desperation.

She chewed on her lip and she walked towards the stables. Most of the stable lads were fast asleep in their beds. Only one leaned up against the far wall, dozing.

Finding her favorite beauty, Lorelai finally smiled as she stepped up to the stall.

"There you are," she cooed.

The horse neighed and kicked her foot.

"Don't get too excited. I just came to talk." She scratched it between the eyes and ran her fingers down the soft nose. "I don't know what I'm doing anymore."

The horse snorted.

"You're right. It's ridiculous. I came here for a reason."

A warm nose nudged her arm and she raised it to tangle her fingers in the silky mane.

"I wasn't supposed to care." She looked into the horse's unblinking stare. "He's a good man, and I ..."

"Don't tell me you've fallen in love with the King," a voice sneered behind her.

Lorelai spun to face Thom. She'd been so entranced by the

horse that she hadn't heard him come in despite the loud steps of his horse. Yet, he'd heard her. Every word.

He glared at her from the door to the stables and then walked forward, pulling his horse in behind him. He put the beast in the empty stall beside her and began to remove the saddle.

"I hate arriving at night because I've got to take care of this thing myself." Thom grunted as he lifted the saddle and carried it to a hook on the stall.

Not for the first time, Lorelai marveled at her uncle's ability to place his people within the palace of Dreach-Sciene. Thom was one of the most trusted messengers of King Marcus. He had free reign of the palace and could come and go as he pleased.

"Think the King is still awake at this hour?" Thom asked, finally looking at her again.

"He's not."

"Right." His lips curled up as his eyes roamed over her lecherously. "I guess you would know." He laughed and it just confirmed what she already knew.

To her uncle's other agents, she was a joke. She was a whore for the good of Dreach-Dhoun. It wasn't the first time her uncle had sent her to someone's bed to gather intel.

Clenching her jaw so tightly it hurt, she squared her shoulders. A small growl sounded behind her and she turned to find the horse baring her teeth to Thom. That caused a harsh laugh to push past Lorelai's lips.

"The horse has good taste," she said.

Thom scowled as he pulled a scroll from his pocket and held it out to her. "One of the King's messengers met me with this."

He didn't mean King Marcus.

"Did you read it?" she asked, taking it from him.

"Of course."

She untied the ribbon holding it together with trembling hands and unrolled the parchment. One phrase was scrawled in thick black ink.

Tá sé in am

"It's time," Lorelai whispered. "Do you know what this means?"

"I have a guess." He leaned against her stall and pushed dark hair out of his tired eyes.

She knew exactly what it meant and for the first time, she couldn't bring herself to hate Thom. She had one more task to complete and he was the only person in the palace on her side.

She patted the horse's neck once more and left the stables behind. Her vision from before was on her mind. Was she the catalyst? Was this the point that sent Dreach-Sciene descending further into darkness?

She shouldn't care. It wasn't her realm.

But she did.

She didn't go back to the King's room that night. Instead, she went to her own. She lay in her large bed with the canopy overhead feeling a hollowness in her chest.

The crushing loneliness from her childhood returned, and she was still crying when she finally fell asleep.

Morning came too soon. She hadn't slept well as memories from her vision haunted her dream. She sat at her dressing table, twisting her pale hair into a long braid. Out of the corner of her eye, she caught the shine of jewels and reached forward to grab the hilt of the knife King Marcus had given her.

He'd been right. She'd never felt unsafe in his palace.

She twisted the beautiful jeweled hilt in her hand and touched her index finger to the point of the blade. A bead of blood appeared. It was a sharp blade. She'd barely felt a thing. Closing her eyes for a brief moment, Lorelai imagined she was anyone else. She opened them to stare at the crystal blue eyes in the looking glass. She didn't know when she stopped recognizing herself.

Maybe it was the first time she'd taken a mission for her uncle. She'd been sixteen and tasked with helping her uncle infiltrate Dreach-Sciene. Too young to be a spy. Too young to know any different.

Maybe it was the first time she used her body to deceive a man.

Maybe it was when the first drop of blood had spilled on her hands.

She flinched and the blade clattered loudly to the dressing table as she wiped her hands furiously against her skirts.

The feeling of blood never goes away.

"You're going crazy, Lorelai," she mumbled to herself. "Get ahold of yourself."

Tá sé in am.

No, not yet. It couldn't be time.

Tá sé in am.

Her heart beat rapidly and she stood on shaking legs before collapsing back onto her bed.

At one point in the day, someone knocked at her door. She ignored it and curled further in on herself.

The light receded across her floor until it was no longer streaming through her windows and night descended. A calm came over her as she thought about the next few days. Her mission was almost complete and then she could return home and stop pretending.

· · ·

HOME. She longed for the familiar. Her uncle may have raised her, but her mother would be there as well. In her lucid moments, she was even kind.

There was no use waiting for the inevitable.

Lorelai stood in front of the looking glass and fixed her appearance. When she was satisfied, she tucked the King's knife at her belt and went in search of Thom.

"Tonight," she said when she found him.

"Tonight," he repeated, a look of relief crossing his face. "I will have the horses ready."

"Plural?"

He looked around to make sure no one was listening. "I've been ordered to bring you back to Dreach-Dhoun. King Calis has put others in place here for when we leave."

"Who?"

"He didn't tell me."

Her uncle was always so secretive.

"Just do your job," Thom said. "I will have everything else ready just as we've planned."

She shot him one final look and left him in the courtyard. Her eyes didn't take in any of her surroundings on the way to the King's rooms because her mind was too full of her one purpose.

The guards let her pass and she knocked lightly on the door. A surprised king opened it.

Despite his obvious shock, a smile spread from one side of his mouth to the other. "Lorelai. I was not expecting you since you've been absent all day."

She forced her lips into a smile. "Are you going to let me in?"

He chuckled and held the door wide.

She ducked under his arm and spun when he shut the door.

He stalked towards her like a cat and gripped her about the waist.

"I've missed you." His words cut off when he pressed his lips to hers. They stopped moving abruptly when his hand brushed the hilt of the dagger at her waist.

She stilled, holding her breath.

"What's this?" he removed the knife from its sheath and stared at her for a long moment before a laugh rumbled low in his chest. "Careful, Seer. You don't want to accidentally stab your king."

She released a tense breath as he threw the knife on the table beside the bed.

Her heart was racing frantically and not because of his closeness. When he kissed her again, it began to calm. He walked her back towards the bed and she let him undo the laces of her dress. She shimmied out of it and pulled it down over her hips to pool at her feet. She hadn't worn anything beneath it and his gaze trailed heat across her skin.

He laid her down and his gentleness caused tears to come to her eyes.

King Marcus Renauld was a good man. That was all she knew in that moment. All thoughts of going home fled from her mind as he made her feel more than any mission ever had.

A few minutes later, she laid her head on his chest and curled her fingers into the hairs there. He kissed the top of her head.

"I received word today that my son and daughter have reached the Isenore border. They might just save us all." He smiled against her head.

The pride in his voice gutted her. To everyone else, Trystan and Rissa were the Toha and the Princess. To the King, they were his children. He loved them in a way she only wished her mother loved her.

He mumbled a few other things about his children and even Davion before drifting off.

Finally, she thought, tears streaming down her face.

His chest rose and fell steadily and she imagined his dreams were peaceful. It was the only way she could go through with this. His arm held her protectively. She picked it up off her stomach and set it on the bed. The blanket tangled in her legs and she almost fell to the ground face first, but she caught herself and stood up. The moonlight streamed through the window, casting a glow on her pale skin as she walked to the other side of the bed.

The knife sat there, inviting her to grip its jeweled, golden hilt.

Her hand shook as she lifted it. It was an archaic way to kill, a knife. In Dreach-Dhoun, their magic could be used for dealing death blows.

Dreach-Sciene had to resort to cruel, painful, bloody methods.

Her fingers curled around the hilt tightly.

She could go home.

She climbed onto the bed.

In Dreach-Dhoun, she'd have more magic than just the sight.

She climbed over King Marcus and straddled him, telling herself to remember the big picture. This was for her realm.

Her eyes found the spot on his chest that would be quickest for him. Only moments ago, her fingers had played with the hair that would soon be stained red.

Tears dripped from her face and her eyes followed them until they dampened the King's skin.

She sucked in a breath as her chest heaved traitorously. Would her uncle ever truly understand what she'd done for him?

She raised the knife. It was time to choose her allegiance.

Before she could bring it down, the King murmured her name and slowly opened his eyes. It took him a second to realize the situation. His gaze darted from the knife in her hands, to her legs straddling him, to her tear stained face.

His eyes widened, but he didn't push her off.

"Why?" he croaked.

"I have to." She wiped at the tears on her face with one hand while the other still angled the knife above his chest.

"Lorelai." His eyes hardened. "How long have you been betraying me?"

"I can't betray you if I was never yours," she snapped. "Dreach-Sciene is not my realm."

Understanding lit in his cold eyes and he finally threw her off him with one movement. She landed beside him on the bed but didn't release the knife. He jumped from the bed and faced her.

"My own knife?" he asked, a deep hurt in his words. "My own freaking knife."

He circled the bed to face her.

She suddenly didn't feel so confident. Her mission was lost the moment he woke, the moment she was forced to look into his eyes.

Her fingers released the knife and it hit the stone ground with a loud clang. A sob broke free of her and her legs gave out. She dropped to her knees and folded over them, her blonde braid falling over one shoulder.

"I'm sorry," she whispered, looking up at him. "I ..."

He knelt in front of her and shocked her when he pulled

her into his strong arms. His bare skin was warm against her icy flesh and she sagged into him.

"I didn't have a choice," she cried. "I came here with a mission. I didn't expect to ..."

"I didn't expect it, either." His fingers traced the ridges of her spine, sending a shiver through her body. "I don't know what to do now. You're a traitor to the crown."

She cried harder.

"I'm going to give you a few minutes to collect yourself and get dressed before I call in my guards to question you." He took the knife from her feet. "And I'm taking this." He looked like he was going to stand and back away from her, but thought better of it. He pulled her to him once again as if he never wanted to let go.

He placed a kiss in the crook of her neck and then jerked against her, his eyes going wide.

A groan gurgled out of him and he sagged against her. Lorelai looked up in alarm to find Thom standing over them and a knife sticking out from between the King's shoulder blades.

It happened so quickly. The King's eyes glazed over and blood leaked from his mouth, staining Lorelai's skin, as he fell sideways.

"We need to go," Thom said coolly. "Get dressed."

She dressed in a daze as cracks formed in her heart. Marcus was dead, but not by her hand. The kind king would never again look at her as if she was beautiful, worthy.

She hadn't thought to wipe the blood from her skin and it now made her dress stick to her. Outside the door, they stepped over two unconscious guards and tried to walk as calmly as they could to the stables. Thom said they must not arouse suspicion because they needed to be long gone before anyone found the King.

Their horses were saddled and ready to go with saddlebags full of supplies. They left through a less used side gate and galloped away from the palace. She didn't once glance back because inside she knew.

She'd just helped the prophecy of darkness come to pass.

There'd never been a choice as to which side she was on. She spurred ahead of Thom and pointed her horse's nose towards the road that would take her home.

The mountains had a rugged beauty to them from afar, but up close the rocky crags and sheer cliffs sent a chill over Rissa. This mountain range was all that stood between them and Dreach-Dhoun. All that stood between them and their mortal enemy on the other side.

For days now, Rissa had been dealing with this uneasiness that had burrowed deep into her bones and refused to let go. Ever since they left the woods behind. She shouldn't feel this way. She should be ecstatic. She'd never imagined telling Davi how she felt or that he'd feel the same way. She stole a glance at him now and as if sensing her perusal, he looked back and sent her a dimpled smile. Heat flamed in her cheeks.

Still, the uneasiness wouldn't let up. If Rissa had to describe the restlessness that plagued her, it would be the feeling of being watched. Like right at this moment there were eyes watching their every move. Watching and waiting and plotting against them.

A low moan echoed from the foothills and a cool breeze drifted down through the valley and along the plateau they traveled. The wind lifted Rissa's hair on her neck and a shiver racked her body. Above her the mountains loomed, blocking the sun and casting them in shadow. She pulled the hood of her cloak a little tighter around her neck.

For two days, they'd been traveling this mountain path. Well, not a path per say. More of a well-worn track cut between the boulders and dead trees, probably back from the time when far more animals had lived and trekked across this range. Most of the trail had been fairly passable but the higher they climbed the harder it became for the horses to keep their footing on the loose shale. After her mount stumbled for about the fifth time that morning, Rissa called out to her brother who was leading the pack.

"Trystan, we should stop. My horse and I need to rest."

"I agree," Briggs joined in. "Breakfast was hours ago and my stomach is about to eat its way through my tunic right about now."

Trystan looked as if he would deny the request, but with an abrupt nod, he reined in his horse and Rissa sighed in relief.

The little band of joking misfits that had sat around the campfire only two weeks ago was replaced by a more somber group as they shared the last of the stale bread and dried meat. Rissa knew she would have to hunt again. There was nothing left of their supplies. Hunt what, was the question. The mountains looming to the left of them had shown nothing so far in the way of wildlife and the dead forest up ahead promised little else. Davi wouldn't be pleased but rat was probably back on the menu.

Rissa chewed slowly on her tiny morsel of food as she studied her companions. The closer they got to the Dreach-

Dhoun border, the heavier the pall that hung over them. She was acutely aware of it, even if they were not. Davi still seemed his cheerful self, but his smiles were far less frequent as if something weighed heavy on his mind. Alixa's and Edric's shared grief encompassed them like a black aura. Avery appeared to have aged considerably in the past weeks and even Briggs had toned down his incessant, inane chatter. But it was Trystan who worried her the most. His constant anxiety had manifested itself as a deep furrow on his brow that never went away and dark shadows under his eyes as if sleep eluded him.

He sat quietly next to her now, studying the valley below the plateau in apprehension, the bread in his hand forgotten about. Suddenly, he whirled on the old man across from him and pinned him with eyes as hard as flint. "Are you positive we will find Lonara here in the mountains, Briggs?"

The old man startled at the Prince's question, almost dropping the piece of meat halfway to his mouth. Nodding his gray head, he popped the morsel past his lips and licked his fingers before answering.

"Yes, yes, I'm positive. I already told you so. She's here in the mountains. I feel we are getting close."

"But how do you know?" Trystan insisted.

"How do I know? How do I know when I need to eat or sleep or piss?" the guardian replied. "My body tells me. Just like it's telling me Lonara is here. The Tri-Gard are as one, even if we sometimes wish otherwise. I know she's here, just as she knows I approach. I cannot promise that she'll make herself known as willingly as I did. I'm much more open and forgiving of myself than Lonara. I have a feeling we will have to persuade her much to join in this fight."

"So, you *do* remember what you did? The Tri-Gard stealing Dreach-Sciene's magic. You forgive yourself for that?" Alixa asked. Maybe her distrust was born from finding out her own father had been a traitor, but she regarded the old man with obvious reservation, similar to Rissa's own.

In response, Briggs glanced over his shoulder at his constant, unseen companion. "Yes, I know she doubts us. But she doesn't know, does she? She wasn't there when Ramsey fell under the dark influence."

Alixa rolled her eyes at the old man. "I know that your 'crazy' moments seem to happen quite conveniently when you don't want to talk about something."

Briggs opened his mouth as if to argue but Trystan cut him off. "You can feel her presence? So, does that mean you can feel the presence of the third Tri-Gard member as well? We are very close to the Dreach-Dhoun borders, do we have to worry about Ramsey sensing your approach and warning Calis?"

Briggs laughed at this as if Trystan had told a thigh-slapping joke. "Don't you know anything, boy?" He looked over his shoulder again and grinned. "Boy is as dense as they come. Hard to believe he descends from Marissa Kane's bloodline. Yes. Yes. I know they don't understand." He turned back to Trystan. "If Ramsey was still in possession of his crystal, Calis would not be able to hold him. That tells me it has been taken. Without it, Ramsey is as impotent as a eunuch. Trust me, he isn't aware of our approach."

Rissa was not in the least comforted by this explanation. Especially with the strange unrest that had been plaguing her since the forest still running rampant. "So you mean to tell us Calis has a Tri-Gard crystal? That worries me more so than Ramsey, Master Briggs. Won't he be able to feel your magic near?"

"No, don't worry about that, daughter of Marissa Kane. Calis is not marked as Tri-Gard. Stolen magic, while still strong, is nowhere near as powerful as when used by those destined to carry it. Calis is totally unaware of our search for Lonara. If he'd been able to fully control the crystal's magic or use it to its capabilities, he would have found us years ago."

The speech, while undoubtedly meant to mollify them, only added to Rissa's edginess. Knowing that King Calis controlled one of the Tri-Gard's crystals did nothing to alleviate her fear of failure or danger on this mission. She yearned to garner comfort from the earth, but she couldn't very well do that here in front of the others. They'd probably consider her as crazy as Briggs if they were to witness it. Instead, she brushed the bread crumbs off of her lap and patted her brother's shoulder soothingly.

"Rest Trystan. You'll need the strength. I'm going to hunt."

He nodded and smiled half-heartedly in approval as she stood, crossing to her horse to fetch her bow. Davi followed.

"I'll go with you, Princess," he called to her back, but she turned to him with a slight grin and ran a hand lovingly over his whiskered cheek.

"As much as I would treasure your company, Davion, you're about as graceful as an elephant tromping through the woods. What little prey there is to be found would hear you coming from a mile away and flee. No, stay here with Trystan. His mood scares me. Maybe he needs a little cheering up. Avery can accompany me."

He put his hands on his hips and arched a brow her way. "What I'm hearing is that I would distract you too much. I get it. I'm a very distracting sort of guy. Okay, fine. I'll stay here. But promise me you'll be careful." He glanced over his shoulder, making sure no one was listening as he softly teased. "I just found you, my love. Don't get lost. We have a lot of catching up to do." He placed a light kiss on the top of her nose before turning back to the group. "Avery, seems the Princess prefers your company over mine today."

"Smart girl," Avery drawled, ignoring Davi's frown as she immediately obeyed the command and approached. Rissa laughed softly and threw the bow and quiver over her shoulder, addressing the sword master. "Which way do you think, Avery? The trees in hopes of a rat or the hills for a mountain bird?"

"Doesn't matter either way, Princess. Meat is meat, but I think I'd prefer rat just to see the look of disgust on Davion's face."

"Careful Avery, my feelings are a delicate thing and not to be toyed with." Davi threw a slight frown the woman's way.

Trystan snorted. "Davi and feelings in the same sentence?"

"I guess miracles can happen," the sword-master responded, straight-faced.

What the hell? Did Avery just crack a joke? Rissa's laughter was cut short as the sword-master's eyes darted past her shoulder, drawn by something the Princess couldn't see. The spark of merriment dropped away and her face hardened to stone as she drew her sword, pushing Rissa behind her with such force she almost fell. Stumbling to catch her balance, Rissa's chest seized as the unmistakable sounds of a force moving closer reached her ears. Heavy hooves pounded into the hard dirt. Armor clanged. It sounded as if an army had found them.

She swerved and the sight that met her eyes confirmed her fears. Soldiers, at least a dozen or more, emerged from the trees on robust, well-fed horses. Nothing at all like the skin and bone animals they were traveling on. The first indication these soldiers were not from Dreach-Sciene. The gold and black tunics with the dark, circled triangle sigil confirmed it. This was a Dreach-Dhoun contingent of troops.

"Wow," Davi breathed.

Rissa froze, going as still as the mountain behind them. Briggs's tiny squeal of panic established that the rest of the group was aware of the new arrivals as well. That spurred Rissa into action. Her muscles tensed and she tightened her grip on her bow, nocking an arrow on instinct. Davi and Avery flanked her on either side, swords already in hand.

The horses lined up, forming a formidable barrier between them and the forest, as the soldiers atop studied the weary travelers in silence. Rissa, Davi, and Avery were joined by the rest of their companions, weapons at ready. Minutes passed, still, no one spoke. Finally, one of the soldiers, the troop's captain perhaps, nudged his horse a little further ahead and gazed down at the ragtag group before him. Broad-shouldered and thick-bellied, he viewed them in irritation as if they were no more bothersome than pesky children. "Unless you're all blind then I believe you've already ascertained that we outnumber you two to one. The King wishes your presence, so please spare any bloodshed today and come with us willingly."

"Your king is no king of ours. We will be accompanying you nowhere today." Trystan's response was resolute and Rissa couldn't contain the small moment of pride that overrode her fear.

"Trust me, Prince Trystan, you do not wish to fight us today. And if by some slight chance you do manage to best us, there are dozens of other soldiers searching the mountains and forest for you. You will not make your destination. You will lose." There was no boasting or pride in the man's voice. Just a matter of fact statement and Rissa feared it would be true.

"You know who I am?" Trystan asked and he failed to hide his surprise. So much for Briggs's belief that Calis was unaware of their approach.

"King Calis knows all," the captain responded. His eyes fell on the old man. "He is especially eager to meet you, Briggs Villard."

Rissa desperately tried to contemplate a route of escape, even as her arrow stayed steadfast on the captain. She knew the mountains on one side and the sharp drop to the valley on the other were not options. They could try and make a run for it and lose them in the forest, but the soldiers astride their horses made a daunting line between them and the trees. Another option would be to go back the way they had come and try to outrun them, but she doubted very much their malnourished animals could outrun the soldier's healthy horses. Her hand shook slightly as the only obvious solution came to mind. They would have to stand.

"King Calis is a fool if he thinks he'll take any of us alive," Avery snarled, coming to the same realization and brandishing her sword in threat.

"So be it," the captain sighed and elevated his hand in a slight wave. Rissa caught movement out of the corner of her eye and pushed Avery aside with her hip as the thrum of a bowstring reached her ears. The arrow sailed by the sword-master, missing her by a thread. Instead, it struck the horse's flank and the animal reared, squealing in pain as it galloped off. Rissa didn't have time to worry about her mare. Instead she fired back, two quick rounds, catching the hidden archer in the neck and the chest. He stumbled from the trees and slumped to the ground. Dead.

The shock of just having killed a man registered on some level with Rissa, but it was outweighed by fear as the deed galvanized the rest of the soldiers into action. The captain leaped from his horse, surprisingly nimble for his girth, and the rest followed his lead, growling as they charged.

Trystan's shout of "For Dreach-Sciene!" was echoed by Davi, Avery, Edric, and Alixa as they surged forward to meet the charge. Rissa fell behind knowing she needed distance for her bow to be effective, Briggs close on her heels. She sent off more shots, taking out a couple of soldiers at the back of the pack. She nocked another arrow and turned her attention to the captain and the other soldier targeting Trystan.

The captain moved fast, closing the distance as Trystan met him head on. The Prince's sword swung up in defense, stopping the captain's blade as it aimed for his chest. The two blades collided with a shrill clang, but the captain was the first to break contact as he whirled and attacked low, his sword now aiming for Trystan's ribs. The prince dropped his blade and deflected this blow as well. His attention occupied by the burly captain, he almost missed the second soldier's attack. Rissa cussed in desperation as her brother leaped away from the soldier's sharp edge just in time, only to block her from taking her shot.

Trystan parried blow after blow from the young soldier and the captain, but Rissa knew he wouldn't be able to keep up the pace forever. She tried in vain to take the enemy down, but they were too close to Trystan and she feared she would hit her brother. A scream stuck in her throat as the soldier landed a lucky shot and grazed Trystan's arm, slicing him open. Blood spurted out; soaking his sleeve but Trystan's only response was a grunt as he nimbly dodged another slice. She needed to do something to help him, and fast.

Blocking out everything else around her, she targeted the captain as she drew the bowstring taut. It released with a loud twang and arched through the air, straight for the captain's back. Just before the moment of impact, he swung low at Trystan and the arrow that should have pierced him between the shoulder blades struck him in the side instead. It broke his momentum, throwing him off balance and he staggered as Trystan narrowly missed being eviscerated.

Trystan's look of horror mingled with relief as he threw a grateful look Rissa's way.

"Look out," she screamed at him as the other soldier leaped past the captain, his sword held high above his head. Trystan pulled his weapon up just in time as the other slashed down and the two blades crashed with enough force to send the prince stumbling back. Rissa heard his growl of frustration as the burly soldier forced the Prince's hilt closer to his body, but Trystan refused to back down. Putting all his weight behind his blade, he jerked it up and his hilt connected with the opposing sword, tearing it from the other soldier's grasp and sending it flying through the air. The Dreach-Dhoun soldier had no time to react. Trystan's attack bit into flesh and bone and the man screamed in pain as the sword tore in his chest. Trystan didn't hesitate. Planting his foot firmly against the soldier's right side, he pushed him off of his blade and sent him stumbling backward into another soldier, knocking them both off their feet.

With this second threat eliminated, Trystan whirled on the injured captain, a savage smile of victory on his face. Rissa tore her eyes away from her brother. She'd given him the upper hand by disabling the captain. He could handle it himself now. She had to help the others.

Searching the chaos for any sign of Davi, her heart jumped into her throat as she found him surrounded by a trio of attackers. Yanking up her bow, she targeted the one furthest from him but her hands shook so badly, the arrow fell out of her grasp.

'Dammit,' she growled as she grabbed for another arrow,

her eyes never leaving Davi's face. Raising her bow once more, she zoned in on one of the soldiers but didn't make the shot. A primal scream of rage echoed in her ears as Alixa attacked the soldier from behind, running her thin blade through his back. The look of shocked surprise never left his face, even as Alixa yanked the bloody steel back out and rushed to Avery's aid before his body even hit the ground.

Alixa had evened out the odds and Davi was skilled, but so were the two remaining soldiers. Every move Davi made was countered and one soldier was even smiling, almost as if he were enjoying himself.

Rissa couldn't contain the small cry that fell from her lips as the tip of a blade pierced Davi's shoulder and a pool of crimson began to stain the white fabric. Davi glanced down in surprise at the wound, as if he couldn't believe such a thing had happened. The moment of inattention was all the soldier needed and he slammed his foot into the back of Davi's knee. He hit the ground hard, his sword flying out of his grasp. Rolling instinctively onto his back, he jerked away just in time as a blade, as heavy as a guillotine, fell near his head and ripped a jagged slash in his cheek. The wound must have hurt like hell but Davi didn't make a sound as he stared at the steel edge half an inch away from his eye in shock. The soldier lifted his sword once again, and holding it upright he thrust the hilt straight down toward Davi's head. It wasn't meant to be a fatal blow. Even Rissa could tell that. It seemed the soldier only meant to knock Davi out, but he never made contact.

Before Rissa could target the man, Edric rushed by her and attacked from behind. The soldier paused almost in disbelief as Edric's blade punctured the back of his neck and erupted in a splash of bloody debris through the front. He dropped his sword and grabbed at the protrusion as if he believed he could remove it. Finally, his knees buckled and he slid off the sharp edge to hit the ground, barely missing the prone Davi.

Davi bounced to his feet, blood pouring from his cheek and gripping his blood-stained shoulder, but through his pain, he shot Edric an extreme smile of thanks. It lasted all of two seconds before an arrow glanced off of Edric's thigh and he crumpled to his knees for a moment in shock.

"No," Rissa screamed. This needed to end.

"Briggs," she yelled at the Tri-Gard member cowering behind her underneath the cover of a huge boulder. "Do something. You need to do something."

He looked back at her, shocked etched deep into his face. "I....I can't, Princess. If I do magic, they will know I'm here."

"They already know you're here. Do something!"

Rissa was stunned into silence as Avery stumbled into her, nearly knocking her to her knees. A small knife protruded from Avery's shoulder and blood gushed from the wound. Rissa dropped her bow and arrow and tried to catch the sword-master from slamming her head into the ground. "Avery," she pleaded but the woman's eyes were not on Rissa. Instead, they were seeing something that carved fear in her face.

"The prince," Avery whispered as she pointed a bloody finger. Rissa followed the sword-master's gaze.

Trystan had somehow lost his battle with the captain and was kneeling on the ground between the stout man and another burly soldier. Blood covered his face, whether it ran from his nose or mouth, Rissa couldn't tell. She was too horrified to even care. The captain's hand was wound tightly into Trystan's hair, holding his head back at an awkward angle while the other hand held his honed steel against the Prince's neck.

"Trystan," she shrilled in horror, searching for her bow. No. This couldn't happen.

Where the hell was her bow?

"Briggs." Her scream was pure frustration as she watched the captain reverse his sword to raise the hilt before bringing it down on Trystan's head. "They're trying to take him."

The next few moments passed agonizingly slow as if time had stood still. Rissa's scream was still echoing in her ears as Davi ran like a madman past her and threw himself in a blind leap at the two soldiers about to drag Trystan away. He collided with the heavyset captain, sending him careening into the second soldier and taking them both off of their feet. He rolled with them over and over, down the slight incline and toward the grove of dead trees---and more advancing soldiers. Drawn by the sounds of battle, another contingent of Calis' army emerged from the copse like gold clad angels of death. More soldiers.

We are all going to die.

They heard the ground break before they were thrown off balance. A loud thunder, like a thousand angry gods shouting their disapproval from the mountains above. It echoed around them, over them, through them, reverberating in their bones. These same gods then slammed their fists into the very ground, making it vibrate and pulse under their feet.

The rockslide began with a few rolling pebbles past Rissa's feet, but she knew what it meant. She turned back to Brigg's. His eyes had rolled back in his head so that only the whites showed. As white as the crystal that had come alive with magic in his hands. He was muttering under his breath and Rissa strained to hear the words he seemed to be repeating, over and over.

"Crystal of the Tri-Gard. Awaken the earth."

The pebbles gave way to stones and Rissa glanced up at the peak. Fissures were forming in the stone wall, spreading rapidly like cracks in the lake ice. Briggs was planning on bringing down half the blasted mountain!

She saw Trystan struggling to gain his balance even as the ground shifted under him like it had a life of its own. Running to his side, she threw her arm around him and practically dragged him out of harm's way from the rocks that had now progressed into boulders. Dropping him into Alixa's capable hands, she pivoted and ran back the way she'd come, Trystan's voice calling out for her to stop ringing in her ears. But stop she couldn't. Davi was still in danger. She needed to get to him.

Briggs had severed the danger effectively, stranding them on one side of the falling boulders and the Dreach-Dhoun soldiers on the other, but in doing so he'd also stranded Davi. Rissa tried to keep her eyes on him as he was now being dragged by the two soldiers he'd taken out and was relieved to see him struggling since it meant he was still alive. She tried to call out to him, to tell him she was coming, but a boulder the size of her body smashed by, nearly squashing her like a bug. It was soon followed by another and Rissa screamed in frustration as the ground underneath her feet split with an agonizing groan forcing her to stumble back, away from the ragged crevasse.

"Davi," she yelled as the soldiers dragged him to his feet. They had to do something. They had to save him. She knew now the soldiers weren't about to kill him. They planned on taking him prisoner. She tried to run again, to leap over the newly formed ravine if she had to, her desperation making her reckless. Landslide be darned. But hands restrained her.

"Trystan," she turned to her brother, her face contorted with fear and pain. "Trystan, do something. You heard what

Calis does to his prisoners. We can't let them take him. We can't."

Her gaze averted back to Davi, willing him to break free. Instead, she was shocked at the sight that met her eyes. Whereas only moments ago he'd been struggling against his captors with the strength of ten men, his fight had now ceased. Soldiers flanked him on either side dragging him back, his face a mask of resignation as his eyes sought out Trystan. Rissa's heart squeezed in her chest and her body went numb as he mouthed familiar words towards her brother, "Truwa, Brathair."

Trystan's eyes widened as they stayed on his friend, his brother. He shook his head slowly. "I can't," he mumbled, his words choking him. Rissa was the only one close enough to hear.

Tears streamed down her face. "What are we waiting for?" She spun around. "Briggs, use your magic, dammit! Get me over there."

Briggs stared at her in terror. "I ... I can't." His shoulders slumped in exhaustion.

"You're the Tri-Gard. You're supposed to be able to do something."

Briggs began to shake, the effects of using so much magic raging through his body. His eyes rolled up into his head and he dropped like a stone, ripples of magic spreading out to shake the earth.

"No." Rissa turned to her brother who was still watching Davi as they finished tying him up. She ran to the edge of the newly formed canyon, testing the distance.

She didn't have her bow, so she picked up a bloody sword that lay on the ground.

A hand clamped around her arm. "Princess," Edric said, his

voice bursting out as his teeth clench in pain. A broken off arrow still protruded from his leg. "You won't make it."

She punched at him. "I don't even know you. Let me go. Davi!"

"Ri." Davi's voice flew across the chasm and she turned to see him take a fist to the gut for his trouble. It didn't stop him. "Don't, Ri."

Her legs collapsed beneath her and she dropped to the ground, the impact jarring through her. As she hit the dirt, her earth connection tried to calm her, but as the warmth soaked into her, she ripped her hands free. She didn't want to be calm.

"Trystan," Davi yelled before they could stop him. "You promised!"

Tears clung to her lashes as Rissa looked up at her brother, his face twisted in agony. He glanced toward the ground, searching. Finally, he walked a few paces and bent to pick up the bow and arrow Rissa had dropped in the battle.

"What are you doing?" she cried. "Trystan." Her chest heaved and she scrambled to her feet to face him. "We can get him back, Trystan. You and me. Davion is our family, we'll save him."

He nocked an arrow. She tried to push the bow down.

"I promised him, Ri." He wiped tears from his face. It gutted her. This was real.

"Please, Trystan. Don't do this."

Avery hobbled up behind her and wrapped her arms around Rissa, more out of restraint than comfort. She knew.

"No."

"Trystan," Davi yelled again desperately as he was lifted into a wagon. He started to struggle against his attackers.

It was only a whisper, but Rissa felt her brother's words in the air around her, cloaking her in despair.

"Truwa, Brathair."

He'd never been a good shot with a bow, but the arrow fell so short a novice would have done better.

He'd missed on purpose.

"I'm sorry, Davi," Trystan breathed. His eyes latched on to Davi and he raised his voice, yelling across the expanse between them. "I'll come for you."

His words held a hope that none of them felt in that moment and a love that crushed them all.

Davi jerked his head to the side and lunged away from his captors towards a sword that had fallen on the ground. Chaos erupted amongst the Dreach-Dhoun troops.

Rissa was frozen to the spot, a scream clogged in her throat, as she watched Davi press the tip of the short sword to his chest and plunge it deep in one swift, final movement.

His body jerked and his hands fell free of the sword as he fell sideways into the arms of a soldier nearby.

He'd given himself a warrior's death.

The soldiers around him scrambled in alarm and started firing arrows towards them.

"Run," Avery yelled as she released Rissa and clutched her arm, herding the horses who hadn't run off ahead of her.

There was no time to think. Edric slung Briggs over his shoulders and Alixa pulled on Trystan's hand to snap him out of his daze. He looked at the bow in his hand in shock and then took off.

Rissa grabbed the bow from her brother to cover their retreat. Her skill did not disappear with a shattered heart.

The newly created canyon prevented pursuit and arrows began to drop just short of them as they made it out of range. They didn't stop to catch their breaths until they were around the bend and hidden.

Rissa slid down against a boulder and buried her face in her hands, sobs shaking her shoulders as her grief poured out. "I love you, Davi," she whispered, thinking that maybe he could hear her.

She couldn't look at her brother as she came to a harsh realization. Trystan almost killed Davi. She didn't understand why Davi had done it. They could have rescued him if they made it into Dreach-Dhoun.

No one spoke as they tended to their wounds, all dealing with their own grief. Finally, Rissa's sobs eased as a numbness encased her. She dried her face on her sleeve and climbed to her feet, walking over to stop in front of her brother who was hunched over on the ground.

"When did you realize we would fail, Toha?" Her voice was icy. "When did you lose faith in us?"

There was such pain in Trystan's eyes as he looked up at her and all she wanted to do was cause him more, but a tear traveling the curve of his cheek stopped her.

"You don't understand," he said, his voice thick. "Davi knew. Both of us did. The imprisoned Tri-Gard is the priority. Davi didn't want us risking the realm for him, only Ramsey."

"We could have gotten them both."

"I'm sorry, Sister. We have but one chance to set things right."

"Then why'd you promise to rescue him? Why'd you lie to him."

Trystan shook his head, letting more tears fall, as he hid his face. "I didn't lie, Ri. I would have risked it all for him. It would have been wrong, but I would have done it. I am the prince of Dreach-Sciene and I would have doomed my people to save my brother." He buried his head in his arms and pulled at the ends of his hair. "And Davi knew it."

246

Rissa couldn't hear any more. She had to get away from her brother and his grief that threatened to swallow her own. She walked away, ignoring Trystan's plea of, "Ri, stop." She didn't stop. She kept walking until she could no longer see the rest of them behind her. Putting her hands on her head, she breathed deeply as her eyes began to water again. "I need you, Davi. I'm so scared to do this without you."

She sank down and curled around herself. The sun set and she knew she should find the rest of the group. The mountains were dangerous, but she couldn't bear to be with any of them.

She didn't know how long she cried there, but a full moon hung above the mountains when she finally looked up.

Feeling eyes on her, she spun around.

A woman stood watching her. The hood of her cloak was drawn up around her head as she stood out in the darkness.

She moved closer and bent down. "Princess, are you okay?"

Rissa wiped her face. "I'm no princess."

"No need to lie to me, child. I know who you are and I mean you no harm. I guess I should introduce myself." Her voice had a musical quality to it that soothed Rissa's heart. "My name is Lonara Stone."

"The second Tri-Gard member," Rissa whispered.

"You can call me Lona."

EPILOGUE

The sounds of a castle in daytime could be called symphony or chaos.

Metal ringing against metal in the practice yard.

Armor clad guards stomping through the stone walls.

Maids scurrying to and fro as if their menial tasks were the most important of their lives.

People lived and people died behind the high walls that belonged to the King of Dreach-Dhoun.

Ramsey Kane knew he would never make it beyond the stone towers that were rimmed with steel spikes. He'd never make it across the vast expanse of land between the impenetrable gates and the nearest village.

Not without his crystal – the same crystal that hung at the throat of his keeper, the King. Ramsey's strength was returning to him as he lived in his gilded cage, his ornate prison.

He pulled himself from the four-poster bed and stood at the window, believing his eyes to be deceiving him. He gripped the bars across the window so tight his knuckles turned white.

The color was draining from the once vibrant palace garden. Right before him, the grasses were drying, the flowers dropping, the trees sagging low.

How was Calis doing this?

He released the window bars, prying his fingers free, and stumbled back as he rubbed absently at his wrist. His tattoo that marked him as Tri-Gard was fading without his crystal. A Tri-Gard's crystal held many powers.

A thunderous pounding sounded on his door before it was thrust open. Calis stood there with his hands curled into fists and two unconscious guards at his feet. His hands glowed and sparked and everything became clear to Ramsey.

He'd drained the land surrounding the garden of magic.

No normal man could hold that much power before his body started to overload and break down. But Calis wasn't a normal man. He was a man with a Tri-Gard crystal.

Ramsey's eyes zeroed in on the swirling white gem that was now glowing as well.

Calis' eyes darted around the room as he switched from foot to foot, trying to keep the power he'd drawn from overwhelming him.

"What have you done, Calis?" Ramsey refused to move closer.

Calis misunderstood and looked at the two guards on the ground. "They allowed it to happen. Death was too good for them, but I didn't have time."

"Death ... you killed your own men." It shouldn't have surprised him. "Allowed what to happen?"

Calis' eyes blazed blue. "Come."

He whirled around and Ramsey had no plans to follow, but

a sudden force pulled him forward. He tried to fight it, but Calis jerked his hand and Ramsey was pulled up next to him. His feet didn't touch the ground.

"Calis, let me go," he growled. "How are you doing this? How do you have this much power?"

Calis didn't seem to hear him before he started speaking. "Fifteen years ago, I had you pull memories from a young child as only a Tri-Gard can."

"You mean when you forced me to wipe an innocent mind? Screw you, Calis."

Calis stopped outside a door and Ramsey was lowered abruptly. His feet slammed into the ground and he stumbled. He knew what was coming next. Calis couldn't perform the magic himself because he didn't know exactly how. All the power in the realm couldn't make up for the skill the Tri-Gard possessed.

"You are here to wipe that mind again."

"Wait, the child is here? They would have to be ..."

"Twenty years old."

"Even if I did obey you which is unlikely, I can't just erase the memories of a full-grown adult. I could scramble the brain completely. The memories are much more embedded at the older age."

"You will do it. You know I can force your hand."

"You've never been able to before. I don't care what you have to do to me. I won't help you."

"Uncle," A pale woman with almost white hair and pursed lips stepped from the room. "We're ready."

"Lorelai," Calis said fondly. He reached out to touch her cheek, but she jumped back as his fingers sparked against her skin, her eyes wide in fear.

"Ramsey." Calis grabbed his arm, searing it with his magic.

Ramsey grunted in pain.

"Meet my niece. The girl who only recently fulfilled her mission of killing my greatest enemy and your grandchildren's greatest protector." The King leaned in close, his touch growing even hotter. "You will do as I say because I'm going to hunt down your grandson and granddaughter and one day soon, you will be begging me to have mercy on them."

He released Ramsey, shoved him back and entered the dark room. Ramsey stayed behind to catch his breath, but the force from before yanked him inside and slammed the door behind him.

The room was lit only by a circle of candles. At first, he thought the King and his niece were the only two people there, but as he was pulled closer, he made out a shape laying on a long table in the center of the circle of candles.

Ramsey gasped. "Is he ..."

"Dead?" Calis finished. "Yes."

The King leaned forward to push dark hair from the smooth brow of a young man who looked like he'd been handsome in life. His face was somewhat distorted with bloat now.

Calis didn't seem to mind. He touched the man's forehead, murmuring words no one else could hear.

The flames of the candles blazed higher, reaching towards the ceiling. Calis had the young man's shirt open and pressed his palms to his chest. His skin began to glow and the hum of magic surrounded them.

Ramsey watched in horrified fascination and he looked up to see the same look on Lorelai's face. Her jaw hung open as the air whipped up around them. Their hair flew about their faces, but the flames didn't even flicker.

The young man's body shook, rattling the table, and Calis

yanked the crystal from his own neck to hold it against the man's.

All at once, the flames extinguished, descending them into darkness. The wind died and silence followed.

"Uncle?" Lorelai whispered.

A green glow began and Ramsey realized it was coming from the crystal in Calis' hand. The glow illuminated the man on the table as he sucked in a breath.

He'd known the power of the crystal, but the Tri-Gard never played with life and death like this. They didn't play God.

Calis had no such reservations. Dread filled his heart as he bore witness to the King controlling death as he controlled everything else.

"Ramsey." Calis snapped his fingers and Ramsey was pulled forward. "Now."

The man's head was damp with perspiration as Ramsey rested a hand on top of it. New perspiration, he thought. Because the dead man lives.

A shiver ran through him and he held his hand out for the crystal.

Calis hesitated before placing it in the Tri-Gard's palm. Even though the King maintained contact with the crystal, power surged through Ramsey for the first time in twenty years.

He channeled his power into the man's mind, picking out the threads of memories. As he saw them in his own mind, he knew exactly who the man was. He closed his eyes for a brief moment but couldn't stop the tear from escaping.

What he was doing was unforgivable just like his actions all those years ago. And yet, he continued.

He gave the man a blank slate and a mind that was easily moldable. He'd fill the role Calis wanted him to fill.

Ramsey thought of the boy he'd wiped clean all those years ago. Would this man live his life as a pawn? Having his mind crafted and altered at will?

Ramsey sighed and stepped back as Calis' hand tightened around the crystal as it stopped glowing.

With a nod of the King's head, the candle came to life once again before the King sagged forward with exhaustion.

A low moan came from the man as the bloat disappeared from his body. His clothes were bloody, but his skin showed no sign of battle. He truly was made new.

The man opened his blue eyes and stared at Ramsey in confusion. Calis pushed him out of the way with a cry.

"Davion." He took Davion's hand in between his own and squeezed as he let out a laugh.

Lorelai's soft cries carried to him as she crossed to the other side of the table.

Calis grinned down at the bewildered young man. "My boy." His magic was depleted now and his legs threatened to give out. "Welcome home, my son."

Calis Beirne, King of Dreach-Dhoun, collapsed to the ground, twitching before going still.

>>>The End<<<

∽

Want to find out what happens next?
Pick up a copy of A War for Truth!

Visit michellelynnauthor.com/memoryofwar

ABOUT M. LYNN

M. Lynn has a brain that won't seem to quiet down, forcing her into many different genres to suit her various sides. Under the name Michelle Lynn, she writes romance and dystopian as well as upcoming fantasies. Running on Diet Coke and toddler hugs, she sleeps little - not due to overworking or important tasks - but only because she refuses to come back from the worlds in the books she reads. Reading, writing, aunting ... repeat.

MichelleLynnAuthor.com

LEGACY OF LIGHT

A War for Magic

A War for Truth

A War for Love

ABOUT MICHELLE BRYAN

Michelle Bryan lives in Nova Scotia, Canada, with her three favorite guys; her husband, her son and her crazy fur baby. Besides her family, her other passions in life consist of chocolate, coffee and writing. When she is not busy being a chocolate store manager or spending the day at her computer, she can be found with her nose stuck in any sort of apocalypse book.

MichelleBryanAuthor.com

ALSO BY MICHELLE BRYAN

THE CRIMSON LEGACY TRILOGY

Crimson Legacy

Scarlet Oath

Blood Destiny

The Waystation - a Crimson Legacy novella

THE BIXBY SERIES

Grand Escape (Strain of Resistance Prequel)

Strain of Resistance

Strain of Defiance

Strain of Vengeance

THE LEGACY OF LIGHT SERIES

A War For Magic

A War For Truth

A War For Love

POWER OF FAE SERIES

The Lost Link

The Lost Magic

The Lost Prince

STANDALONE

Clash of Queens